Tom Wasp and the
Newgate Knocker

TOM WASP AND THE NEWGATE KNOCKER

AMY MYERS

FIVE STAR
A part of Gale, Cengage Learning

GALE
CENGAGE Learning

Detroit • New York • San Francisco • New Haven, Conn • Waterville, Maine • London

GALE
CENGAGE Learning

LIBRARY OF CONGRESS CATALOGING-IN-PUBLICATION DATA

Myers, Amy, 1938–.
   Tom Wasp and the Newgate knocker / Amy Myers. — 1st ed.
     p. cm.
   ISBN-13: 978-1-59414-870-5 (alk. paper)
   ISBN-10: 1-59414-870-8 (alk. paper)
   1. Great Britian—History—Victoria, 1837–1901—Fiction. I. Title.
PR6063.Y38T666 2010
823'.914—dc22   2010003990

Published in 2010 in conjunction with Tekno Books and Ed Gorman.

Printed in Mexico
2 3 4 5 6 7 14 13 12 11 10

To Alma
Encourager and friend

AUTHOR'S NOTE

I have recounted Tom's story as he told it to me in my head, but of course as a nineteenth-century chimney sweep, his use of English sometimes varies from standard grammar and reflects his own idiosyncrasies. Fortunately, Tom had much more schooling than any other sweep in his trade would have had at that time, thanks to his patron, Lady Beazer, who paid for him to attend a Ragged School after he appeared in her hearth by mistake during his climbing boy days. Thankfully, by the time Tom was operating himself as a master sweep, the use of climbing boys was dying out, thanks to the new regulations following Lord Shaftesbury's long campaign.

Besides Tom himself, my thanks are due to David Priestley, of Priestley & Ferraro, for his help over Kwan-yin, and to Doreen Kendall, of the East London History Society, for information on Victoria Park and for the Society's publication, *A Pictorial History of Victoria Park.* I hope they approve of the use to which I have put their information, and any errors are down to me alone. I am also very grateful to Five Star Publishing and to Alice Duncan, who edited this second Tom Wasp mystery as sympathetically as its predecessor. As always, a big thank you to my agent, Dorothy Lumley of Dorian Literary Agency, for all her faith in Tom Wasp.

CHAPTER ONE

The great door of Newgate prison clanged behind me as the warder pushed it shut. As I hobbled into the porter's lodge, there was a loud rumbling as the key was turned, and the huge bolt shot home. I felt like a convict myself, closed in by stone walls, iron spikes, bolts and bars.

Fortunately, the officer in charge once again graciously decided that a chimney sweep of my years was unlikely to be planning the escape of any of the miserable souls incarcerated there. In any case, there are so many twists and turns to its dark and silent passageways that they'd never find the way out.

"Wasp, Tom," he roared for a turnkey to come to fetch me. "Cleared for solitary. Female."

Before her trial, I used to talk to Eliza through the iron rails of a narrow fenced-off area in the female exercising ground. Yellow-faced, bedraggled creatures had eyed us warily as we talked, as though I were St. Peter himself sent to judge them and Ned his gatekeeper—Ned being my chummy or sweep's apprentice. Poor souls. If I were St. Peter, I'd have been tempted to release the lot of them. Just being here was punishment enough.

This would be my last visit, and I paid it alone, for tomorrow morning, Monday, 5 January 1863, Eliza Hogg would take the Dead Man's Walk to face the hangman's noose. Today there was no exercising ground for Eliza. She was in the dark cell in the basement of the women's wing, there being no cells reserved for female murderers as there are for male. The heavy chill of the grey stone began to depress me even more, as we descended the staircase into the dark corridors beneath. This wing was remodelled only recently, but nothing could change the gloomy atmosphere of the Newgate corridors, or the echo of the sound of the iron bolts as one door after another shut behind us.

"Eliza Hogg!" shouted my turnkey as he reached the two dark cells set aside for solitary confinement. "Sweepie to see you again." He turned to me, gloating, "She won't see yer. She won't see no one. Turns 'em all away."

"Let 'im in."

I heard Eliza's croak, and so did the turnkey. He glared at me, but in we went. This was a rare privilege for a prisoner condemned to death, and two female wardresses guarded her at the entrance. These dark cells are so named because there are no windows, and the only light came from the turnkey's lantern. The brightest paint in the world can't disguise the smell of death looming over such places as this, and I was glad that I had decided to leave Ned outside, for he and Eliza had been friendly. It would have upset him too much to see her on the eve of her execution. The doorway was left open to aid the dim light, and as Eliza peered out at me I could see her face was gaunt, under the now grey hair. To my surprise, however, she looked not only pleased to see me, but almost excited.

"You've been a good friend, Tom," she told me.

Had I? Visitors are not encouraged at Newgate but I had come when I could since Eliza had first been arrested, although she'd never shown much interest. She was housekeeper at the Gables where I swept the chimneys, and she'd seemed happy enough there at first. The Gables is near the church of St. George's-in-the-East on the Ratcliffe Highway in London's East End, not very far from where Ned and I live, although a world away in grandeur. The Gables was nearly opposite the church in a very salubrious street, for it runs down to the notorious Highway. I'd always enjoyed a good chat with Eliza, listening to her jokes and the few woes she then had. She did a fine line in pies, to which Ned is particularly partial. About two years back, however, in 1861, her soldier husband returned from the wars, and after that she had been a changed person. Her face had hardened, and her smile and generous nature disappeared. When she could not take his beatings and brutality any longer, she murdered him.

"They found you guilty then, Eliza," I had said when I saw her after the verdict at the Old Bailey in December. I had hoped the judge would be lenient and give her life and hard labour, or transportation, but her attitude must have put them off. No remorse for Eliza.

" 'Course they did, Tom," she'd replied. "I killed the brute, and I'd do it again."

It's at such times that I'm glad I'm not St. Peter, for how does he balance cause against punishment, or what's in the heart against what is done by the hand?

Her husband had been of the opinion that Eliza was there chiefly to look after him, and only grudgingly had permitted her to work for the household that paid her wages. Being an invalid—he had a limp from a Chinese pike—he made sure that others did his own work as a general manservant. He seemed to organise most of it from Paddy's Goose, the nickname of the pub in London's Ratcliffe Highway where every major and most minor crime in London is planned. One day last year Eliza had had enough of him. She put rat poison in his dinner, enough to kill him several times over, and he died a day later. If she'd taken a knife to him on the spur of the moment, the judge might have been more sympathetic, but that wasn't Eliza's way.

"I wanted him dead, Tom. You won't get no last-minute tears from me when they come to take me to the hangman."

11

That was what she said then, but now the day was almost upon her. I had thought she might have changed her mind, but she hadn't, I could see that. Instead of fear, she still had that excited look in her eyes. I shivered at what she'd face tomorrow.

Executions are held in public; some folk even bringing their kids to watch as though it were a family outing to the pleasure gardens of Victoria Park. There is a lot of concern about that now, with many folk, including me, believing hangings shouldn't be held in the open yard before the prison but behind closed gates. So I wouldn't be coming tomorrow, and I certainly wouldn't have brought Ned. Ned is halfway between believing what he's told at Sunday school about the right way of life, and belief that the quickest way of earning a coin or two is the best. This is not, in his opinion, by cleaning chimneys, although he humours me in my odd ways of preferring this method to taking money off unsuspecting people without their consent.

"Say goodbye for me, Tom. To those who remember me," Eliza said awkwardly.

I knew this was as far as she would go toward emotion. It had been an easy household to work for. Mr. and Mrs. Periwinkle were good employers and the butler, housemaids, footmen, odd job boy and gardener were a happy bunch—even though they had their funny ways. But then, who doesn't?

Eliza's eyes were still excited. "I've got something to give you, Tom."

She was whispering but the wardresses and the turnkey heard and rushed in to restrain her, as they saw her hand stretch out. " 'Ere," said the turnkey indignantly, "you can't do that."

"Gonna hang me for it, Bert?" Eliza jeered. All the same she gave what looked like just a scrap of pink paper to him first.

This pleased him, so he turned it over, examining it carefully, as though it contained details of how she might vanish through the bars to freedom. Satisfied at last, he handed it over to me.

"What's this, Eliza?" I asked gently.

"Nothing much, Tom, but it's all I got. No one else is going to have it. He didn't care nothing about me. I pinched it from him, and hid it in the best place I could."

"But what is this, Eliza?" I was still puzzled. It still looked only like a small piece of thick pink paper.

A cackle. "I don't know and that's the truth, Tom. I don't know *why*, that is. But *he* guarded it like gold dust, so I made sure he couldn't get it back. Nor no one else either. Everyone was asking me there at the house. Strangers even. So it is something, Tom. You find out. You have it. That's"—she glanced at the turnkey and the wardresses who were all paying very close attention—"what caused it all. He whacked me, and then I knew what I had to do. Last time, George, I said. Last time you do that. He laughed in my face, but that was for the last time too." Another pause. "You coming tomorrow?"

"No, Eliza," I said. "But at seven in the morning I'll be praying for you, asking our Lord to take into consideration all you've done in the way of pies for me and Ned and so many others."

She managed a sort of grin, then turned away as the turnkey said it was time to go. I was glad for I could feel salty tears on my cheeks.

"Why is she called the Newgate Knocker, guvner?" Ned asked me.

I found him shivering outside on Newgate Street, standing by our horse and cart, and never had I felt so glad to be out in the air. It was a raw January day, that Sunday, and I could hardly see his small figure through the heavy fog. This was freedom though, and the horrors of Newgate prison were behind me, with only the thought of poor Eliza to follow me home. Luckily the fog wasn't dense enough to be a London particular, or else we wouldn't have got home that evening. We had to crawl our way gas lamp to gas lamp along the roads we knew so well.

"Black as the Newgate Knocker, that's what they say, Ned. Meaning," I added, "those who leave the path of goodness are like the black knocker on the main door of the prison."

That was true, but poor Eliza didn't just get the name that way. Eliza had been a handsome woman with a mane of black hair, although it was grey now. She had carried herself proudly at the trial, so I like to think that's how she got the "Knocker" attribute, rather than its other lower meaning of being a judy working the streets or otherwise distributing her favours. New-gate Knockers are sideburns too, which made the joke all the more amusing for the bright patterer or newspaperman who thought up this name for her. It had caught on quickly.

"She's given me something, Ned," I told him when we got back to our palatial lodging in Hairbrine Court. Palatial isn't a word widely associated with this part of London, even though the Tower of London is but half a mile or so away. Still closer, however, is the stink of Rag Fair, or Rosemary Lane as it's properly called, and in the other direction are the swarming ant holes of the docks. Hairbrine Court sounds grand, but it is only one of the hundreds of little yards approached from the street by a narrow entry. Within them, tumbledown houses hide their faces from the main thoroughfare of life, skeletal human beings usually sleep eight or ten to a room, and in the central yard the communal muck gathers, as London's delicate dustmen never venture inside. Hairbrine Court is by no means the worst of courts however, and so when good fortune came our way last year in the way of gold coins, because Ned and I had rendered some service to the gentry, we were able to improve our circum-stances.

"We could move to Buckingham Palace, Ned," I had joked. "Or we could stay here. Or move out to the country." Wherever that might be. I'd never been sure how far away it is.

Owing to his background, first as an anybody's child and then as a climbing boy enslaved to the Walworth Terror, Ned likes his security, so I guessed what his answer would be.

"Here, guvner," he had immediately piped up. "It's home. We can spend the money on pies."

We compromised, and instead of two rooms we now have four, and our landlady Mrs. Parsnip was given money by our benefactors to install a small laundry and wash room at the back of the house. This made her the Queen of Hairbrine Court in her neighbours' estimation, even though the water only runs in our part of the world for twenty minutes a day, and never on Sundays. Nevertheless, just having a wash room greatly pleased her. Only Ned wasn't delighted, since that meant that washing has become much easier than before, and Ned and water don't agree—which I put down to some happening in his past when he was with the Terror. Mrs. Parsnip, however, thinks she's running one of those model living places; there was even enough money to turn part of the backyard where the privy is into a miniature garden with a bush or two.

With the extra rooms I had persuaded Ned with difficulty to have a sleeping room of his own. He didn't like this idea one bit, liking to be sure that if the Walworth Terror came roaring through the window to get him, I'd be right there to scare him off. I pointed out he could have a book or two of his own, but he was not impressed by this offer. However, the idea of having a *bird* of his own in his room appealed immensely, so we paid a visit to Leadenhall Market especially to purchase one. I'll say this for Ned, he has good taste. No showy birds for him. He took a fancy to a linnet. He's a pretty little bird called Jack for some reason known only to Ned. He was a dull little thing when we bought him a year ago, but not long after that something magic happened and he grew the loveliest crimson breast with a red patch on his head to match. Ned thought this was all due to him, so was disappointed when he eventually turned brown again. Like us all, Jack longs for spring and his coloured plumage again.

"What is it, guvner?" Ned asked eagerly, as soon as I mentioned Eliza's gift.

His face fell as I produced the scrap of pink paper I'd been given. I think he had some idea it might be a longtail—that being a valuable banknote—but I quickly put him right on that score. I saw it had a number written on it, 247, and the name J. Doolittle, Nelson Street, Commercial Road, in heavy letters and realised it was a popshop ticket. I had seen too many to mistake it. That's where Eliza had hidden the valuable thing of her husband's. Pawnbrokers being pawnbrokers, and Eliza's hanging due to take place tomorrow, I knew the sooner I got there the better, or whatever she or her husband had pawned would have disappeared. We'd go first thing tomorrow. The ticket might even have expired already, for Eliza had been in prison for many months, so I told Ned not to expect too much.

"It has to be something," he said obstinately.

This was true, of course. Eliza had hinted it might be valuable, and that couldn't be the ticket itself, only what it represented. To Ned, whatever it was, it meant something that could be sold. Even in winter, we sweeps are usually out and about ringing our bell and calling the streets well before seven o'clock but this morning we had been delayed while we thought about Eliza. I had a notion that Ned was praying more for what Eliza's ticket might produce than for Eliza herself, but perhaps I was wrong for as we drove our old horse Doshie and our cart to the Commercial Road he was very quiet.

"Where is she now, guvner?" he asked at last.

"Explaining to our Lord why she murdered him, Ned."

A pause. "I meant her body."

I'd been hoping he wouldn't ask that, but Ned always likes to know everything before he'll let something go.

"They bury them, Ned, under the flagstones of the corridor leading to the yard. Dead Man's Walk they call it."

"There wouldn't be enough room," he objected immediately.

I didn't want to have to explain to Ned about quicklime, so I said hastily, "Keep your eyes skinned. We're coming to Commercial Road. Look out for Nelson Street." The fog had lifted today, but it was still misty and grey.

He thought over what I'd said for a while and then informed me, "They probably use quicklime, guvner."

"Maybe you're right," I agreed.

There are pawnbrokers and pawnbrokers in this merry old town of ours, ranging from the dolly shop fences to the more respectable who see themselves as helping not only themselves but the poor through tricky times. There are more of the former than the latter in this part of east London. The receivers of stolen goods mask their trade by fronting it with a pawnshop, and as Mr. Doolittle's establishment wasn't known to me, I wondered which sort I would find.

Nelson Street is a turning off Commercial Road, which is a busy road and tramway with quite grand houses in between shops and offices. Nelson Street is not nearly so grand, however, and from the look of it Doolittle's was unlikely to be handling stolen high-class goods, although looks can be deceptive. I wondered why Eliza had chosen to come up here, when several pawnbroker establishments would have been closer to the Gables. I recalled again what she'd hinted about the ticket being for something of value, at least to her husband. From my memories of George, he wasn't the sentimental sort, and so valuable must mean in money terms—something I was stupid enough to convey to Ned.

The window of J. Doolittle Pawnbroker was full of enticing objects such as old clothes, pots and pans, bibles, secondhand candlesticks and oil lamps, even half-used candles. A faded sign announced that nothing would be turned away and that honest prices were always given.

Ned spotted a battered magic lantern in the window so we were delayed for a few moments while I pointed out the unlikelihood of its being in working condition and of being able to afford the pictures to use it with. Then we went in.

Mr. Doolittle didn't bat an eyelid at our sooty faces, which was unusual to say the least. He was an immensely thin and tall gentleman, rather like a chimney himself, especially as he was clad all in black.

"I've a regular chimney sweep already," said he, as though he genuinely regretted his misfortune in not being able to employ us. I took to him immediately. He had a long, mournful face and sad eyes, and seemed in need of companionship, judging by his general lost expression and shabbiness. He had a patient look to him, too, which for a genuine pawnbroker would be a help, him having to listen to hard-luck stories all day long, only some of which would be genuine.

"We've come on other business," I explained.

"Back shop business?" he enquired warily. A more direct uncle (that being a pawnbroker) I have never met. Most uncles do most of their trade in the back shop with stolen goods. I was not surprised at his nervousness, as chimney sweeps, particularly lads of Ned's age and younger, are well known for their connections to the underworld. Mr. Doolittle was safe with me. I prefer to rest my hopes with the Upper world.

"Front shop," I assured him, conscious of Ned fidgeting at my side. I was tense too. After all, how much money was I going to have to find to redeem this valuable object?

Mr. Doolittle frowned as he looked at the ticket. I thought he was going to say it was already sold, time-expired. Then he consulted his ledger, which impressed Ned, who is inclined to think that book records are a waste of time. To my relief, after turning back quite a few pages, Mr. Doolittle looked at me with a pleased smile as if he'd have been really upset not to oblige.

"Ah," said he. "Name of Betsy Pigg."

"Yes," I said quickly, recognising Eliza Hogg's name in this, and thinking the fewer explanations the better—at least until I'd seen what this ticket would produce. "Betsy's ill."

"Sixpence," decreed Mr. Doolittle apologetically, "that's with the twenty per cent interest." He looked as if he knew full well that Betsy was more than ill, but pawnbrokers don't live to a ripe old age by asking unnecessary questions.

I was relieved. Sixpence, although representing the income from two chimneys, was not an impossible sum—although that suggested Mr. Doolittle could hardly have considered it a valuable item, even if George Hogg had. He went over to his store of goods awaiting redemption, which looked even less desirable than his window display. He came back with a large and very ugly doll in what might once have been a sailor suit; now the jacket and hat were missing and threadbare canvas could be seen in some parts of this brave sailor's anatomy.

I could see Ned's face falling as I thanked Mr. Doolittle politely and paid my sixpence. Then we left for our day's work, complete with the doll. The sky seemed brighter now, and there was even a hint of January sunshine, which made us feel better about our disappointment. We stuffed the doll out of sight under the seat of the cart. Ugly as it might be, anything gets stolen around these parts and I didn't want Eliza's gift, however unappealing, to disappear on the very day of her death. It wouldn't be respectful.

"Why would that bloke George think a dirty old doll valuable?" Ned asked crossly, after we reached home that night. He must have been very disappointed, to brood on it all day. I took it as one of life's little hiccups, which are all over quickly if you hold your breath for a moment. Probably the doll had belonged to George in his youth, and that was why he valued it, though why strangers should apparently have been chasing after it was a mystery. I put this idea to Ned, but he would have none of it.

"You said he wasn't the sentimental sort," he reminded me, and I was silenced.

Once back at Hairbrine Court, we propped the doll up in one of the two old armchairs by the fire. We had bought them from Rag Fair market with our newfound wealth last year. Once they'd been red plush, but it had suffered over the years. Nevertheless, they looked homely enough set next to the fireplace, and to my mind that's the purpose of a chair. Some of the chairs I see in my work look as if they're daring even their owners to sit on them, let alone chimney sweeps. Besides, Ned had found a silver fourpenny piece between the cushions of his, so he was delighted with our purchase. Not with this doll, though.

"Do we have to keep this thing, guvner?" he asked, giving the doll a vicious punch.

"For a while," I said. "In respect for Eliza."

So that doll sat there for a week or more. I could see Ned eyeing it thoughtfully, as if wondering whether it might suffer an accident. And sure enough one occurred. The contents of the slop pot that he keeps under his bed so he don't have to visit the privy in the pitch of the night somehow got tipped over it. I eyed Ned sternly, and decided to teach him a lesson. "It's only the head got messy," I said. "Take it to the washroom and clean it up."

He was so annoyed he gave the head a sort of twist as if to tear the thing apart. To our surprise the head came straight off.

Ned laughed in delight, seizing hold of the trunk as if to tear off the limbs too. I seized it back, but looking inside the neck I realised that it wasn't just stuffed inside with straw.

"There's something stuck in here, Ned."

"A fortune, guvner?" Suddenly the doll didn't seem so bad to him after all. Ned promptly slid his hand inside, as I held the doll. He brought out a wad of newspaper, wrapping up some object or other.

"The crown jewels," I said solemnly, and Ned looked excited. Her Majesty Queen Victoria could rest easy, however. Whatever we had, it wasn't diamonds or gold or silver. When he unwrapped it, there was only a dirty little china figure, maybe twelve inches high, of a seated lady. She was sitting with her knees spread out under her draped gown, her lower legs tucked out of sight and her hands folded in her lap. Her delicately moulded headdress adorned carefully sculpted hair. The lady wasn't even young or pretty, even though I could see this was fine workmanship, and when I rubbed a bit of grime off her she was a nice ivory white colour. She was looking down and gently smiling, not as if she was about to burst into laughter, but as though . . . well, I couldn't sum it up for a while but then I tried to do so.

It was as if she thought the world was good, and no one was really evil. All she could see was peace, and that was what she gave.

"I like her, guvner." Ned was staring at the lady as though she were another singing bird, as in her way she was. I could even hear his linnet piping up in the next room as though Jack knew we had something nice in here.

"So do I, lad, so do I." I felt a lump in my throat, though why I don't know.

"I don't mind if we keep her," Ned said anxiously, his eyes on me, in case I might want to put the lady back inside the doll and rush her off to sell her in the market.

"Nor do I, Ned."

We tried several places for the lady to live: we tried the

mantelpiece, the upturned box where we leave our working boots overnight, the top of the box where we keep our clothes, and the food cupboard. She didn't seem happy anywhere. Then I thought of somewhere else. I tried putting her by the window. It was a fine cold day, so the evening sun just caught her, before it sank for the night. It's low at this time of year, but between the roofs of the houses opposite came a glimpse of gold. The lady seemed to come alive, saying to us:

"Time for you to have your pies. You've earned them. Sleep well."

Perhaps Ned didn't feel the same way, because he was shifting from foot to foot as if dissatisfied with something. At last he told me what it was.

"I think she'd like Jack for company, guvner."

He was making the big sacrifice. Without a word from me he disappeared into his room and brought out the linnet in his cage. He placed him on the table by the windowsill so that he too could see the sun. Oh, my word, Ned did look satisfied then. So did the lady—and so did Jack, who began to tweet most melodically.

The only person who wasn't completely satisfied was me, Tom Wasp. This lady must be what Eliza's husband had believed valuable. The doll itself couldn't be worth anything either in money or otherwise now, but what about its contents? Eliza had said something was going on at the Gables. Was the lady something special?

And if so, shouldn't I be enquiring what it was?

CHAPTER TWO

I had battled with myself for a week over what to do about this. What I wanted to do was to forget all about the china lady's origins, and just enjoy the happiness she brought to Ned and me. What I *should* do was make sure that whatever was going on at the Gables had nothing to do with Eliza's lady. Duty eventually won, but it was a hard decision.

There was no way Ned would be left behind where that china lady was concerned, and so off we went together on Wednesday, 14 January, "down the Highway"—these words pack a lot of meaning for us who live here. The Ratcliffe Highway must have been our Lord's experiment for the world. You meet an assortment of every race under the sun, quarrelsome Americans, Italians and Greeks, Orientals, Lascars, Romanies, and of course our own sailormen. Every shade of villainy can be found (usually led by those born right here in the east of London). Among the villains and drunks are respectable folk struggling along as best they may among the shouting and screaming roisterers and fighters.

Our Lord wouldn't have planned it this way, but the Devil also puts his hand in the mixing pot, and nowhere more visibly than on the Ratcliffe Highway. To me this is a natural way of things, regrettable though it is; it's when I get to villages like Kensington that to me it seems most unnatural. The scum and the poor are swept out of sight where villainy can breed even more fruitfully. Out on the Highway everyone fights it out in the open, tumbling out from gin palaces, swaggering out of public houses and penny gaffs and packing out the pie shops, which I try to drag Ned past. The Gables is not very far from the Highway, but it's a step into a different world.

A gentleman named Hawksmoor designed St. George's Church, so I heard. It's a grand building, and naturally likes grand houses around it. It had lots of them years ago when the gentry thought they'd like to move out from London's smoke. Then they found there were worse smells than smoke so they left again, leaving their grand houses behind them. The Gables is one of them. With its turrets and imposing black beams, it looks like a medieval palace, but it's a welcoming house even so. In my trade, I tend to sniff each house I enter to see if it has a welcome smell or not. Every house has its identity, just as we humans do, and the Gables gives me a friendly greeting. I had wondered whether it would go on doing so, after the tragic events that took place here, but so far it had.

Ned and I crunched over the gravel to the tradesmen's entrance. It was one of those raw January days when however fast you try to walk, you never seem to get warmer. We'd had no wash this morning for the water from last night never came through, being frozen, but that didn't worry us because people are used to sweeps not smelling of roses. Fires would all be lit by this hour but often there were smoke-jacks to be cleaned, or a chimney causing trouble that had been left unlit in the hope of an obliging sweep passing by. This morning my reception at the tradesmen's door was unexpected and far from friendly.

"No sweeps needed," snapped the lady who opened the door. This was Mrs. Davy, Eliza's successor, as I knew from earlier visits, but she wasn't usually so brisk. She was a stately lady, head and shoulders taller than me, and her face was as bleak in welcome as mine was in soot.

"I'm your regular," I informed her pleasantly. "I wanted—"

"That's as may be, but not today."

"Might Mr. Tomm be in?" I persisted, seeing that I had other missions than cleaning chimneys to discuss.

"We've the police here," she answered, stepping back to close the door in our faces.

Ned was a lot quicker than she was. He ducked under my arm and leapt into the path of the closing door. "My guvner's a pal of the police. That's why we're here. We've got information."

I wasn't sure this was true but it served to gain a grudging entrance for us. Luckily once over the step and into the corridor, I could see Mr. Tomm in the servants' hall on the left. This was a grand name for what in this case was a room opposite the kitchens; it was friendly enough, although on the small side.

Mrs. Davy wasn't happy about this, but as the butler outranks the housekeeper (just) she couldn't say much, except that her look of disapproval would have swept the chimneys by itself. No self-respecting speck of soot would stay around in her presence. Mr. Tomm is a tall, mournful-looking gentleman. He once told me that his Christian name was Harrison, after the gentleman who invented longitude as Mr. Tomm's father was a naval man. Ned argued that longitude was there already and didn't have to be invented, but Mr. Tomm wouldn't have it, and butlers always have to be right. His name causes some confusion. As butler, he is usually addressed as Tomm by his employer, which to those unaware of his status sounds as if he is merely a footman. If called Harrison, however, he would *feel* like a footman, knowing it to be a Christian name.

"I get most distressed about it, Mr. Wasp," he had confided to me.

I could understand that. If you live and work all day and every day in the same place, you need to be sure who you are— and even more importantly, who others think you are. Fortunately, as a sweep, I have no problem this way. My face and smell instantly proclaim it to everyone.

Mr. Tomm rose to meet me, as we went into the servants' hall, which was in great disarray. Drawers were half pulled out, and cupboard doors open. Inside them the contents were jumbled together, and some of them lay in piles on the floor. Normal work had obviously been suspended.

"A sad state of affairs, Mr. Wasp." Always polite is Mr. Tomm.

"The police?" I ventured. "No trouble I trust?"—hoping this would draw the right response.

"Thieves," piped up Jemima obligingly.

She's the eighteen-year-old housemaid, and a favourite of mine, with a pretty face, lively manner and a disposition to match. She had been fond of Eliza, and the only one I saw shed tears for her. "Shocking, it is," she continued. "It ought not to be allowed," she added virtuously, an eye on Mrs. Davy. The other housemaid, unlike Jemima, looked agog with excitement at this departure from the usual routine. Housemaids have a long, tiring day from six A.M. in the morning right through till ten or so at night, working continuously through the day from blackleading stoves and whitening steps early in the morning, then to dusting, cleaning and cooking the servants' meals right up to late in the evening, and so they appreciate a distraction or two.

I nodded gravely. For some time I have had a shrewd suspicion that Jemima Johnson might be related to Billy and Doll Johnson, the couple who run the Rat Mob, one of the two biggest thieving gangs in the east of London. We'd never spoken of it, but if I was right, it was odd that robbery appeared to have taken place here, as, like birds, thieves don't foul their own nests. That made me suspect this was the work of the Rat Mob's rivals, the Nichol Gang.

"Has Mr. Periwinkle lost a great deal?" I asked sympathetically. I could see Mrs. Davy eyeing my soot bag as though I had only brought it along to stuff it with Periwinkle prized possessions. I couldn't entirely blame her. Chimney sweeps are a decent group by and large and mostly trusted, but there are some bad 'uns amongst us who get us a bad name and so housekeepers tend to dog our footsteps every step of the way while we are about our business.

"Not a thing," Mr. Tomm replied to my surprise.

"None of the china, jewellery, or other valuables are missing," Jemima added with pride, as though she had foiled the thieves single-handed.

"What are the pigmen here for then?" piped up Ned, as I hesitated over asking this delicate question.

"Because *we* was done over ourselves," a footman volunteered.

"Fancy the servants' quarters being burgled," sniffed Mrs. Davy. "I don't know what the world's coming to."

"Very few of us are rich enough to have the luxury of being burgled, Mrs. D," quipped Mr. Tomm. "We should be honoured."

"The butler's pantry was disturbed?" I asked. That was surely the only room this side of the green baize door to offer temptation to burglars. "The key to the cellar, perhaps?" I was very curious now. The servants' quarters at the Gables were comfortable compared with those in most large establishments, but even so, to choose to rob them rather than the Periwinkles set my mind a-thinking.

"No," snapped Mrs. Davy indignantly, "but it's a wonder we wasn't murdered in our beds. Having wrecked the servants' hall, while we were at breakfast they came back and did over Mr. Tomm's pantry and even *my* room."

It was hard to refrain from a smile, as I pictured those thieves hiding in the garden till the servants were safely occupied elsewhere and then running in again for another try at finding their booty.

"Not a lot lost, I hope?" I asked, enjoying the thought of an East End gang making off with a pot of quince jam.

"It was the damage," Mr. Tomm explained heavily. "Especially in the Cottage."

"Where Mr. and Mrs. Hogg used to live?" My ears pricked up at this. I remembered that being a married couple they were allowed to live in this separate small building by the old stables. The former groom used to live there, but nowadays most London families have given up carriages of their own, and hire them from livery stables when needed.

"Clever," Mr. Tomm remarked gloomily. "I always said you were clever, Wasp. That's right. Hasn't been used since The Day It Happened." He emphasised these words very heavily to indicate that the word *murder* was inappropriate for a house such as the Gables.

"The shame of it," Mrs. Davy proclaimed indignantly. "If I'd realised this was the house where that murder took place, I would never have come."

It was my private thought that that's exactly why she had applied to come here. The notoriety of the murder would give her a certain standing in the neighbourhood.

Jemima went pale. "I can't bear to remember it. Eliza was so kind to me."

"A murderess," declared Mrs. Davy. "You should be ashamed of yourself, Jemima. In front of this child too."

Ned was endeavouring to look like an innocent child in need of a pie, but only the last part rang true.

"Anything missing from the Cottage?" I asked yet again. I was beginning to feel very uneasy. If there was something stolen, then the burglary might be less likely to be something to do with the Hoggs themselves.

I thought Mrs. Davy was going to say it was none of my business, but Mr. Tomm replied, "Not that we can see, but they've made a wreck of the place. Furniture ripped to pieces, floorboards up, even bits of that nice flowered wallpaper torn off. Ghouls, that's what they are. Come to take a souvenir of the house where murder took place, just as if we were Margate."

This drew another reproachful look from Mrs. Davy, who obviously did not like her place of employment being compared to a mere seaside holiday town, to which Londoners travelled by railway excursion trains.

There was a silence, this having fixed our minds on Eliza again. Even James looked subdued. "Mr. and Mrs. Periwinkle called us all in for a prayer at the time Eliza . . ." Jemima broke off and then burst out: "It was all that husband's fault."

"You hadn't been here long enough to judge the situation," Mr. Tomm told her reprovingly. "He'd suffered, had George. Fought for his country."

"No reason for him to go bashing his wife about though," Jemima said defiantly.

I decided to say nothing about our china lady, although as Eliza had said her husband was so fond of it, it had to be a possibility that that's what the thieves were looking for. I couldn't believe gangs would be sent out to tool a sailor doll. If I mentioned the lady to the pigmen, though, they'd have the whole Metropolitan Police Force descending on Hairbrine Court quicker than it takes Ned to eat a pork pie. No, far better to look into this myself.

At that moment, to my surprise Sergeant Wiley came in to the servants' hall, blue coat, pot hat and all. I knew him of old and my surprise was because the sergeant is with the River Police, not the Metropolitan who would normally be watching over the Gables, and nor is he one of those detective gentlemen in the Criminal Investigation Department in Scotland Yard, although he'd like to be. He stopped short when he caught sight of me again, and his eyes narrowed—and they're small enough to begin with. Mean is Sergeant Wiley—until you get to understand his ways, that is. I'm partway there, and he with me, so we treat each other with caution. After all, he helped save my life last year, when my poor friend Bessie was murdered, and I am much obliged to him for doing so.

"Wasp," he said, his shoulders heaving, as if a laugh might get out if he didn't take care. "That's if I got the face right under that black." This is Sergeant Wiley's idea of a joke, so I took it as such.

"Most humorous, sergeant," I said cheerily.

Then I saw to my astonishment that Mr. Periwinkle himself was following him into the room; like all gentlemen in his position, he very seldom trespasses in his servants' domain, and nor does his family. Today I could even see Mrs. Periwinkle's crinoline advancing round the edge of the door behind him. As crinolines are often larger than most doorways, they have to bend themselves egg-shaped to pass through, thus preceding their wearers.

I had had the pleasure of meeting Mr. and Mrs. Periwinkle several times on my previous visits to clean chimneys, and seldom have I met such a delightful couple. Mr. Periwinkle is a member of parliament and all I can say that if House of Commons were all filled with gentlemen like him, the country would be a much happier place to live in. They were much alike in their short height, with the same beaming, round faces. Even today they managed a small beam when they saw me.

"My dear Mr.—" began Mr. Periwinkle.

"—Wasp," his wife finished breathlessly for him as usual, her crinoline swaying as if in agreement that that was indeed my name. I had last seen them at the New Year's servants' hall dance, to which Mr. Tomm had kindly invited me at their suggestion. They led the first dance themselves before returning to their own guests in the small ballroom, and were a fine sight twirling like Harlequin and Columbine, only somewhat fatter.

"I've brought Mrs. Hogg's last greetings to you," I told them, "but very sad I am to see you in such turmoil here."

"Ah." Mr. Periwinkle's face sobered. "A tragedy. I attempted to visit Mrs.—"

"—Hogg in Newgate," Mrs. Periwinkle contributed anxiously.

"—but she would not see me. Poor soul, poor—"

"—Eliza," ended his wife sadly.

It might sound as if Mrs. P was constantly interrupting Mr. P but it was not that way. They have a way of finishing each other's sentences as though the two of them share exactly the same thoughts. They bill and coo together like a pair of turtle doves.

"Had Mrs. Hogg not readily confessed her guilt, I should not have believed it possible. Some violent disagreement took place, no doubt." Mr. Periwinkle shook his head in perplexity, as if it were unknown for husbands and wives to fall a-fighting.

"Blood everywhere," the footman supplied, eager to be in on this unusual dialogue between employers and servants, especially with police present. Considering George Hogg died by rat poison, I realised the story must have grown over the months.

Sergeant Wiley cleared his throat. "I 'ad to arrest her," he said awkwardly. "No choice."

"How could you not?" exclaimed Mr. Periwinkle. "I fear George Hogg was not a very nice fellow. A soldier, you know, invalided over two years ago after Lord Elgin's second Chinese expedition. He took part in the storming—"

"—of the Summer Palace in Pekin." Mrs. Periwinkle took over, seating herself on one of the uncomfortable Windsor chairs. Added to Mrs. Periwinkle's full figure, the crinoline ensured that the chair entirely disappeared from the onlookers' sight.

"Of course that was a dreadful and foolish decision," Mr. Periwinkle observed. "My friend Sir Laurence Mallerby, the famous—"

"—traveller—"

"—who was with Lord Elgin on this expedition and talked to George when he visited us," Mr. Periwinkle continued seamlessly. "There is no doubt that the Chinese tortured our captured soldiers abominably, but whether the chosen retribution was wise, I doubt. Sir Laurence took the view that diplomatically speaking it could have been disastrous, and only time will tell. Other steps might have been taken. Imagine if Buckingham Palace were to be burned and looted in retaliation for our execution of Chinese prisoners of war. Of course, it is true—"

"—that we should return to our muttons, Mr. Periwinkle," his wife gently suggested.

"My dear, muttons it shall be," her husband beamed. "Sergeant Wiley, what is to be done about this outrage in our home?"

I listened to Sergeant Wiley beginning his usual speech of the wonders that the Thames River Police could perform in the way of tracking down culprits, and it emerged that the reason he was here was that a couple of Oriental sailormen whom he was after for crimes committed on the river were thought to be involved in this burglary. Something else interested me too. I thought I had seen Jemima's head jerk up at the mention of Sir Laurence Mallerby and wondered why, especially as Sir Laurence had talked to George Hogg. I reasoned, however, that if our little china lady was anything to do with this looting of the Chinese Summer Palace, then Sir Laurence would surely have known about it, and if it was important he would have insisted on taking the figure with him. He wouldn't have allowed George to keep it, even inside a sailor doll. I began to think she was more probably a personal memento perhaps given to Private Hogg by a Chinese judy and naturally he would want to keep that out of Eliza's sight. But if that was the case, what were the thieves looking for in the servants' quarters and the Cottage?

Sergeant Wiley still had his eye on me. "What are you doing here, Wasp?"

"Hoping to clean chimneys," I said innocently.

"We don't . . ." began Mrs. Davy, but Mr. Tomm's eye was on her and she subsided.

"Splendid," said Mr. Periwinkle heartily. "Can't clean them too often at this time of year."

The servants would naturally disagree with this, as it puts their lighting of fires timetable out. Chimneys can't be cleaned with fires in the grate, and the bad old days when a fire in the grate "encouraged" poor climbing boys to go up quicker are over, thanks to Lord Shaftesbury who worked hard to get new laws passed through parliament. But practice always lags behind new laws, and I'm sorry to say that many master sweeps still continue to use boys to climb up the flues. But now there is new hope as Lord Shaftesbury is still persevering. The government has set up an investigation to see how the old law is working and is said to have found thousands of cases where it is being broken.

At Mrs. Periwinkle's urging, I made an arrangement with Mrs. Davy to call on a less busy day, and turned to go—only to find that Ned had gone missing.

"In the garden, I expect," said Jemima quickly, jumping up and following me outside, even though it seemed an unlikely place to find Ned. I couldn't see him in the garden, but as the stables lay beyond it, I guessed where he was. He likes horses. I said nothing because Jemima obviously brought me here for a reason. Even in her morning black dress, she looked a pretty picture, with strands of her brown hair peeping out under her cap. Her usual smile was absent, however, and she still looked upset.

"What is it, Jemima?" I asked kindly. "Do you think you know who carried out this crime? The Rat Mob?" I asked innocently.

She looked shocked. "No, Mr. Wasp—" She went very pale. "It was what Mr. Periwinkle said about Sir Laurence Mallerby."

So I had been right, and this was very interesting. "Yes?" I asked encouragingly.

"My sister works there. He lives at Claremont House, over by Victoria Park."

Victoria Park was called "the lung of London" when the land was turned into public pleasure gardens about twenty years ago. It's Hackney way, and gives a nice open area of green, so we can all breathe a bit more than smoke and grime. There are one or two very grand houses built by it on the western side, so I hazarded a guess that Claremont House was one of them.

"What about your sister, Miss Jemima? Something to do with this burglary, is it?"

She looked genuinely surprised. "Oh no, Mr. Wasp, but there's something odd about the place, so Dinah says. Something going on."

"Any idea what that might be?" I was disappointed that it wasn't related to Eliza, but felt obliged to do my best.

"She didn't say, but—"

I could see Ned coming toward us, but I waited patiently.

"Could you help her, Mr. Wasp? She's scared," Jemima blurted out.

"Of someone there?" Housemaids were easy prey for unscrupulous employers or even other servants. The path from

34

housemaid to workhouse was all too speedy for the unwary, as dalliance leads to babies, which lead to the poor girls being turned from the house with no chance of other employment and with nowhere to go but the workhouse.

"No. It's worse," Jemima said. "She thinks someone might try to kill her."

"Well, Ned," I said, watching him feed Jack later that day when the dark had fallen and we were back home. "I've promised Jemima we'll pay a visit to Claremont House just to see what's going on and help her sister if we can." The way Jemima looked at me, with anxious dark eyes, had made this seem a simple matter, though if I was right about her parents, it might have been a foolish step.

Ned looked doubtful, and I guessed what he was thinking.

"With Doshie and the cart," I added and he brightened up. Victoria Park is a good step from here, three or four miles, and Ned doesn't believe in walking when there's no good reason.

"It's the boots, guvner," he always says.

We buy boots twice a year from Jack Higgins' stall in Rag Fair. Here you can see all the scruffy boots and shoes laid out along the road as if about to walk off if you don't hurry up and buy them. They're cast-offs of course, probably several times over from the state of some of them, and that's why we go twice a year. Last year when we came into our bit of money I was going to buy us both *new* boots, but Ned pointed out this was a waste of money as new boots get worn down and get old, so why not buy old ones to begin with? I pretended to agree with him, but really I know he just likes going to the whelk stall in Rag Fair.

"What did you see in the stables, Ned?" I asked him, reverting to the Gables and hoping to catch him off guard before I cooked us a bit of supper. Ned likes choosing his own time to talk—but that can be never on occasion, and this time I needed to know.

"Nothing, guvner."

"Now tell me the real story."

"Nothing much," he amended.

"Tell me about the much."

"Saw the gardener." Ned fidgeted with the carrots I was about to boil up. "Told me that not long before Mr. Hogg was murdered there was a couple of sailors from out East hanging around here. Chinese, he thought. He found them in the old stables and saw them off. Not a word of English, he said. Bet they had. They're clever, guvner."

"What did he think they were after?" I didn't like the sound of this. These must be the men that Sergeant Wiley was looking for.

"After Mr. Hogg, they were. They came back after he died. Only the pigmen were there because he'd been murdered, so they ran away. And," Ned added, "they had another try, with crowbars."

"Does this gardener friend of yours reckon it was the same men that did the burglary last night?"

"Dunno."

When Ned gets that look on his face, I know that's that. He'd nothing more to say—or wasn't going to. I wasn't sure what his news meant except that I still had an uneasy feeling that the china lady was something more than a present from a Chinese judy. I looked over to where she sat so serene and peaceful at our window. It didn't seem right that such a lovely lady should be fought over, and I hoped now she'd found some peace with us.

Next morning Doshie seemed reluctant to be going Victoria Park way. He prefers routes he knows and this was out of his usual routine. Moreover, it was frosty, and Doshie disapproves of that too. Still, he responded well to the remains of the carrot Ned had brought with him and plodded on. The scene around us changed as we slowly made our way north. Cosmopolitan dockers and sailors gave way to respectable struggling weavers and other tradesmen, and every now and then there was even a glimpse of prosperity on Commercial Road. This was a world away from the Nichol rookery, the docks, the Highway and the two-up two-down crammed lodging tenements I knew so well.

I could now see well-kept small houses lining the streets, and not sure where we were, I stopped a whistling postman, who was out delivering the post in his scarlet coat and shiny pot-hat. Everyone, he told us, knew Claremont House, but he was kind enough to describe where it was. This was on the west side of the park, not far from Old Ford Locks on the Regent's Canal, which runs along the park boundary on this side. When we reached the driveway to Claremont House, we tied Doshie up to a gas standard in the lane, and set off through the gates.

We couldn't see the house at first, for the imposing gateway and trees beyond it still hid it from our sight. Once we'd walked up the drive, clutching our credentials—those being cards stating our services, our brushes and our cleaning machine—to the tradesmen's entrance we realised why everyone knew this place. It was gleaming white, a huge stone building with a rounded dome and several turrets, no doubt from which to fire the cannons to repel any invaders who might take it into their heads to run across the park with bows and arrows. There were more crenellations to be seen than on a real castle and I half expected a moat and drawbridge too, but there was none. Instead, there was a long colonnade of white pillars leading to the front door, with stone walls in between them rising to half the height of the columns. I could also see that on the wall were what looked like shiny tiles with different colours making up pictures. Very nice, but it was unusual in London's grey old city. However, the strangest thing about this house was that it fitted into the landscape quite well.

In fact, like the Gables, it looked a welcoming sort of place, rather like those one-man-bands with instruments sticking out all over. With my professional eye, I looked up at the chimneys, which were not at first visible over the crenellations. Fortunately, as we walked along the side of the house, stepping back, I could see them tucked together, several four-flue chimneys as big as little rooms in themselves. I was relieved, just in case I had to sweep the chimneys here. I once had the misfortune of sweeping the chimneys of another house with a large dome, in which to avoid the ugly (as the owner considered) sight of chimney stacks all the flues fed into a large, tastefully shaped smoke receptacle on top of the dome. This meant I had to drop an iron ball and brush down each flue; Ned was down below hauling ropes up and down to effect the cleaning while I sat aloft, feeling halfway to heaven, doing the dropping. Never again, I vowed, with which Ned was in full agreement.

What worried me here was that if Claremont House was so unusual on the outside, what might it be like inside?

I never did discover that—not then anyway. A footman who looked as if he was about to cry when I enquired for Dinah made way for a familiar face.

"Not you again," Sergeant Wiley snarled. "For your information, Miss Dinah Johnson was found strangled in Victoria Park early this morning. Hop off, Wasp."

CHAPTER THREE

I took the hint and hopped off. I'm not one for giving up on a chimney without taking away its soot, but on this occasion it seemed wise.

"Ned," I said, clambering up on to our cart. "There's times in life when wriggling back down is more sensible than shinning up."

He still looked as if I'd snatched a meat pie out of his hands, and even Doshie looked reproachful, as thought he'd been expecting a nice quiet rest grazing while we worked. The horse looked even more reproachful when Ned jumped up after me and took the reins. I couldn't oblige Doshie today by taking over. I had too much to think about. Here in London's East End death hangs over us all the time like the black fog from the fumes of London chimneys. Babies, children, men and women are deprived of life by disease, starvation, brutality and the general misery of their situations. All the workhouses and charity organisations in the world can't overcome that, while drink and violence offer easier exits than fighting onward with our Lord's help. But for a young woman like Dinah to die at the hands of another has a brutality of its own.

"Are we going to tell Miss Jemima, guvner?" Ned ventured to say.

He looked hopeful, and I knew he had free pies in mind, rather than the grief of a sister. But I couldn't blame him. Death doesn't bother to hide its face from us, and we had not even met Miss Dinah. Ned was too young to grieve for humanity itself. I knew why I was taking this so hard, however. Because I'd been asked to help her, and I hadn't.

I shook my head, knowing the police would do that. "This is a rum one, ain't it?" Ned said, having read my face correctly.

"You've put your finger on it, lad, as usual. Very rum." Was it only by chance that yesterday we had called at a house where there had first been a murder done, then a burglary, and where I'd been asked to prevent another death—only to find I was too late? "Chimneys are all different, Ned," I observed. "This flue of ours could join up with another at any moment. We'll just have to keep climbing up it."

"But we might get stuck," Ned whispered as if to himself, and I saw him shiver. I knew he was thinking back to his early years before I knew him, and the terror of climbing up those dark spaces, so narrow only small children could climb them and then only with difficulty. Some of them are less than nine inches wide, and the boys—and often girls—had to slant it.

I remember from my own days as a climbing boy what that was like. Elbows and legs were no use as support in the narrowest flues; you went up in the angle of the chimney where it was widest, with one hand pressed to your side, and the other hand up above your head pressing and groping onward. Many of the boys got stuck, and some never saw God's light again. Like my friend little Charlie. Lobster we used to call him, for his hands were skinned down to black skeletal claws; he was dead at six years old. I felt my eyes moisten at the memory, even all these years later. Lord Shaftesbury is a truly good man for trying to put an end to this evil. There are still many master sweeps who keep to their wicked old ways, and Ned knows who they are. When he passes them, he clings to me, for all he's about twelve years old. Now Dinah too had been taken before her time.

Never fear, Charlie. Never fear, Jemima. I'll find out who did this thing.

"No, lad, we're not stuck," I said gently. "We just have to find the right flue." There were three of them troubling me now: whether the china lady was connected to the burglary at the Gables; whether the Gables burglary had anything to do with Dinah's death; and who killed Dinah and why. Was her death a separate chimney or another flue branching into ours? The only link so far was that Jemima and Dinah were sisters. So far as I knew, Jemima had nothing to do with Eliza's gift to me, and so I couldn't see how Dinah could have had any connection with the china lady.

Ned had been brooding. "If we sat on top of the chimney, guvner," he suddenly piped up, "and looked down it, we could see if your problems joined up."

"That's our Lord's job," I pointed out. "We have to do it the hard way and work our way up, just hoping He'll throw us a friendly helping hand from time to time."

He must have heard me, because He promptly threw down an interesting thought or two. First, Mr. and Mrs. Periwinkle were friendly with the owner of Claremont House, this Sir Laurence Mallerby, who was in China at the same time as Eliza's husband. Coincidence? Possibly. Second, there was yet another flue to consider, and a most unwelcome one. If I was right, Dinah and Jemima were the daughters of the Rat Mob king and queen, Billy and Doll Johnson. And if the Rat Mob was involved, there were sooty chimneys around—ones I didn't fancy sweeping.

All that day I pondered on this problem. Ned and I had called at the Gables to convey our condolences to Jemima. We didn't see her, but Mrs. Davy said she'd pass them on, as Jemima had been given the day off after the news reached her. I was worried about her, but felt better after I was told that Constable Peters had broken the news to her.

That interested me, as I know Constable Peters, who used to work for Sergeant Wiley. He is a bright lad, and now works in the Detective Department in Scotland Yard. If his department, as well as Sergeant Wiley, was concerned in Dinah's murder I could well be right about very nasty soot lurking in unexpected corners.

"Look," Ned said joyfully, after we had reached our lodgings and lit the oil lamp. "Jack's belly is turning red."

The little bird gave a hopeful tweet at this encouragement, but as it was only January, I doubted whether this was the case. "It's just the light glowing on him," I said.

Ned wouldn't have it. "The lady's smiling at him," he said obstinately as though she was bringing spring nearer all by herself.

I sighed. "Let's get something to eat, Ned. Then maybe we'll all be smiling." I was low spirited, as if I had let Jemima down, even though I knew there was nothing I could have done to prevent the dreadful fate that overtook poor Dinah. Even so, when I caught the china lady's eye she seemed to be looking at me as reproachfully as Doshie.

"What can I do?" I asked her out loud rather crossly. Ned looked surprised, taking this personally.

"Cook a few spuds, Gov," he said. "I'll get the fire going."

It was just as well we moved quickly. Luckily there was enough of yesterday's hodgepodge to heat up—today's variety being potato soup with anything else we could throw in, like the scraps of mutton we bought cheaply in Rag Fair. We had just taken our last mouthful and sipped the last of the beer we get in jugfuls from the alehouse, when there was a thunderous knocking on our door.

Ned's usual reaction to this summons is to hide, assuming

the police have caught up with his latest slip from perfect grace. As I've hinted earlier, Ned is always torn between believing his Sunday school dictates (which point out that our Lord helps those who help themselves) and whether that includes permission to help himself to the occasional tempting wallet or kingsman. So as I hobbled to the door, I wasn't surprised to find myself alone in the room. I expected it to be Big Matthew, one of our neighbours, a coal heaver at the docks, who has appointed himself head of Hairbrine Court and objects to falling over the occasional bag of soot in the yard overnight. Normally we store it in the cellar until we can arrange with the night-soil men to take it away; they sell it to smallholdings to keep insects away from the crops.

It wasn't Matthew.

It was a stranger, and a most unusual one. Of medium years and height, and inclined to portliness, his stove hat and mournful face and formal (if ancient) clothing gave him the status of an official. Not an unpleasant one. There were no jemmies or knives to be seen about his person, and yet he didn't strike me as a missionary. Despite being mournful, he had a look about him that was most human—and that is unusual in Hairbrine Court. This man had pink cheeks and mild kindly eyes, which are not often seen in these parts.

"Mr. Thomas Wasp?" he enquired loftily.

I gave him a courteous bow for this formality. "I am, sir." The mournful face remained unmoved by my ceremony. "You require a sweep?" I added.

"By no means. I require *you*, Mr. Wasp. At once, if you please."

I was confused. Was this someone's butler? "You want me to sweep your master's chimney?"

He was most indignant. "I most certainly do not. I, Mr. Wasp, am Benjamin Chuckwick, Bug Destroyer to Her Majesty Queen Victoria."

I blinked. "Her Majesty wants a sweep?" I knew those chimneys in Buckingham Palace from my own days as a climbing boy. The worst place in London for dead flats, those being our name for horizontal flues, the bane of a sweep's life.

"Her Majesty," Mr. Chuckwick informed me gravely, "does not require a sweep. Regrettably, nor," he added, "does she require any bugs to be destroyed at present. Are you aware, Mr. Wasp, that had my services been called on earlier, the tragedy that beset Her Majesty in the death of her husband, the esteemed Prince Albert, might well have been averted?"

I was impressed, but at a loss to know what such a distinguished gentleman was doing at my humble door so late in the day. He soon told me.

"You are required at a most important meeting, Mr. Wasp."

"With Her Majesty?"

He shook his head. "It is doubtful whether Her Majesty will attend in person, but you may rest assured that she will be keenly interested in the outcome."

The word "but" is one I am wary of, although I decided not to query this. "Is Ned's presence required too?" I sensed that Ned had emerged and was lurking behind me somewhere.

"No such instructions have been issued. Nevertheless, kindly present me to Mr. Ned," Mr. Chuckwick requested.

I hauled Ned out from behind the chair where he had taken refuge, and he was duly inspected from head to toe. Ned returned this favour with a suspicious scowl.

"Mr. Ned," I introduced him. "Meet Mr. Benjamin Chuckwick." Ned has no known surname so Mr. Ned he had to remain.

Bows were exchanged, rather jerkily on Ned's part, although he now seemed as fascinated by our visitor as I was myself.

"Mr. Ned," pronounced Mr. Chuckwick after some contemplation, "may accompany us."

44

"Thank you, sir." Ned appeared overwhelmed with the honour, perhaps because something about Mr. Chuckwick seemed to demand it. We promptly put the guard round the remains of our fire, took our coats and ventured forth in Mr. Chuckwick's august wake for our most important meeting.

To my amazement, a four-wheeler growler awaited us in Blue Anchor Yard, the roadway outside Hairbrine Court. This was indeed doing things in style. Not entirely to my surprise, however, when the cab reached Ratcliffe Highway the cabbie turned left and not right, indicating to me that Buckingham Palace was not to be our destination. To look on the bright side of the matter, however, nor were we about to be thrust into the Tower of London for high treason. Nevertheless, I was somewhat uneasy and rapidly ran my mind over anybody I might have offended. Only Sergeant Wiley came to mind, but he would not have paid for a growler to convey me to his police station in Wapping.

The Highway was not yet at the height of its evening "jollity," although lurching sailors and their bawling women were already spilling over the roadway, their gaudy clothes making a contrast to the gloom beyond the pools of light afforded by the few gas lamps. Behind them were dark shapes emerging like moles from the gin-shops, unlit courts and alleys. Ratcliffe Highway resembles the path to paradise only in one respect: it's unwise to take any side turnings, for there hell reigns supreme.

When the growler passed St. George's Church, my worries as to our destination grew, and to my dismay it stopped outside Paddy's Goose. Not surprisingly the cabbie seemed extremely anxious to get rid of his passengers and be gone. No wonder Her Majesty was unlikely to be present at this meeting. I only wished that Ned and I weren't to be there either. My faith in Mr. Chuckwick was disappearing rapidly.

"I'm not taking Ned in there at this time of night," I told him firmly. Ned knows this den of iniquity well enough by day, since the pub is a regular customer of ours, but I try to make sure he doesn't go there by night.

"Do not be dismayed, Mr. Wasp." Mr. Chuckwick's face, illuminated by a lamp, displayed a beaming smile. "Follow me if you please."

What, I asked myself in trepidation, was a bug destroyer to Her Majesty doing in a place like this—or any purveyor of goods to Her Majesty, come to that? Nevertheless, we had no choice but to follow him into the alley by the side of Paddy's Goose. The word "no" could bring out the entire drinking assembly within the pub to persuade us otherwise.

The alley was unlit save for the dim light coming from the Highway, or from the occasional window on either side. I don't like alleys, and I certainly didn't like this one. Even in daylight, it's usually hard to see more than six inches in front, let alone what you're walking over. It might be supposed that as we chimney sweeps are dirty with ingrained soot all the time, we do not mind walking through the filth and stench of the byways of London, but this is not so. Each person is used to his own dirt and smells; it's only those of others that offend, and there were plenty here.

Fortunately, we had not far to go. A dark shape suddenly loomed up before me, and for a moment I thought a garrotter faced me, but he brushed past me with an oath just as Mr. Chuckwick opened a side door and pushed us through. It was a tumbledown extension to Paddy's Goose that I had never visited in my professional capacity. I had always been told not to bother sweeping the flues in this part of the pub, and consequently as we entered my nostrils immediately sensed sooty smoke.

To my surprise, however, when Mr. Chuckwick showed us with great ceremony into a room leading off the corridor, it looked most homely, with two armchairs drawn up round a cosy fire, and several others dotted around the room. I could hear noise and raucous laughter from the next-door room, but here there were only three people, all of whom were strangers to me. Silence reigned as they examined the two new specimens of mankind who had arrived in their glorious presence.

A shifty, keen-eyed man in shirt and waistcoat, who looked not much taller than me, was seated in an armchair by the fire opposite a tough, sturdily built lady, with her legs thrust out before her, displaying boots and stockings; the huge crinoline she wore was rearing upward as if trying to escape from its wearer. Instead of the mark of gentility such garments are thought to convey, this one had the air of a weapon of war against anyone who crossed her.

Standing by the window in a most menacing way, as if blocking a possible way of escape, was the third member of the group, who could have made a tidy living as a giant at a fair's sideshow. He looked twice as wide as me and half as high again. I looked at the muscles bulging through his shirt, and decided I'd agree to anything that was said to me. When he saw me looking at him, he grinned, but the grin didn't reach his eyes. It suggested he was assessing which of my limbs he'd tear off first.

I was beginning to have a shrewd suspicion of who these people were. Mr. Chuckwick seemed to have vanished, and here was another fellow now guarding the door, who looked like an out of work dustman judging by his apron, fan-tailed hat and expression of general disgust with life.

"Pleased to meet you, Mr. Wasp." The keen-eyed man opened proceedings. "Billy Johnson's the name. And this is my wife, Doll."

I froze, for all I had guessed their identities correctly. Friendly greetings from a bad 'un can strike more fear than a knife held to your throat. Billy looked like a fox begging to be let loose in a chicken run, and his wife hardly the sweetheart from which her nickname had presumably come.

"Pleased to meet you, Mr. Wasp." Doll didn't look at all pleased; her face looked very grim, and no wonder as she was Dinah's mother, poor soul. All the same, I had to bear in mind that grieving parents though they were, they were also leaders of the Rat Mob.

"A great sadness for you today," I said sympathetically.

Billy cleared his throat. "It is, and you'll be right to wonder why we called you today. It's a matter of business, Wasp. Doll and I can grieve alone. You can't help us there. No one can."

"Billy's right," Doll said sternly. "Billy and me have a job to do, and you're going to help."

I didn't like the definite nature of this simple pronouncement, but I liked the look of the Giant even less. Billy saw me glance at him. "That's George," he said pleasantly. "Don't cross him, Mr. Wasp. He don't like that."

I assured them all that crossing anyone was far from my mind. This met with an invitation to sit down, which is a compliment most sweeps never get. Our clothes aren't suitable for most households.

"Who's this?" Billy demanded, looking at Ned.

"My apprentice."

Billy looked Ned over and Ned seemed to get clearance, for he too was allowed to sit. Another compliment since it must have been painfully clear to him that Ned and washing don't agree.

"Your business is to find out who done this thing, see, Wasp?" Billy kindly explained.

"All I've heard is that your daughter was murdered, Mr. Johnson, and a real tragedy that is. I'm most sorry." I've never had children of my own, not living ones that is. My woman and I had two babes that our Lord took back as soon as they saw this sorry world. Maria died many years ago of the cholera, so there'll be no more; but I thought of Ned and how I'd feel if he was taken so cruelly from me, as Dinah had been from these two. Villains or saints feel the same in that respect.

"You told our Jemima you'd help her," Doll took up the story.

"I'll do that, Mrs. Johnson. Pardon me, though, but the story goes that you've a lot of helpers already." The rumpus from the adjoining room grew even louder. "I'm only a sweep. Can't they do more than me?"

"No bleeding way, Wasp," Billy informed me. "Now look you here: we heard about Bessie Barton and how you sorted that business out last year. Just you do the same for Dinah, see?"

"You don't know—" I began, getting alarmed now, and wondering what the penalty for failure might be. Giant George seemed to be pondering that as well, but from a different viewpoint.

"You know pigmen," Billy cut in graphically. "Jemima told us about that. Now that—" tapping his nose thoughtfully "—is a situation I'd normally be most cautious about. But in this case I'd be glad of it. We need to know what's happening. Me and Doll and Mr. Chuckwick and George and them lot"—he waved a hand toward the noise—"we don't talk to pigmen. We ain't got much in common."

I saw his point. The Rat Mob not only ran most of the small crimes round here and many of the larger, but the story was at Paddy's Goose that they were spreading their wings into international matters, which is easy enough so close to the docks. That wasn't to everyone's liking, so I'd heard, particularly to the Nichol Gang.

"I don't do business with sweeps as a rule," Billy growled. "That's my mates' job."

I knew only too well what he meant. We sweeps acquired our bad name with the public because a few act as spies for thieves as they go about their trade. Most of us are honest, but like any line of business there are rotten cabbages amongst us.

I realised Billy needed encouragement to proceed and didn't care to think about what might happen if I didn't provide it. Ned and I had seen too much to walk away. I gulped as I entered a chimney that might never reach the light.

"Feel up to telling me about Dinah?" I asked gently.

Billy grunted that he did. "Know Victoria Park, do you?" When I nodded, he continued, "Know the fountain?" Again I did. It had recently been donated by the philanthropically inclined Baroness Burdett-Coutts.

"Our Dinah was found early this morning lying at its side. Strangled last night."

I had an immediate point to make. "In January?"

"I knew you was a leery cove," Billy said approvingly. "Me and you are going to get on, Wasp. Dinah was walking out with a young German chap, Erich Mayer. Plays in one of those German bands."

These have a poor reputation in our part of London, as they are wrongly thought to harbour villains, and their music to be inferior. Many German people have come to live here since my youth and they live here peaceably enough. As for their music, to my ear they play in a more lively fashion than the English bands.

"It was her evening off," Billy continued, "and she and this Erich went to the Eagle pub by bus. She never came back after the show. The house was locked at eleven o'clock as usual, the servants thinking she was back, but she wasn't."

I've heard of the famous Eagle in the City Road, which is a fine place for young couples. More than a public house, it's like one of these pleasure gardens, where customers can stroll around and watch plays that are a step up from the penny gaff on the Ratcliffe Highway. Of course, this being winter there would have been less temptation to stroll around outside, but no doubt there was entertainment inside instead. I was wondering how to phrase my next question, but there was no need.

"I can see what you're thinking, Tom. That our Dinah lost her head and spent the night with this Erich. Dinah wasn't like that."

"She was a good girl," Doll growled. "And so's Jemima. We brought them up that way."

I let this intriguing statement pass.

"But the police have arrested this Erich," Billy went on doggedly, "reckoning he did it, after he'd persuaded her into the park for a spot of canoodling."

"In January?" I asked again. It wasn't snowy this year, but in the evenings there were bitter frosts enough to chill the warmest ardour, and the fountain was a fair step from Claremont House—and I was sure the park was locked at nights.

"We think alike, Wasp. And our Dinah was smart enough to keep bad 'uns at arms' length."

"If the police are sure this Erich killed her," I asked, very puzzled now, "what might you want my services for?"

"You might well ask, Mr. Wasp. The reason is that Doll and me, we don't think this Erich did it."

This was a facer all right. Normally parents are all too eager to agree with the police once someone is arrested.

"You knew this Erich?" I asked.

"Never set eyes on him," Billy declared.

"Then why don't you think he's the one they're after?"

Billy fiddled with his glass as though wondering what to say next. Ned was sitting upright in his seat, not moving a muscle in case someone's attention was drawn to him and he was sent packing.

Billy looked at Doll for approval before he spoke. "There might be other reasons our Dinah was killed, Wasp. You tell him, Doll."

Doll obliged. "Jemima knew the servants at this Claremont House, through going visiting. Dinah told her one of the footmen, Joseph his name is, tried to take liberties until he found out who her dad was. That stopped that."

"He sent me round," Giant George boomed proudly from his great height.

"Joe took it that amiss, it seemed," Billy explained. "George's friendly words can upset some people. Dinah didn't have any more trouble from Joe, but he was always what you might call lurking. Awaiting his chance."

"Why would he want to kill her though?" I asked reasonably.

Billy scowled. "I'm disappointed in you, Wasp. Obvious, isn't it? She comes home from the Eagle, this Joseph lets her into the house, decides he's in a good position, persuades her to come into the park, it being so near, and when she won't do as he wants he kills her."

"It's possible," I conceded, but far from truthfully. This explanation raised a few questions. "The inclement time of year is still a barrier."

"It is," Billy agreed luckily, "and mind you, Dinah never said it was Joe she was scared of. It's an odd sort of place, that Claremont House. Heard of Sir Laurence Mallerby?"

That name again. I nodded.

"Got an eye for the ladies," Billy continued. "And his son too. And ladies include housemaids."

"Could it be him that Dinah was scared of?" I didn't fancy this idea. Sweeps didn't go up to knights of the realm and ask whether they'd been interfering with the housemaids, familiar situation though it was.

"Dinah never said he was hot for her," Billy said regretfully, "but then she wouldn't tell us if he was. Mark my words, Wasp, there's plenty to strike a light here, so you get yourself moving. Tell your pigmen mates that they've got it wrong. I'll make it worth your while."

Money wasn't my first consideration. Wiley was. I could see his face if I informed him he might have arrested the wrong man. There was no point telling Billy this, as Giant George would rapidly persuade me otherwise. Moreover, I sensed there was something here I wasn't getting, and my guess is it was the full story. Billy and Dutch didn't strike me as being the sort to care whether or not justice was being done to the right person. Did that mean the reason for Dinah's murder was *very* near home? Had Dinah been killed not because of anyone at Claremont House or even by Erich Mayer but because she was Billy and Doll's daughter, and they knew it? In which case the soot was already tumbling down nicely in my mind. Billy and Doll might be worried that Jemima would be the next victim. And they might well be right. This was a sobering thought, for if they were, then I had to prevent it.

I summoned up my courage. "I'll do that. Anyone been threatening you—"

"What the hell and tommy do you mean by that?" Billy roared. Doll echoed him and Giant George tensed ready to pounce on me.

"If Dinah was killed because of who you are," I quickly pointed out, "you would have been warned that she might be killed."

We were still at daggers drawn. "Especially," I added, desperately hoping the Lord was keeping His eye fully open for me, "if Dinah ever did jobs for you." Housemaids in some big houses made extra on their scanty wages by slipping the word about valuables to be found. "Working in a big house it's natural she might have chatted to you about what they had there—"

I came to a sudden end—nearly physically as well as conversationally. Billy and Doll were on their feet, and Giant George was lumbering toward me ready to yank me up by the scruff of my sooty neck and drop me from a high window. The dustman was carefully looking in another direction and Ned was under his chair, trying to look invisible.

"Could you be suggesting," Billy said menacingly, "that our Dinah was a nark?"

"She was an honest girl," Doll said belligerently, "and so's our Jemima."

"And so am I," Giant George roared, obviously liking to be included in whatever was going on.

"Not like the Nichol lot." Mr. Chuckwick's voice came from behind me, but I was too busy watching my front to turn round.

"Of course," I said hastily. "Everyone tells me how honest the Rat Mob is."

"Yeah," Billy growled. "We're honest, and don't you forget it."

Everyone has his own idea of what that word means, and I doubt whether more than a handful of these definitions meets God's standards. But honesty by your own lights is good enough for most folk. I'd seen enough of Billy and Doll to think they really believed what they said.

At last they calmed down and Billy slumped back in his seat. Ned crept back on to his seat again, and Doll pacified her crinoline again, although she still kept suspicious eyes on me. "You seem an honest bloke," she said grudgingly. "We're honest too."

"Yeah," George assured me again.

"Honest." Billy brought this point to an end by banging his fist on the arm of his chair. Then he leaned forward and stared at me as though he would scrape the last bit of soot off my face to be absolutely sure of my own honesty. Finally, we seemed to be in agreement that we were all honest—and it was then that Billy told me the truth.

"Know anything about the Nichol Gang, do you?" he asked

almost in a whisper as though he even dreaded to speak the name.

I did of course, but decided to be diplomatic. "Who?"

Billy licked his lips nervously. "The Nichol lot. Rival gang. They do the big jobs, we do the clever ones. See?"

I saw. I longed to ask who chose which were which but decided on discretion.

"Vicious, they are," Billy continued. "We've lost three to them."

"Jobs?" Ned piped up.

"Dead 'uns, youngster," Billy said matter of factly, and Ned quickly fell silent again. "They work out of Wapping, down by the river there. A cove called Dabeno runs it." Billy was white-faced at the effort of speaking about the dreaded gang.

He was right to be. I knew what the nickname Dabeno meant: the Bad One.

"You think this Nichol Gang might have killed Dinah?" I was liking this less and less. "Why would that be? To get at you? You took jobs they wanted?"

Billy almost blushed. "Might have done. We've picked up one or two odd jobs they might have reckoned upon being theirs. They've got connections, see? Stuff coming in from the coast and run through London up north. Plenty of work for all, so Doll and me think, but the Nichols don't see it the same way. But Dinah's murder ain't about that. You've got it all wrong, Wasp. It's worse." He glanced at Doll.

"Tell him, Billy," she ordered.

"What?" I couldn't imagine anything much worse than pinching jobs from the Nichol Gang.

"We think Dinah might have found out something."

"About a job?" I was getting lost—and nervous.

"No. About who someone is."

I was mystified. "What someone?"

Billy gave a desperate glance around. "Tell him, Billy," Dutch said again.

Even then Billy hesitated. After a moment or two he almost spat it out. "The putter-up."

Dead silence greeted this admission. Even I knew what a putter-up was. The putter-up of the Nichol Gang would be about as evil as you could get. The putter-up of any mob is sometimes the Billy Johnson figure, the visible leader of the gang, but in really big mobs, he remains anonymous and in the background, often independent of the gang and an apparently respectable member of society. In fact, he's the organiser with his own tried and trusted small team, the maker and breaker of deals, the man who sends out death orders, the man who collects the money. He could be working down here in the East, he could be up West, he could be running the Bank of England, or skulking in a Limehouse den. Only his number two would know, and he wouldn't dare speak the name if he had any sense. If Dinah had suspected or had evidence as to who the putter-up of the Nichol Gang was, there was good reason indeed behind her terrible death.

And so, I realised with foreboding, would there be for the death of anyone she might have told. Her sister, her parents, her friends—and *that* might mean the whole mob could be on the list for sudden death too. Including anyone working for them—such as me. The carousing from next door began to sound like the last trump.

"This," I said carefully, "is a nasty little job you're expecting me to do."

Billy was ingratiating now. "We'll support you, Tom old cock. Don't worry about that. Mr. Chuckwick is assigned to look after you. He'll never be far from you. Will you, Mr. Chuckwick?"

On the whole I'd rather have had Giant George to look after

me, and so, assuming Mr. Chuckwick was now back in the room, I turned round to say this would not be necessary. Mr. Chuckwick wasn't there. Only the dustman, lounging by the door.

"Certainly I will," he remarked in Mr. Chuckwick's voice.

"You're not Mr.—" I stopped. The voice was the same and the clothes, save for the apron and hat, but as I looked closer the dustman's face and demeanour seemed to change before my eyes, and there, now clapping his stove hat on to his head, was Mr. Chuckwick.

"My dear sir, pray do not be alarmed. I am indeed Mr. Chuckwick at your service."

"Bug Destroyer to Her Majesty?" Ned piped up bravely.

"Of course. I might also be a costermonger, a bonegrubber, a docker, a foreign prince, who knows?"

With each pronouncement the face changed like India rubber. "Pray do you not let it alarm you," he continued. "I am an impersonator, educated in every fairground of the land, a most useful apprenticeship for my current position."

Now it was Ned's turn. "And you, lad." Billy's eyes fell on him. "I've got just the job for you."

Ned looked terrified as Billy roared, "Young Nipper!"

After a moment, a youth slouched through the door. He must have been with the crowd next door, the rest of the gang, I presumed, but it looked as if he had dropped from the cherub club in the heavens. He was fair-haired, blue-eyed, and the most innocent and upright young lad I have seen for many a long year. Or was he the deadliest? I wasn't sure I took to him, especially the way he looked Ned up and down—and *then* smiled.

"Pleased to have you on my team, sir."

Ned looked most gratified, but I was far from that. When a villain smiles, he's more likely to be seeing a fly-flat (or what he

57

thinks is gullible prey) rather than offering you the hand of friendship. "Temporary assignment only," I said sharply. "Understood?"

Ned needed no encouragement to follow the path of wrongdoing, and although this path he was being told to take was for the best of reasons, I feared the mud might stick as hard as the soot. What's more, I have a nose for soot, and the smell of this case so far told me two things. The first was that for all Billy's and Doll's affability, they didn't become leaders of the Rat Mob for that reason, and second that the way to solve this case did not lie through Sergeant Wiley. It was going to take me to the Metropolitan detective department in Scotland Yard—quickly.

CHAPTER FOUR

It's not often that I set out to call the streets before dawn on a rainy Friday morning in mid-January and find a hansom cab awaiting my pleasure. When Billy Johnson said he'd be making arrangements, I had in mind that he would be passing the word around that no one should garrotte me, but Ned had returned from feeding Doshie in his stable at the Black Lion in a state of great excitement, his eyes as big as harvest moons when he told me what awaited me. I'd told Billy I'd be calling on Constable Peters first, but had expected to be going in our old cart.

"Jump up quick," the cabbie snarled. He was a most unpleasant-looking individual with glaring eyes and sinister whiskers, and perhaps he thought correctly that the less time he spent round here the better in case his horse was pinched from between the shafts.

Jumping is something I can't manage, owing to the bowed legs from my climbing boy days, but Ned pushed me up and off I went. I was sad to leave Ned behind, but this was something I needed to approach alone. It's a fair step to Scotland Yard from here and most grateful I was that Mr. Johnson had made his "arrangements" this way. Then it occurred to me that this might be the Nichol Gang's plan, not Billy Johnson's. Perhaps I was going to meet my doom, but as we clip-clopped past the Tower and I saw all the people scurrying to work, I began to feel safer. Indeed I began to feel like a lord myself in my new elevated position on the cab.

I'd have enjoyed the ride more, however, if it wasn't for the task that lay ahead of me. As it was, when the cab turned into Whitehall Place and across into Scotland Yard itself, and I saw the fine building awaiting me, I felt like that lady in a story I'd read years ago. Cinderella stepped down from her coach in her pretty gown to meet her prince, but it would only take a wave of the fairy godmother's wand for her grandeur to turn to rags and the cab back into a pumpkin. Scotland Yard itself was like that. I remember it when it was just another London rookery courtyard teeming with poverty-stricken people crammed into vermin-ridden lodging houses, without money, food or hope. Now they've vanished without leaving a trace on the world. Progress? Oh yes, but where are *they?*

My cabbie seemed more fitted for a pumpkin than a golden coach. The surly fellow snarled that he had orders to wait for me to return. Well, that was nice of Mr. Johnson, uneasy though I felt at being beholden to him.

The gentleman who met me as I entered the door of the police building in Scotland Yard looked down on me from a great height:

"Round the back for you, sweepie."

"Constable Peters, if you please. The name's Wasp," I said quietly.

It took a while for him to stop laughing and take me seriously, but at last he sent someone to fetch the constable. At first I didn't recognise him, expecting to see him in uniform, as when he was with the River Police, but he appeared in everyday clothes, trousers, coat and waistcoat, as apparently all such detectives do. He was still the bright young lad I remembered though, with nice big ears and rosy cheeks, so working in the Yard can't be too bad a fate for him. After all, they get two extra shillings a week for being a detective, making thirty in all, although that's not a lot these days when even the cheapest tenement rooms take five of them.

He looked pleased to see me, which was gratifying. He then looked anxious to get rid of me, which was natural enough. He also looked surprised, which indicated that he had no prior warning of my visit from Billy Johnson, whose arrangements evidently stopped at hansom cabs—to my relief. Collusion between the Criminal Investigation Department and the Rat Mob would have been highly suspicious.

"It's a matter of murder, Constable," I told him. He looked at me sharply, especially when I went on to say, "At Sir Laurence Mallerby's house. The death of the housemaid."

That did it. He fairly pushed me up the stairs before him. He's a lad after my own heart. It's the smell of the problems that's important, not the smell of the sweep. He took me into a large room where several other young men were sitting at tables. As they didn't need to be detectives to tell I was a sweep, a certain amount of objection was immediately made, and Constable Peters took me into a small room next door, full of files and boxes. It was only cheered up by a grand photograph of what looked like every single pigman in the Detective Department proudly presented in three rows outside the building's entrance.

His eyes were alight with eagerness. "What have you got to tell me about this murder, Mr. Wasp?"

It was more what he could tell me, but I did my best. "I heard you'd arrested the poor girl's sweetheart, Erich Mayer."

"Not us. The Metropolitan uniform police," he said too quickly, and it was my turn to look sharply at him. "And Sergeant Wiley's helping them."

"So you're not involved?" I asked.

"Looks that way," he said carefully.

"You think Mayer's guilty?"

"Sergeant Wiley reckons he wanted his way with the girl, she fought back and he strangled her. From the way she was found with her clothes all torn," he said delicately.

"The body was by the new fountain, wasn't it?"

"It was. Lying by one of those small ponds surrounding it. The lamplighter was doing his round at eight o'clock, and chatting to the lodge keeper as he opened the gates to the park. They fell to talking about the new fountain, and had a bet of a pinch of baccy on the words carved on it. Not being a drinking man, the lamplighter swore they were to do with temperance, and the lodge keeper that they were for God and Country. They strolled in to settle the matter, and found the body. They're not under suspicion. Besides, she'd been dead more than an hour or two when the police got there. Seems straightforward enough anyway."

"No doubts then?" I noted the "seems." I didn't know the park that well, but I knew the Victoria fountain was a fair step from Claremont House. It's not far from the Royal Gate on the north side of the park, where the lodge keeper and lamplighter must have walked from, but Sir Laurence's house is on the western side.

The constable looked undecided whether to speak or not, but then took the plunge. "As the gates were all locked, it took a lot of determination to get in there last night. And what a night!"

I nodded, pleased we still thought alike. The fiercest of passions would be quenched by locked gates and January chill. It was still cold this morning, and to me it felt as if snow was on the way.

"The butler at Claremont House locked up, thinking the girl was safely back, but she wasn't," Constable Peters continued.

"How did the police know who she was?"

"Lamplighter recognised her."

This was possible, I supposed. Housemaids do get known that way. They have trips to post-boxes, errands to shops and so forth, and he might have seen her then, as in winter the lamp-lighters have to carry out their job earlier in the afternoon. In the mornings when he passes to extinguish the lights, the maids are often out whitening the steps, so that was another time when he might have passed a word or two with her.

"To my way of thinking, constable, it's an odd place to go if she was frightened of her young man. She doesn't seem to have been scared of Mayer." (I hoped he wouldn't ask me how I knew.) "But she does seem to have been uneasy about one of the footmen, Joseph, who was pestering her. He seems more likely than Eric Mayer, and she told her sister she was scared for her life."

"Did she?" He eyed me carefully, waiting for me to say more.

I obliged. "Her sister Miss Jemima works at the Gables near St. George's. A burglary took place there the day before yester-day."

The constable shifted uneasily in his seat. "What's your inter-est in this, Mr. Wasp?"

"I was at the Gables to give them Eliza Hogg's last respects, she having worked there as you'll recall. Miss Jemima told me about Dinah being scared, and it seemed only right I should follow it up. So I called at Claremont House and found out the girl had been murdered the night before. What's so interesting to me, Constable Peters, is why *you're* interested."

"It's murder," he said awkwardly, his cheeks an even rosier pink.

"But you're still interested even though Sergeant Wiley seems certain who's to blame, and would be only too pleased to settle the case without you."

A pause, then: "Yes." I said nothing, and then it all came in a rush. "You've heard of our sergeant here, Mr. Wasp. Sergeant Williamson?"

I had. He was said to be a genius at this new art of detection, sorting out all the little points of a problem and putting them into a pattern.

"A real gentleman he is," continued Constable Peters in awe. "You should listen to him. He don't look much and he don't speak much, but what he says—phew! And he's really interested in this murder. Well, not the murder so much as it's pretty clear who did it, but, as he says, there are angles of interest because of who she worked for." He swelled up with pride as though he alone were privy to the great man's thoughts.

"Sir Laurence Mallerby," I said, to show I knew my stuff.

Constable Peters looked taken aback. "No secret about it, I suppose," he muttered. "Sir Laurence has friends in high places. He's a friend of the Prince of Wales himself. He was in his party to visit Venice and Trieste last year, so the Sergeant said. He's on calling terms at Sandringham, and approved by Her Majesty herself. When Sergeant Wiley found out where this housemaid lived, Sir Laurence must have notified the Prince of Wales because His Royal Highness has asked to be kept informed."

"Over a clear-cut case of the murder of a housemaid?"

This set me thinking. It was rumoured that the Prince of Wales, who was shortly to be married, had an eye for a pretty girl, whether a housemaid or duchess. Constable Peters must have been thinking the same way because he blurted out: "Nothing like that, Mr. Wasp. It's just a friendly gesture to make sure all's well. Sir Laurence is an important gentleman, and he's sent for us himself, to talk about Erich Mayer."

This made me think even harder. The constable seemed anxious to ignore the idea that Sir Laurence might have had more interest in Dinah than her merely bringing up his hot water of a morning, although I knew it must have occurred to him too. Was that because the detectives here thought it might be true, or because they knew it wasn't?

He caught my eye. "It might not be a bad idea, Mr. Wasp,"

he said brightly, "if you were to clean the chimneys at Claremont House. You never know."

I agreed. My suspicions were confirmed. Sergeant Wiley had been afraid Sir Laurence might be involved. I had had every intention of sweeping those chimneys one way or another, but it would be easier with the constable's help. "Would that be the chimneys in the main house or the servants' domain?" I asked blandly.

He looked disconcerted. "Both," he said bravely, looking overcome at his own decisiveness. "I'll fix it for you."

How, I wondered, but decided not to enquire too far. "And the burglary at the Gables?" I added almost as an afterthought.

"Nothing stolen," he said hurriedly. Then even he seemed to realise that this displayed a knowledge of events beyond the Detective Department's remit, for he blushed and looked away.

"What about the housemaid there being Dinah's sister?"

I didn't need to spell that one out, and he replied straightaway. "If Erich Mayer's guilty, there's nothing for her to be scared of."

I thought I detected a slight emphasis on the word *if*. "Where's he being held?"

"Newgate." He avoided my eye again.

I nodded. Newgate has reception cells for those awaiting trial in the Old Bailey next door to it—and being there rather than in one of the other houses of detention, such as Clerkenwell, indicates guilt—in the police's mind anyway.

"Can I talk to him?"

The constable went bright red. "I'll see what I can do," he said weakly, which indicated that wasn't likely to be very much. It wouldn't be easy for him to explain to the awe-inspiring Sergeant Williamson that a sweep was doing part of his job for him, albeit unofficially.

Tom "Cinderella" Wasp returned to his pumpkin carriage

aglow and it still looked a golden coach to me. It seemed as if my job for Billy was nicely on its way. I was driven back to Hairbrine Court to where I hoped Ned was still waiting for me, and the cabbie pulled up with a flourish. I descended with his help and looked up to thank him despite his churlishness. He wasn't a cabbie, of course. It was Mr. Chuckwick, who thought his masquerade a fine joke.

The butler at Claremont House when I called early the next day took his duties even more seriously than Mr. Tomm at the Gables. Mr. Longfellow, as I discovered his name to be, did not earn his name through his height, which was only medium, but his face was the longest and gravest I had seen since Prince Albert's funeral. I began to wonder if he could be Mr. Chuckwick too, as I had seen no sign of my guardian that morning. Apparently not, for Mr. Longfellow knew this house well. As I thanked him for agreeing to employ me, he told me I had been recommended by a Mr. and Mrs. Periwinkle to Sir Lawrence. He then looked at me grimly.

"It's not what I'm used to. I like to choose my own sweeps. Nor," he added even more severely, "am I accustomed to murder taking place a mere two months after my arrival. It's been a great shock."

I'd had time to do some thinking about this case. Although the swells, being Sir Laurence and Sergeant Williamson, had some interest in it, it seemed to me that only the heaving ants' nest below their level was going to produce results in finding out who murdered Dinah. Even if the swells were involved in her death, the way to the truth was to mend the sewers of life, not to glide over the top. There would be no use my going to Sir Laurence and asking, sweep to swell, "Were you involved in Dinah's death?" If he had been giving the poor girl a hard time, then I would only find the answer through her family and her fellow servants. On the other hand, if this Erich murdered her, one of them might know something about it, whereas Sir Laurence would not.

Anyway, Billy and Doll didn't think he was guilty, and I wasn't being employed by them for my contacts with Her Majesty. It was my job to empty the soot bag, not take tea at the fireside with the swells.

Mr. Longfellow led me to the servants' hall where breakfast was in progress. Ned and I were promptly escorted to a corner where our sooty smells would not offend so greatly. I've seen many servants' halls in my time, and looking at the people seated there at the long table I could pick out who did what here. That was the housekeeper all right, Mrs. Poole I'd been told. In black silk with her keys dangling from her waist, she was the guardian of the tea chest and precious spices and more or less everything else that the butler didn't claim. Mr. Longfellow's keys gave him command over the silver, and the wine cellar.

Most housekeepers are well-sized ladies, but Mrs. Poole was not. She was an angular, sharp-looking woman, and I guessed that the *Mrs.* was the usual courtesy title. I needed to be on her right side or I'd get the order of the sack before I began my sweeping. I'd set Ned on that task. He has a fine line with housekeepers, almost rivalling Mr. Chuckwick in his swift change of face whilst pursuing his free pies. He has a range of expressions from starving orphan to handy boy to have about the place.

The young girl at Mrs. Poole's side was in black, which indicated she was another housemaid. She still looked shocked, and was taking no part in the conversation. One of the two footmen in livery must be Joseph, who had a lech for Dinah, and I decided he must be the bigger one of the two, since his sullen and drawn face looked as if he was suffering, whereas the other one was a sallow youth who looked scared out of his wits. A rounded lady was so contented-looking that she put herself into the cook's role. The young lad must be the odd-job boy, and a lady with wispy hair, whom I recognised as Miss Twinkle, a lady's maid who looked familiar.

Mr. Longfellow wasn't the sort to dominate the room by grand gestures, and yet all eyes were on him.

"Sir Laurence has recommended this new sweep, Mrs. Poole."

The barriers went up. This was a point of honour to be fought over. "The fires are lit," she snapped at me. "Come back tomorrow."

"They ain't lit, Mrs. Poole," the housemaid said nervously. I had picked up that her name was Mary. "I only done the morning room and kitchen and bedrooms because Sir Laurence said not to do the others."

From the look on her face, I thought Mrs. Poole intended to challenge Sir Laurence's right to interfere with her decision—and she did. "Understandable, Mary, but they must be lit *now*. The sweep will be coming back tomorrow."

"A *ramoneur* at such a time as this? Impossible," cried Miss Twinkle. It came out as a shrill squeak rather than a tinkle. I knew this word to be what Frenchmen call a chimney sweep, but she was no French lady for all she'd like to be thought so, judging by her aloof, sour expression.

"I'm not one of these ramon people," I answered her genially. "I'm just a sweep, not as grand as a lady's maid such as yourself."

"A lady's maid? I am a travelling seamstress, much sought after in all the best houses," she snapped.

That reminded me where I'd seen her before, and that gave me my opportunity. "Including the Gables, miss?"

"Correct. Lady Mallerby was kind enough to recommend me to Mrs. Periwinkle."

"That's where the murder took place," Joseph said suddenly. "Eliza Hogg."

"It was," I said immediately, relieved now the subject was out in the open. "She was a good friend to Ned and me. You must all know Miss Jemima who was Miss Dinah's sister and housemaid at the Gables, and their parents too, no doubt. I'm most sorry to hear of Miss Johnson's death."

A general silence suddenly fell and anxious looks were exchanged. Miss Twinkle observed that the death was very sad, but young girls today often put themselves in positions of danger. Joseph agreed with her, Mary did not, and Miss Twinkle took exception to this. Then authority intervened.

"If Sir Laurence requested the chimneys to be swept today," Mr. Longfellow said, "he must have had good reason. He can probably smell soot and fears a fire in the chimney."

There was reluctant acceptance of this, but to me this didn't have the air of a servants' hall at peace with itself. One look at Joseph's sullen face told me that. It was the kind of face I was accustomed to seeing early in the morning on the Ratcliffe Highway from those who had been indulging too late into the night. There was something in this room that needed further investigation on my part, but this would not be possible, as everyone was now unexpectedly eager for me to sweep chimneys.

I was looking forward now to seeing whether the interior of the house was as unusual as its exterior, and set off with great curiosity, escorted by Mary, who was shy and tearful—as well as anxious that I didn't make off with anything I shouldn't.

"This murder has been a shock to you all, I can see that," I said.

"He did it, Mr. Sweep. That awful Prussian man." Mary began to cry in earnest.

"Do you know him, Miss Mary?" I asked gently.

"He came to the tradesmen's door sometimes. He wasn't

supposed to, and we didn't like him much, even though he was handsome. Full of himself he is. So's Joe but not as bad as him."

"Joseph is the footman?"

"Yes. Joseph Belt. He's ever so upset. You should have seen him yesterday when the news came. He couldn't even shave properly and he looked as if he'd never smile again. He was proper sweet on Dinah, you see, but she turned her nose up at him as soon as that Erich came along. We're not supposed to have followers," she added belatedly.

"Especially in the same household, eh?" I wondered if this rule was very strictly applied in Claremont House, with the master of the house seeing all his female staff as his own private prey. I told myself I must stop thinking that way. I hadn't even met Sir Laurence yet, and my suspicions could well be unfounded.

"It's difficult," Mary said shyly. "Our half-days don't agree, you see. Lady Mallerby doesn't mind. Mr. Longfellow does though. He's new here and I wish we had old Bents back again," she volunteered in a rush. "He was the old butler and ever so nice. But Mr. Longfellow ain't that bad," she added hastily. "A stickler, though."

"What about Sir Laurence? A good master, is he?"

She stared at me, rather pink. "Oh yes. He's . . ." She came to a halt over her enthusiasm for Sir Laurence, and instead quickly added, "Lady Mallerby's nice though. And Miss Jane. And Mr. Alfred—that's the young master, but he's not here often and . . ." She went on talking as I put the tuggy cloth over the dining room fireplace. The odd-job boy, whose name I discovered was Charlie, was busily following us, putting sheets over the furniture. As well as listening to them both I was wondering what Mr. Longfellow had to complain about. This room was like one of those gentlemen's clubs in St. James's—I once swept the chimneys at one—all formal chairs and portraits of old gentlemen glaring down at you like sentinels to ensure you don't put a speck of soot wrong.

"What was Dinah like?" I asked chattily, while doing my job with the machine.

This floored her for a moment. "She was older than me. She knew what was what."

"In the ways of the world or in the ways of men?"

"She was merry," Mary unexpectedly replied.

I was still confused. "In what way?"

"Very sure of herself. She laughed a lot. Even Mrs. Poole giggled at her jokes. Dinah could get away with anything."

Except her life when she met her murderer. "Was she pretty?"

Mary considered this. "No," she admitted, as though this was running Dinah down. "But she had one of them faces, if you know what I mean."

I did. I daresay Mr. Marc Antony would have said the same about Queen Cleopatra and King Charles when confessing to his liking for Miss Nell Gwynne. It could be that possession of such a face was why poor Dinah was lying dead in a mortuary at this very moment. Erich Mayer could well be guilty, but I never like to clean a chimney too quickly The best brush in the world can miss an important patch of soot, and a patch of soot can set a chimney on fire.

Was one patch of soot Joseph? Was another Sir Laurence or his son? Or could it be Erich or someone else she'd met? Perhaps Dinah was a dollymop on the side, unknown to her parents, one of the lassies who give a good time in return for receiving one in the form of a dance or other frolic. I couldn't see Billy and Dutch standing for that, unless of course Dinah had been a nose for them, as I'd suggested. But that meant Jemima might be too and that I could never believe.

Ned came running back from having checked from outside

that the brush had reached the chimney top. We collected the soot bag and tuggy cloth and walked upstairs with Mary to the next flues. The painted doors looked normal enough and so I was unprepared for what happened when Mary opened the first door.

Here was I, Tom Wasp, in the middle of the desert. I have never been there myself, but I had no doubt of what it was from pictures and from what I had read and been told. It was very *yellow*. Yellow carpet, yellow walls, with strange plants painted on them, and real such plants dotted around the floor. The rest of the room was given to a huge white tent, like they have at fairs, and the ceiling was painted blue. Inside the white tent were a few cushions, but nothing else, no seats. I enquired doubtfully where the chimney might be. Mary giggled, seeing my expression, and led me behind the tent to the flue, which was white-tiled, not black-leaded as usual. I half expected the soot to be white or yellow too, but it wasn't. Black as ever. Behind me, Ned seemed flummoxed over where to put the covering cloths but the odd-job boy was in no doubt. Over the tent.

"A nursery, is it?" I ventured.

Mary shook her head. "No, Mr. Sweep. Mr. Alfred and Miss Jane are grown up now. It's a drawing room."

I could say nothing, but I thought that Ned and I did better with our withdrawing room at Hairbrine Court; we could at least afford chairs of a sort.

Mary watched nervously until I had collected the last speck of soot from the white grate, and I hoped the next grates would be decently black, as white grates worry me.

Luckily they were, but the rooms themselves were like a visit to a peepshow of the world. Only a few steps away from the desert was Italy. Italy appeared to be full of water, indicating Venice I presumed, which I'd heard was full of canals. Here these were troughs sunk into the floor to hold water. There was even a miniature boat on one, but I stepped over it without comment.

All in all, by the time I had swept the chimneys of Africa, India and China I was thoroughly bewildered. And bewitched, I must confess. Especially by China. I had thought the jewel-studded draped room for India dominated by pictures of a building called the Taj Mahal and a stuffed tiger in the corner was interesting enough, but China outdid them all. Even Ned stopped his chatter, as we gazed at small temples, mountains and flowers, painted on the walls with charming Oriental ladies standing on little bridges. It made me think of our china lady back in Hairbrine Court. She had probably come from the land of China, and would be at home here. It looked a peaceful place.

"What's Lady Mallerby think of this?" I asked Mary curiously. She must be a very patient lady, unless all this was her idea.

"Oh, she thinks it's very nice," came the unhelpful reply. Mary might have enlightened me further, but instead, having taken me back to the first floor, she said awkwardly, "the master says I can leave you here. He wants to see you but no need to do the chimney."

I was most gratified to hear this sign of trust, and having dispatched Ned outside to await the appearance of the last chimney brush, I wondered what might lie within this closed door. Was it a dungeon? Was there a snake-pit inside ready to catch unwary sweeps? Or would it just be an empty room?

It was none of these. As I went in, I saw the chimney—plain, black. But that was the only thing that was plain. All around me the walls were a mass of colour painted with exotic flowers and lovely maidens—at least I presumed they were maidens, since there were no gentlemen painted next to them to tempt them.

They were holding out baskets of fruit, and guarding them was an array of peacocks, with tails spread in courtship ritual. I've seen peacocks in Jamrach's Menagerie on Ratcliffe Highway, but they were poor specimens compared with their painted cousins here.

"I call it the Peacock Throne Room," chuckled a deep voice to my left.

I swivelled round to look at the silken-draped throne raised on three steps running most of the length of the side wall and decorated with more peacocks and jewels.

"Prester John," said the throne's occupier, clad in white with white headdress. "Sitting here gets me thinking. Ever heard of Prester John, Tom Wasp, master sweep?"

I had, for I had been well taught at the Ragged School, thanks to my patron, Lady Beazer. "He never existed," I said.

"Good man," crowed Sir Laurence—for it must have been him. "But the fellow who invented him pulled the wool over everyone's eyes, didn't he?"

"He did, sir." So far as I recalled it had had taken several hundred years before scholars, travellers, priests and kings of Europe had come to the conclusion that their potential powerful ally in the East, with his magical powers and his jewels, had never existed. It had all been a joke dreamed up by a lonely monk.

Sir Laurence ruminated. "That poor girl's death. Appalling, Wasp, appalling. Come and sit down."

As I have said before, this is an invitation not often extended to sweeps, especially when it is to share a peacock throne swathed in delicate silk.

"Soot, sir," I explained. "I'll sit at your feet, if I might."

He laughed. "I like you, Wasp. Now, poor Dinah. Sergeant Peters tells me you know her sister."

"I do, sir."

"She works at the Gables, the home of my friend Mr. Periwinkle."

"Yes, sir."

"Where George Hogg was murdered by his wife. You know that, do you?"

"I do, sir. I knew Eliza." I was sitting so I could see his face, and I saw his eyes gleaming under that white headdress.

"Did you know George? Like him?"

Where was this leading? I decided to take care. "No, sir. An excellent soldier, I'm sure. Did you know him?"

His eyes narrowed. "Talked to him once, but that's all. I was out in China with Lord Elgin's first mission a few years back. Bombardment of Canton. Bad business. Elgin thought so. I thought so. Know Eliza well, did you?" This last remark was shot at me out of the blue, perhaps to take me off my guard—although why he should wish to do so, I could not even begin to guess.

This was leading us well away from Dinah, but nevertheless could give me the opportunity I needed, and I decided to go further. Even if Sir Laurence in his private capacity was given to pursuing housemaids, he could surely be trusted in his public role. Furthermore, he knew about China. "She gave me a ticket for a pawnshop."

"What for? A bottle of gin?" He was jesting, but he seemed interested.

"A doll that belonged to her husband, but inside was a statue that reminds me of your China room here."

"What's it like?"

I described it to him as best I could. His interest came over as very casual, but I had a feeling it was far from that. "I've taken a fancy to it, sir, but if it's valuable I thought I should tell someone . . ."

I stumbled on, wondering what Ned would say if Sir Laurence demanded I handed it over to the authorities. To my relief, he laughed. "No, Tom—if I might call you that. It does sound Chinese but there's a lot of stuff produced there that's made cheaply for soldiers and visitors. I think I know the model you mean. You keep it, if you like it. Thousands of them around. Hold on to it, though. You never know, it might be worth a bob or two in years to come."

I was greatly relieved. Being an expert in China, Sir Laurence would quickly have demanded its surrender if the little statue was of value. Now I had a question though. "Why did you agree to my coming here, sir? It's not as if I knew Dinah."

"The police arrested Mayer far too quickly, in my opinion," he said easily. "I'd like to be sure they're right. I agreed with Sergeant Williamson that there are things you can do that neither the police nor I could do as well. Do you follow?"

I did. This was also confirmation that the name Wasp had reached the great Sergeant Williamson. "Some tongues might be loosened to me that wouldn't be to you."

"Correct, Tom." Sir Laurence beamed, but his face clouded again. "I've requested that you become our regular sweep for a while. You'll be paid well and fed well, and that should give you time to loosen tongues. And I'll recommend your services to any household you feel you need to know better."

My mind grappled with the thought of Her Majesty summoning me to clean her chimneys, but this was unlikely with the prince being set on his wedding in March and Her Majesty far too busy arranging it as mothers always do.

Then I grappled with another thought. If Sir Laurence was encouraging me to investigate Dinah's death, he was unlikely to have had anything to do with it. Then I remembered he was a diplomat and therefore a clever man. Perhaps that was just what he wanted me to think. Perhaps what he didn't want me to think was that Dinah's murder was anything other than a domestic tragedy between a girl and her follower. And yet it had been he who mentioned the Gables.

While I waited for Mrs. Poole, who was grudgingly seeking the money to pay me my shilling (double rates as Sir Laurence had apparently requested), I chatted to Joseph Belt. I did most of the chatting, for Joseph for all his good looks was still looking haggard and sullen. He was a big, burly young man, however, quite capable of overcoming a young woman if he chose to. He eyed me suspiciously when I offered my condolences over Dinah.

"I loved her," he hurled at me, as if I had claimed otherwise.

So might Mr. Shakespeare's Othello have said of Desdemona, I thought, and so I believed him. "Girls are flighty," I sympathised. "They will go off with these foreign fellows and then find out their mistake."

"That Prussian's a skunk," he said. "The sooner Jack Ketch gets him the better. She should have listened to me."

I was not so sure. Dinah seemed to have been a bright, lively girl, and Joseph hardly looked a match for her in that respect. Furthermore, Erich Mayer was some way off from meeting the hangman yet, and I'd like to be sure he deserved it before I agreed with Joe.

"Do you know Dinah's family?" I asked.

"No," was all he said to that, and cast me a nervous look, daring me to question it.

There was no point my doing so. If he did, he wasn't going to tell me the truth. From his drawn looks, he seemed to be truly grieving—but that didn't mean he hadn't killed Dinah in a fit of jealousy. I needed to find out more about Claremont House and its servants. The servants' hall was not a happy one, and I had to find out why.

Mrs. Poole appeared at that moment, and Joseph took one look and made a speedy departure. She had come to present me with my money and also to tell me that Constable Peters was waiting for me by the tradesmen's entrance. I found him eager to talk to me. "That Newgate suggestion of yours, Mr. Wasp. The sergeant thinks that might be a good idea."

I was very pleased, though I needed to clear up one point. "Sergeant Wiley or Sergeant Williamson?" I asked carefully. It made a big difference. Williamson was an honour, Wiley could be up to something.

"Williamson. He thinks Mayer might let slip something to you that he might not say to a policeman. He wants to know everything Mayer says. Do you see, Mr. Wasp?"

I wasn't sure I did, but it seemed an easy request to fulfil. All I had to ponder as Ned and I set off home in the cart was when to start cleaning this particular chimney. It had been a strange day so far, and I didn't much like the smell of it.

"Guvner," said Ned, as we turned onto the Highway, "there's a hansom been following us all the way from Vic Park."

"Don't you worry, Ned. That will be Mr. Chuckwick."

"No," said Ned seriously. "He's in the growler following the hansom."

CHAPTER FIVE

The porter eyed me with great suspicion when he saw me waiting on the Newgate prison steps on Monday morning. He had the advantage of being able to see all of me, whereas all I could see of him was his imposing boots and official-looking trousers and jacket, because the door is of an even lower height than I am. What with the spikes on its top and having to bend the head to enter, visitors are not made to feel welcome at Newgate.

This time he hesitated so long about letting me in that he must have thought I was eager to take up residence there. He couldn't turn me away, however, as I was clutching an order sent over to me by one of Sergeant Wiley's constables. He had looked most annoyed at having to visit the likes of someone who lived in Hairbrine Court, not normally an address that any constable would go near. Remembering what had happened on the Saturday evening when we returned from Claremont House, I had looked around for any sign of anyone following me as I set out, but on this occasion noticed no one.

"Harry!" roared the porter once I was through the outer door, still reluctant to let a sweep into his lodge, and a warder reluctantly appeared through the heavy inner door with much unbolting of bolts and clanking of keys and padlocks. "Here's that sweep again," the porter said, somewhat unnecessarily, as my face announces my profession. I was minded of that eccentric noble lord, who wishing to be without strangers in his first-class railway train carriage, paid for a first-class ticket for his sweep to accompany him as a means of driving any intruders away.

Harry proved to be the same warder as had been allotted to me when I visited Eliza, but now I had an official permit. Yet another iron bolted door faced us before we were in the prison itself; then I was locked into the gloomy narrow passages, which the recent renovations to the cells had done little to cheer. I expected to be led to the male cells but after a hurried consultation with another gentleman, who appeared frock-coated and heavily moustached through another door, I was taken off to what they call the solicitors' rooms. Here those held in reception cells awaiting their trials can meet their solicitors in relative privacy. Even Mr. Chuckwick wouldn't be able to follow me here.

I was seated in solitary grandeur at a table in a room enclosed with glass panelling through which I was grimly supervised on the outside by no less than three warders. I tried to feel as though I were indeed a solicitor, not a chimney sweep, but I felt more like a prisoner myself. Thankfully after a few minutes, a young man was led in and pushed into the seat opposite me. This must be Erich Mayer, I thought, and I looked at him carefully as Harry left us. He hadn't disappeared, however, because he joined the other three outside, and I could see his stalwart figure, truncheon at the ready, through the glass.

Poor lad. Erich Mayer looked too dazed even to wonder why he was being interviewed by a chimney sweep. From the look of him, he was still in the clothes in which he was arrested, and he looked so scared he put me in mind of a starling deprived of light and freedom, his feathers all scruffy and unkempt. Then I remembered Dinah, and that if he were guilty I should have no sympathy for him. He might well have killed the girl, as Sergeant Wiley was no fool, and I have enough respect for him to know he wouldn't arrest a man just so that he could claim a case was solved.

"Any solicitor been to see you?" I asked cheerily, busy summing Erich up. He was on the tall side, and could have been called handsome if it wasn't for his sallow face and lank hair. Even his small moustache seemed to droop in despair. There was a shifty look to him though, which might have been suspicious or it might have been a sign of a cunning streak, so I decided to go easy at first.

"Yes, but he think I am guilty also. You all do."

"Are you?"

He looked at me angrily. "What does that matter? They will hang me anyway."

"There are some who think you innocent," I told him, but he took no notice. "I'm here to know your side of the story."

"Why?" he asked suspiciously.

I could see I'd have to woo him, so I ignored his question. "Tell me about yourself, Erich."

He looked doubtful at this suggestion, and I began to wonder whether I was the right person for Billy's job. "Where do you come from?" I continued helpfully, trying to draw him out. I thought he was not going to answer me, but finally he said:

"From Prussia." He still looked sullen.

I knew Prussia was the biggest kingdom of Germanic states. Our Princess Royal had married Prussia's Crown Prince, Frederick William, and would someday be queen. So why was Erich hesitant about where he lived?

"You played in a band, didn't you?"

"*Ja.* I play the clarinet. I come to England last year because it is a good place to play music."

"Alone?" I asked.

"With the band. We are seven. Three play clarinet, two play French horns, my friend Carl play the trombone and one play a saxhorn. We play good music."

"And Miss Dinah liked your band?"

"Yes," he said defiantly. "We play in the Chinese pagoda in the park, like the English Royal Marines."

"Very nice too." I'd seen this Chinese pagoda by the lake in Victoria Park. It had once been part of a Chinese exhibition in London years ago, where in my youth I'd seen it at the entrance.

"I saw this beautiful Mädchen listening," Erich said. "I saw her dark hair under a little bonnet. So afterwards I talk to her." I saw tears in his eyes, and they looked genuine to me. But perhaps it was the thought of the gallows made him weep. "*Ach, mein Hertz, meine Röslein.* How could you think I kill her? In the band we play dancing music, but my heart dance for Dinah."

I like a nice band to cheer me up, and I like to hear a nice ballad sung in the streets, but I know these German bands are not highly thought of here. They're cheaper than the English ones, and so naturally the English bands pass the word round that they are villains. Was Erich one, though? Seeing him here, the picture of despair, it was hard to believe.

"Dinah and I walk out together," Erich stumbled on. "On her evening off once a month, and sometimes in the afternoons I saw her."

I wondered how she managed this. Housemaids' lives were not easy, and the rules were strict. Still, Dinah was Billy Johnson's daughter, and she would find a way if she liked Erich enough.

"We go to the Eagle by omnibus in the Mile End Road," he continued, "Dinah wanted to see the play. It was cold, so it was not in the garden."

As I had thought, even the Eagle's dark nooks and crannies would not encourage much loving in January, although they say that love keeps you warm. For a moment I felt my eyes moisten as I thought of my woman, dead these twelve years. No use doing that, Tom, I told myself. That's the Lord's job now. He's keeping her safe till I get there. I tried to get back to Erich Mayer and *his* girl, remembering there was only his word as to where they went that night.

"What play was it?"

Erich burst into tears. "It told of murder. *Maria Marten and the Red Barn*. Dinah make a joke," he sobbed. "She said you wouldn't do that to me, would you, Erich?"

"Maria was Corder's fancy lady, going to have a child," I said casually. "That like it was with Dinah?"

His head shot up, no tears now. "I wanted to marry Dinah."

"Did Dinah want to marry you, though?"

A hesitation again. "Perhaps it would be possible if . . ."

"If what, lad?"

"If I met her father and mother," he finished quickly.

"You know who they are?"

He did not meet my eye. *"Nein."* He banged his fist on the table in anger and two of the warders rushed in waving their truncheons. They were going to drag him out, but I said not to. After a bit of persuasion they left again and resumed their positions, glaring at us through the glass panelling.

Try as I might I couldn't budge Erich on this point and so instead I went back to the fatal night. "Dinah must be in by eleven of the clock," he told me. "We rode back by omnibus and were there by half past ten."

"Omnibus all the way?" I asked, remembering the narrow road by Claremont House and the open land near it.

He fidgeted. "To the corner of the park. Then we walk to the house by the canal side."

"And where do you live?"

"On Commercial Road, with my friend Carl Weber and the rest of the band. But it is the custom in my country to escort a young lady to the door," he explained stiffly, as his home was some way from Claremont House.

"Did you see her right to the door? Or just to the gates?"

"I took her to the tradesmen's door, as you call it."

"Did you see her go in?"

"No. She tell me to go after I kiss her. She watch while I walk away because at the gate I can turn round and see her. She said next time I must meet her parents," he said miserably. "They would call on me, she told me. But I see her no more after that wave."

"There are a lot of bushes in that garden. Did you see anyone else there?"

"No." He looked even more miserable.

"Any reason she would want to go to the park with anyone else?"

For the first time he looked at me with a sneer. "Why would she wish to, Herr Sweep? She was my girl. If she went with another, it was against her will."

This did not sound a good story to me—although that, I thought, was its strength. Erich would have thought of a much better one if he was guilty. But there was something he wasn't telling me, I was sure of that, and I didn't like that sudden sneer of his. And yet he seemed sincere that he loved the girl. Then I recalled that in Mr. Dickens's great work, Bill Sykes loved Nancy—once.

"You're scared of something, aren't you, Erich?" I said. "You tell me if that's so, because I might be able to help you." If he was scared of the Rat Mob—and who wouldn't be?—then I could risk reassuring him that Billy and Doll believed him innocent. When he said nothing, I added, "I'm told Dinah was scared too."

Still nothing, though he was trembling now. "It must look a dark world out there to you, Erich," I continued. "But no one can reach you in here, can they? You've got your life to forfeit, if the trial goes wrong for you. If you're innocent I might be able to save you. So whatever it is you're scared of, now's the time to tell me."

"*Nein, nein,*" Erich shouted with terrified eyes, and all the warders tensed, ready to rush in again. "You do not understand, Mr. Sweep. You understand *nothing.* I trust no one. Not you, not solicitors, no one. I do not know from where this darkness comes."

So it was the terror that strikes by night, as the Bible says, that scared him. Yet what terror could be worse than being in the reception cells awaiting trial for murder?

"Was Dinah scared of you, Erich?" I asked him, hoping to catch him unawares. "Did you try to make her do what she didn't want to that night?"

"Never." In his agitation, he rose up from his chair and the warders prepared themselves again. "I kiss her. I kiss her very much. More will wait till we were married, I say to her." He sank back, to my relief.

"So who was she scared of? Someone in the house where she worked?"

"I do not know that. She was not so happy working there, she told me."

"Did she mention a footman who was troubling her?"

"I think yes. He come outside and threaten me once. Tell me to keep away."

If Joseph was jealous of Erich, I reasoned, he might have argued with Dinah when she came through the tradesmen's door. There were unlikely to be any other servants around at that time, except for the butler perhaps. "Or could it have been Sir Laurence himself or his son worrying Dinah?" I thought to ask Erich.

"I do not *know.* But it was not me who killed her." A fist banged again, and this time the warders were inside quick than soot falling down a chimney. He was led away, throwing over his shoulder, "She say when we marry, she very glad to leave that house."

As I was being escorted out, I was looking forward to breathing the fresh air again. This dark place was like another world. I say fresh air, although London's air is hardly that. Only when you get to Victoria Park can you catch a smell of it. Elsewhere there's smoke and dirt in the air, fog and the stinks of the river. Our government said it was going to do something about that, when the stink of sewage in the Thames stopped Parliament working one fine day a few years back. They're working on the problem now, but the smells haven't improved. The plan is to get the sewage running underground in pipes and not thrown into the river by the night-soil men as at present. One day perhaps pipes might even reach the east of London.

As for the sewage of everyday life, I prefer to see my enemy bold and clear, rather than have him driven underground. That's what I didn't like about Dinah's death. I couldn't see my enemy yet. There was something going on at Claremont House and somehow Dinah got in the way; the most obvious reason for it was Joseph Belt. So far, so good, but how did the Gables burglary fit in with this?

Ned said he would be waiting for me outside the Tower of London, where our next appointment was for today—with our brushes, that is, all set to clean a chimney or two. The snow had been brief and now we were back to rain and gales. I don't mind the rain, for it does its best to make our old town cleaner, but the gales whipped through my clothes and spirits.

As I walked round the high grey stone walls of the Tower, I thought of all that had gone on there and the executions that had taken place in times past. No wonder ghosts are said to walk there, Mistress Anne Boleyn's most of all. All around me were people going about their daily business on this cold January day, dockers, fisherwomen, costermongers, sellers of baked potatoes, pie sellers—all trying to scrape a living somehow or other. Ghosts of the past don't trouble them—or the many people who live inside the Tower precincts. It made me sad to think of those poor dead people who'd been executed there, most of whom died for what they thought was right, and now few of us even think of them. It made Dinah's death seem all the sadder and I vowed I would do right by her.

Ned was waiting for me, as promised. He had his "don't ask me what I've been doing" expression on and I knew better than to question him. If it was something he was ashamed of it would come out sooner or later. If it wasn't, then I didn't need to know. Instead, I told him about Erich Mayer and that although I hadn't taken to him, I thought he was innocent of Dinah's death.

"You never know about people, guvner." Ned often tries to help by pointing out when I might be going astray, but I thought he had something else in mind this time.

"Don't I?" I said, turning him round to face me.

"No," he said defiantly. "They're not what they seem."

I could see something might be coming, so I went on unpacking the brushes from the cart and waited.

"If I was well in with Young Nipper, would that help you?" he asked.

I realised what was on his mind. He was a new recruit on Nipper's team, and didn't much like what he saw. My guess is that Nipper's deft hands extended to more than dipping for the occasional kingsman and probably to much more than Billy knew about. Ned wanted to know how far he should go.

"Put it this way, Ned. Would you murder someone in order to find out who murdered someone else?"

He looked startled, as well he might. "No, guvner."

"Or if we lost something we cared about, like the china lady for instance, you wouldn't break into a house and pinch someone else's statue instead?"

"No," he said a little less certainly.

"It comes to the same thing," I said gently. "You don't solve one evil deed by doing another."

"But—"

"Nipper won't harm you if you say no to anything, Ned. Not while we're on this case for Billy, anyway. You can still work with him like Billy told you, but only on this case. Do you like Nipper?"

"Yes, guvner."

"Trust him?"

"No, guvner."

"So you just say no to his little extra jobs."

Ned went red under the black grime. "Next time."

I fixed him with a look, and sure enough a nice fat wallet suddenly landed at my feet. I sighed. "Looks as if I'd better return this to Constable Peters, eh?"

Ned nodded vigorously, still looking shamefaced. "I've already eaten the pies I pinched."

Not having noticed anything untoward outside the Tower or even at Newgate, I half expected Mr. Chuckwick, not to mention our other anonymous pursuer, to appear down a chimney in the Tower, but neither of them did. There had been plenty of people around, including soldiers from the barracks, and I had eyed each Beefeater standing there with his red costume, ruff and pike, in case one of them winked at me and changed into Mr. Chuckwick. None of them did, although one seemed about to arrest me, and so I had hurried to our appointment in the Martin Tower, where I'd been summoned to clean the chimneys. That's where up until recently they kept the Crown Jewels, and so perhaps they thought I was about to steal them. I'd had an unfortunate episode with a ghost here once, but today all that appeared was soot.

The Tower was a gloomy place in January, and the quicker Jack the linnet could get his red breast the happier I would be. Our duties finished, there was one other call to be made—a sad one, however. It seemed to me that Jemima might well hold the key to this mystery of her sister's death, even if she wasn't aware of it. She would know what Dinah was worried about even more than her parents, and now that Dinah was dead, she wouldn't hold back as she might have done earlier, especially as her parents were supporting me.

As Doshie plodded along toward the Gables, I began to feel more certain of my way forward. I didn't even care who was following me. They wouldn't want me or Ned and anyway, what would they learn from me? They would gain nothing but a few dull waits at houses while I swept chimneys.

"There's a hansom following us, guvner," Ned shouted.

I felt this was unlikely to be Mr. Chuckwick, who would not repeat his tricks. I supposed he might be disguised as one of the watercress girls at the streetside or a hot chestnut seller. Maybe he was disguised as the Lascar seaman stumbling along the road beside us.

As we reached St. George's, we turned left for the Gables, and instantly felt ourselves in a more salubrious area. No Lascar seaman was trailing after us, or even a hansom cab. We were on our own—but strangely I almost missed Mr. Chuckwick's comforting company.

Once we were inside the Gables, however, and I had received Mr. Tomm's permission to talk to Jemima, I forgot all about Mr. Chuckwick in my concern for her. She was a wan figure, for all that as it was now afternoon she was wearing her print dress, rather than the sombre black of her morning uniform.

Mr. Tomm had kindly loaned us Pug's Parlour to talk in—that being the common name for the butler's room—and her face broke into a little smile when she saw me. Then the day seemed a little brighter to me.

"I had the pleasure of meeting your father and mother," I began cautiously. "I'm of your father's way of thinking—that Erich Mayer didn't kill her because of a lovers' tiff. If the matter was a personal one," I add delicately, "then it was probably someone at Claremont House itself. Your parents mentioned one of the footmen, Joseph. He or someone else could have tried to molest her, killed her accidentally when she resisted and then panicked."

"That's possible, I suppose." Jemima did not seem convinced.

"Anything else come to mind?" I asked.

She shook her head so vigorously that the mob cap nearly flew off her curls. This was a mite too quick a response, I thought. "On the other hand," I added casually, "if it wasn't personal, it could have been the Nichol Gang's work."

Jemima went very pale. "I know Pa thinks so, but I'm not sure."

"Why's that then?" I asked gently.

Jemima is an intelligent girl as well as a pretty one, and she understood as clearly as I did that the Nichol Gang could have wanted to take revenge on Billy through Dinah. Billy had protectors guarding him, but his daughters did not.

"They'd need a reason," she answered firmly. "They'd be after something. Something important."

"Billy thinks it could be a warning to him not to move into Nichol territory."

Jemima still was not convinced. "Murdering—" she stumbled on the word "—my sister would be a declaration of war."

"And you don't think there's cause for that?"

"I don't know, Mr. Wasp. I don't really."

I looked into her clear brown eyes, and I believed her. The last point to clear—and the biggest—now came. "Do you think Dinah found out who the Nichols' putter-up is? That's your father's real fear."

She looked very scared now. "I don't know, Mr. Wasp. She didn't tell me, if so."

The danger was, I knew, that the putter-up couldn't be sure of that, but I didn't want to frighten Jemima. Or myself, come to that. The more I was seen to be involved, the greater the risk to me too—a fact that would not have escaped Billy either.

"So where do we go from here, Jemima?" I asked. "In the left flue we have footman Joseph or someone else who killed her because she loved Erich and not him. In the right hand flue there's the Nichol Gang who might want to scare off the Rat Mob. And in the central flue we have a gentleman we'll just have to call the putter-up, who would go to any lengths to protect his identity. Agreed?"

"Yes, Mr. Wasp," she half gasped.

"So which flue do I clear first?"

She took a deep breath. "Not just you, Mr. Wasp. I'm going to help all I can."

My heart lifted, but I had to warn her. "It's a risky job. Not one for you of all people, being her sister."

"Especially for me," she said firmly.

She would not take no for an answer, and so I had another helper. Jemima, Mr. Chuckwick, a chimney sweep and a twelve-year-old boy. It didn't sound a lot to fight the forces of evil, but I daresay David felt the same when he set out with a sling and a stone or two to fight Goliath.

"It's her funeral tomorrow," Jemima said.

"I'll be there to pay my respects," I assured her.

"*They'll* be there."

"Your parents?"

"Yes, but I meant the Nichols."

That seemed strange, as well as sending a few more shivers up my spine. "How do you know that?"

"It's a mark of respect. All the gangs send a representative to a funeral—unless they were involved in the death. So if there's someone there tomorrow, it means the Nichol gang wasn't responsible."

That was a principle I wouldn't want to test too far, but it was a nice thought. "Who will it be?"

"We don't know. They don't identify themselves."

Now this was a contradiction. If they didn't identify themselves, how would one know whether they were there or not? I decided not to press the point, however, and bidding her goodbye until the morrow, I went to detach Ned from his source of pies in the kitchen. I nearly bumped into another sweep leaving the house at the same time. I stood back, and politely tipped my hat to him.

As he sauntered away down the driveway, Ned peered after him while I was seeing to Doshie. "That was Mr. Chuckwick," he said matter of factly.

And so, I realised, it was.

Which turned out to be a pity. Mr. Chuckwick should have remained as guardian of our Hairbrine Court lodgings, not followed us to the Gables. After we had stabled Doshie and reached home, Ned raced up the stairs ahead of me. I heard him give a howl of distress and hobbled up the remaining steps as quickly as I could to see what was wrong. As soon as I walked in it was all too clear. Someone had been here. Our possessions, such as they were, were thrown all over the place, our boots, our clothes, our papers, even yesterday's ashes emptied out on the floor.

Worse, the china lady was missing from her usual place, and

Ned was standing there, silent and white as a sheet.

Someone had wrung Jack's neck.

CHAPTER SIX

After that first great cry, Ned didn't say a word. I made him sit down, took off his working boots, put on his other pair of shoes and told him we'd go out for a pie later to make him feel better. Of course I didn't believe that would help, and nor did he. There are some things that even pies can't cure, and this was one of them. He sat there without a word while I cleared up our rooms as best I could. He didn't even say anything when I picked up the sailor doll that had been knocked off its chair and found to my pleasure that the china lady was inside. Ned must have put her there for safety because of our being followed home that day. But he couldn't have kept Jack safe that way.

I said nothing, but put the lady back in her place before the window. I saw Ned turn his head away. He didn't need to speak, as I knew what he was thinking. The lady couldn't protect Jack, so what was the good of her?

Even to me the lady looked commonplace that evening. There was nothing special about her anymore. I puzzled as to why that should be, and then it came to me. I'd lost faith in her for not protecting Jack, and so had Ned. Then I thought harder. It couldn't just be that. It was more as if I'd lost faith in our Lord because He had let this happen to Ned.

Ned didn't take his eyes off me, as I wrapped Jack's poor little body up in our best tuggy cloth, and put him in a cardboard box. "We'll bury him tomorrow, Ned," I told him. I had in mind taking him to St. George's in Borough High Street,

Southwark, where my wife and lost babies lie. The churchyard had been closed for burials these last ten years or so, so no one would mind a little bird being buried by the hedge.

A slight nod was all I got in return from Ned. Heavy of heart, I lit the fire, hoping it would help, but it didn't. Telling him to keep it stoked up, I went out to buy us some supper. The Black Lion where we stable Doshie makes a nice toad-in-the-hole, and I thought Ned might appreciate it as a treat. It's not far to the pub, but it feels like it, for there's only one gas light here and either side of it lie long stretches of darkness through which shadows move like ghosts until they rear up at you.

Coming out of the pub, clutching my toad-in-the-hole in one hand and a jug of beer in the other, I bumped into a clergyman, judging by his neck cloth drawn twice around his neck and his subdued clothing. He raised his hat to me.

"Good evening, my son."

I was about to return this gracious greeting, when I realised the voice was familiar and his grave features could be rearranged to resemble those of Mr. Chuckwick. I was thankful to see him and told him our troubles, seeing that they had most likely been caused by my involvement in the Rat Mob's affairs. He listened most gravely and asked if he might accompany me home.

Most of the mess was tidied up now, but enough was left for him to see what had happened. Ned was still sitting where I'd left him, stiff and silent.

"The Rats would not have done this," Mr. Chuckwick declared most firmly. "Why would we?"

"Then who killed my Jack?" Ned suddenly bawled out, making us both jump.

Mr. Chuckwick turned to him and gave a deep bow. "I shall endeavour to discover that, Mr. Ned."

"The Nichol Gang?" I said savagely. It was all I could think of. They killed Dinah and wanted to warn me off from looking into the matter.

He looked shocked, as though even to mention this name was a breach of etiquette. "Did they pinch anything?"

"Not that I can see."

I saw his eyes fall on the china lady, but without much apparent interest. Since she was out on the table, he would obviously assume the robbers had ignored her. I was going to mention that, but something stopped me. Could it be, despite what Sir Laurence had told me about her value, that it was the china lady the robbers had come looking for?

Mr. Chuckwick cleared his throat. "There's more to this than meets the eye," he declared grandly. "Pray leave it to me, Mr. Wasp. It is a most puzzling matter."

So far Mr. Chuckwick's protection had achieved nothing, and when he left, I felt more alone than I had since my woman died. I tried to get Ned to eat something, but he wouldn't. He had that closed look on his face that I remembered from when he first came to me five years ago. It had taken a year or more to get rid of it then, but now it was back in a matter of an hour or so.

Next morning, I got up early and went to St. George's to bury Jack. This church lies just beyond the old Marshalsea prison, long since closed, although its high wall still forms the boundary with one side of the churchyard. It always moved me to come here, and after a few moments asking our Lord to pass on a message to Maria and my babes, I went over to the side and dug a little hole for Jack. I vowed I'd find out who carried out this unnecessary and cruel act.

When I returned, Ned asked not a word about where I'd been. He knew all too well. I'd already put on my funeral trousers and jacket, they being my Sunday best, but I found him still in his working clothes.

"Aren't you coming to Dinah's funeral, Ned?" I asked.

"No."

This was serious, but I knew that when Ned had made up his mind he meant it. I'd be going to the funeral by myself. I couldn't understand the lad, as it wasn't Dinah's fault that Jack had met such a sad end. At least Ned took a bite of bread with me, but I still set off to fetch Doshie alone. Did I say alone? Of course I wasn't. I had only reached Blue Anchor Yard when a cart pulled up beside me, driven by an organ-grinder, judging by the equipment he had with him and the monkey on his shoulder. I was about to climb into the cart, assuming this unpleasant-looking individual was Mr. Chuckwick, when the handle of a stout walking stick applied round my upper arm drew me sharply back. Turning round, I saw Mr. Chuckwick's face peering indignantly out of the same ecclesiastical garb he had worn yesterday.

He rushed me down the street, where he had a hansom waiting. I glanced behind to see if the monkey was after me, but both organ grinder and cart had disappeared.

"Oh my," he exclaimed worriedly. "I do seem to be failing you—and failing my own standards of achievement too. That organ grinder was Jimmy Hayes, a most unsuitable person for you to associate with. Known for his accomplishments with the garrotte. I wonder who he's working for." Then an abrupt switch of topic. "How is Mr. Ned this morning?"

"No better. He has his own plans for today."

"That is not good," Mr. Chuckwick said thoughtfully, and I fully agreed with him.

"There's no telling him. He has to find his own way out of this."

"It's more what he might find his way *into* that worries me." Mr. Chuckwick echoed my own sentiments exactly. "I have boys of my own," he confided.

I had never thought that there might be little Chuckwicks dependent on my Mr. Chuckwick. "Is there a Mrs. Chuckwick, might I ask?"

"There is." He beamed. "Dorinda is the light of my life, Mr. Wasp, I assure you."

He looked so happy at the mention of Mrs. Chuckwick, I felt envious, wondering whether I was doing my best by Ned on my own, or if I should be looking for another woman myself. Knowing Ned, I rather thought the answer was no, but then Ned isn't full grown yet, and doesn't realise how long the nights are when one is alone. I am blessed in having Ned and so my duty is to look after him—wherever he is. And this morning I feared for him.

St. John's churchyard is a place of peace, despite its position in the midst of Wapping sailortown. I had sat at the back of the church while the service took place, but to my mind God was waiting out here to welcome Dinah to this quiet place with the yew trees around and the comforting green grass. I listened to the parson telling us we would one day be dust, and I thought of when I should be dead. Soot to soot and ashes to ashes. This cheered me up because God will make no distinction between sooty and clean, as colour will have disappeared by the time I reach the gates of Heaven.

Unfortunately, that made me think of little Jack and of how he'd never got his red breast again, and all the other unhappy things in this world. Sometimes I can understand them, but with Jack, I couldn't. I decided instead to think of Dinah and of what I still might be able to do for her—and of how pleased Jemima would be if I did.

There was quite a crowd around her grave. I could see Billy and Doll standing with Jemima and the parson with all his gang pressing around him. To my surprise I could see Sir Laurence

with his family—or so I presumed—at his side. There too were
Mr. Longfellow and Mrs. Poole, and even the sourpuss Miss
Twinkle had come. I noticed her in particular because at her
side was not only Mary, but Joseph Belt. No livery for him
today but a black coat, which with his broad shoulders made
him look like a sinister black crow set down amidst sparrows. I
shouldn't judge though. Not here, not today.

I wasn't the only shabbily dressed person here. Far from it.
Working men and women in heavy shawls shivered in the cool
air, side by side with men in top hats and ladies in fashionable
bonnets and crinolines. Many funerals are men only, but it
seemed right that Miss Dinah should be attended by her own
sex too.

There was no sign of Constable Peters, but I was interested
to see Sergeant Wiley here—and a gentleman standing beside
him with a heavy beard and whiskers. I wondered if he was the
famous Sergeant Williamson of Scotland Yard's detective department. He certainly had something of the pigman about him.
That's not being disrespectful but in the same way as I'm
unmistakably a sweep, here in the East a pigman is just as
recognisable.

Somewhere here too might be the Nichol Gang representative, perhaps even the great Dabeno himself. I looked for
someone on his own—but would he be alone, I wondered? After
all, to be on one's own, as I was, would set him apart, and draw
attention to him, which he wouldn't want. So he might have
brought a companion, man or woman. To my relief, I couldn't
see Jimmy Hayes, but nor could I see any other familiar face.
Dressed in funeral black it's hard to tell one from another.
Black unifies us all in death whether we be sweep or swell. I
picked out one man, who might be the Nichol representative.
His face was hard and he sported splendid Newgate Knocker
sideburns. That thought made me think of Eliza again, the bit-

terness of her life with George. I tried to think instead of Mr. and Mrs. Periwinkle, and their happy, smiling faces, who brought joy into life, not anger and violence.

I apologised to our Lord for deflecting my thoughts from this solemn ceremony, which looked as if it were now at an end, with the last handful of dust being scattered on the coffin before it was buried. But Dinah wouldn't be out of mind—not mine anyway. I thought of poor Erich in his cell and knew I had to hurry if I was to discover if he was innocent or not before his trial in March. But how was I to set about it?

"Morning, Wasp." Billy Johnson had walked up to me, looking as respectable in his black as the clergyman himself—I took a quick look to be sure the clergyman here really was a clergyman and not Mr. Chuckwick. "Chuckwick told me about your misfortune. Nothing to do with us. You've got to believe that. Who was it, do you think?"

I'd like to know that myself. "What about this Nichol Gang?" I asked firmly.

"What would they be wanting?" he snapped at me, but I noticed he was waiting for an answer.

"To frighten me off from finding Dinah's killer for you." I was not going to mention the china lady to Billy, and in any case how would either he or the Nichol Gang know I had it?

"How would they know about *you?*" He moved toward me in a menacing way, though I could not understand why.

"I'm being followed," I said, "and not only by Mr. Chuckwick."

He considered this for a moment. "Nah. The Nichol lot wouldn't have warned you first. Nor would the—" He had to force himself to say the word and then it came out in a rush and a whisper "—putter-up. They'd both have knifed you."

That was a consolation, I suppose. I gulped and said bravely:

"I'll begin with the Nichol Gang. Where can I find them in Wapping?"

He went very pale, as though I'd asked him to arrange an audience with Her Majesty, and looked nervously around before he spoke. "Don't know. They move around." He put his face very close to mine, then thought better of it, as he confided, "They're here somewhere."

"Where—which one?"

"Could be that bloke," he said hoarsely. He nodded toward the pigman I'd picked out as Sergeant Williamson. "Or the gravedigger."

"How do I find out?"

"If," he said, not looking at me straight in the eye, "they want to, they'll find *you.*"

I did not find this comforting and was glad to be distracted by less daunting people. The Claremont House group seemed to be making their way toward me. First, Sir Laurence himself, who introduced his wife, a very nice lady who didn't seem to think it at all strange to be introduced to their new sweep. Then came Miss Jane, an elegant young lady of about seventeen who *did* think it strange. Then Mr. Alfred, who thought it outrageous to meet a sweep socially and turned his back.

"Mr. Wasp is a connoisseur of Chinese artefacts, my dear," explained Sir Laurence to his wife. "He has acquired an attractive little piece of porcelain. Do you still possess it, Mr. Wasp?"

I take care what I confide in whom, but decided it would do no harm to have it in the open. The burglary at my lodgings could not have been set up by Sir Laurence. The only object of interest to him would have been the china lady, and he had had every chance of obtaining her from me when I first told him about it. And yet who else knew I had it?

"I do, Sir Laurence," I said most innocently, "though someone kindly searched my rooms last night. It couldn't have been for the china statue for no one knew she was there. She was well hidden anyway. Something was taken from us though. My Ned's little bird was deliberately killed."

He looked perturbed. "I'm most sorry to hear that. An act of callousness. Of course, although your statue is a mere trinket, a casual thief might think otherwise."

"Oh, they won't come again now," I said more confidently than I felt. "The word is out that there's only soot around in my rooms." All the same, I was thinking hard as to where I might hide it so that any other thieves wouldn't come across it. It made me realise that my loss of faith in the china lady had only been temporary. I felt most strongly about her again.

"All the same, I'll get Williamson to put a guard on your place."

I was not sure I liked this idea. A policeman could do more harm than good, and I preferred to rely on Mr. Chuckwick. But I could hardly tell Sir Laurence this.

Once Sir Laurence had paved the way, his servants felt able to lower themselves to speak to me as well, and once the Mallerby family had moved away, they too came to speak to me. I felt much honoured at everyone suddenly wanting my company.

"You seem to be everywhere, Mr. Wasp," Miss Twinkle trilled disapprovingly.

"Friend of the Johnson family," I said easily. "Remember?"

Miss Twinkle obviously did for she gave another humph of disapproval.

"Sweeps are usually at weddings," Mary said brightly, "so it's nice to see you, Mr. Wasp."

"I'll come to yours, Miss Mary," I said gallantly, "and that won't be far off, I'll be bound." My mind was on Joseph, however, who without his haggard look was a good-looking man, albeit still surly.

"You still asking questions about that Erich Mayer?" he growled.

"I am," I said gravely. "He could be innocent."

"And he could more likely be guilty," Joseph snorted.

"What do you propose to do about it?" Mr. Longfellow enquired, giving me a superior smile. "Tell the police they're wrong?"

"In my younger days," Miss Twinkle informed me, "sweeps kept to their own station in life."

I retorted smartly, "Like you travelling ladies in a way. We've much in common."

This seemed to silence her, for she stared at me in disdain at this thought, and said no more.

Joseph did. "You think you know everything that's going on, do you?" he demanded. "That's why you're the new sweep, ain't it? You've been sent to report on us."

"Why?" I asked, thinking quickly. "What's to report on?"

I was aware that the Johnson party were coming up behind me, and so was Joseph, for he just said, "You mind what you're doing, sweep. Or that filthy neck of yours could be meeting a nasty end."

Miss Twinkle looked shocked, Mrs. Poole looked as if she'd faint, and Mary gave a small squeak. Mr. Longfellow then exerted his authority to move them away. I could see the Rat Mob moving off too, but Jemima ran over to me, seeing I was left alone. Her sweet face was sad under her spoon bonnet but she managed a smile.

"You'll come to Paddy's Goose, won't you, Mr. Wasp, in Dinah's memory? Pa and Ma would be most upset if you didn't," she added, which indicated that might be understating the case. I agreed I would, and Jemima ran back to join her parents.

Before I left the churchyard, however, I thought I had picked out who the Nichol Gang representative was. There was a man standing by the gateway looking most villainous despite his funeral garb, and since only he and I were left, it seemed a reasonable guess on my part. So the only question was should I wait to be murdered or offer myself for the honour? I decided to tackle this chimney straight up and walked over to him. He looked surprised to be accosted by a chimney sweep.

"What yer want?" he asked.

"Friend of Miss Dinah's, were you?"

"What's it to you?"

"I'd like a word with your boss." I felt much braver now.

"Best come down the station then."

"Station?" I asked, somewhat bewildered.

"Ask for Sergeant Wiley."

I'd make a mistake. Fancy me not being able to tell a pigman from a bad 'un. "I'll do that," I said hastily, but instead set off for Paddy's Goose.

As I said, the churchyard is a haven of peace in the centre of Wapping, and I felt a tremor of fear about leaving it. It's not that far to Paddy's Goose from St. John's, but today it seemed a long way. It was foolish to think myself alone in the midst of the noise and dirt and filth of Wapping, but with all the noise from the docks, the cries of streetsellers, the shouting of drunkards and the milling crowds in the streets and alleys it seemed so. I had even managed to shake off Mr. Chuckwick, wherever he might be. The sound of my boots over the cobbles seemed like the long march to hell. Who was going to notice if Tom Wasp were suddenly whisked off these streets and disappeared forever? No one.

It was the middle of the day and yet as I turned into New Gavel Lane, I felt more fear than I felt on the Ratcliffe Highway itself in the darkness. Foreign faces peered at me suspiciously, and I fancied each one had his heart set on robbing my home or alternatively on murdering me. I told myself I was foolish, that no one in their right mind attacked a sweep. We are well known for having no money. What could anyone want from me? My china lady? No one knew about it, except Sir Laurence, and he was no threat here. My job for Billy? For that I had the Rat Mob to protect me—so why was I alone?

I told myself that Mr. Chuckwick must be somewhere here, and that probably he was disguised as a dockworker, but I could not convince myself. We climb our own chimneys in life and mostly climb them alone, and here I was climbing mine. I looked behind me as I passed between East Dock and the Shadwell Basin, but the group of sailormen behind me seemed to have no other thought on their minds than which gin-shop to visit first.

At last I saw that Shadwell High Street was near, and never had I thought I would welcome the sight so much. I turned into it—then heard footsteps pattering behind me. A glance round revealed a bunch of Lascars and I decided to quicken my step as I crossed the street. The next thing I knew was an arm round my throat, my hands were being wrenched back behind my back, and I was being dragged between my assailants, then half pushed, half thrown into a cart of some kind. Strong hands kept me lying on the floor and when I managed to look up, I could see evil faces glaring down at me. I could not even tell in which direction we were going, back toward the docks or further down the High Street toward Cock Hill.

When the cart stopped, I was hauled to my feet and pulled down to the ground. I saw no fields or green grass, only the decayed houses of men and women who have reached the end of despair. Limehouse perhaps? Or were we back in Wapping? The smell of ships and tar was strong. Groups of men watched us but made no attempt to stop my attackers or rescue me— why should they?—as I was hurled through a gate, across a tiny forecourt covered in bird's muck and human rubbish and into a doorway of what had once been a prosperous mansion. Now it appeared to be a rats' paradise. Or rather, I suspected, a Nichol one. Dabeno had indeed come to find me.

I was pushed into a room, my captors piling in beside him. I realised I was on Red Lion Street, one of the roughest places in dockland. Dominating the room was a giant of a man, even bigger than Giant George and even less friendly, from the look on his face. That was one I wasn't going to forget in a hurry; it was a pugilist's face, from the look of it. Could this be Dabeno himself? I could well believe it and if so, I didn't give much for my chances of winning this fight.

"Well now, Tom Wasp." The pugilist grinned. So this *was* Dabeno. He had a most surprising voice. Deep, very, very gentle and warm. It was the most sinister voice I had ever heard, because underneath it was an edge so marked that I shivered. "What an honour. Not often we get a sweep here, is it, boys?"

The Lascars probably didn't understand a word, but Dabeno's henchman did. In contrast to Billy's, he was a small man who looked as if his speciality was picking the wings off flies or other annoying creatures—such as sweeps. I decided I'd better treat Dabeno's welcome as real. "Glad to be here," I assured him. It came out as a squeak. "I've been looking for you, Mr. Dabeno."

His eyes narrowed. "What you got to say then?"

I didn't feel brave, but I had nothing to gain by letting him see that. "Why kill the bird? You didn't have to harm him."

"What bloody bird?" he snarled, doing a good job of looking bewildered.

"My chummy's. Your mob did over my home last night, but why kill his bird?"

A roar of a laugh followed. "Never went near your place."

"You expect me to believe that?" I was taken aback, because

I'd assumed I'd been brought here to be told what the gang needed from me.

He marched over to me and it was hard to stand my ground, since Dabeno was almost double my size, and smelled of evil as strongly as I did of soot. He grabbed me by the collar in case I missed the point he was trying to make. "Yes, Wasp. I do, and you know why?"

All I could manage was a feeble squawk of a yes, since he had a lot of my neck in his grasp as well the collar by now.

"We didn't do it last night, because we were going to do you over tonight," he hissed, letting me go with a push so suddenly that I cannoned across the room, falling in a heap at the underling's feet.

"What did they pick up?" this gentleman said, with a fingernail poked in my neck.

"What they came for." I managed to get to my feet, hoping this wouldn't bring on another attempt to throttle me.

Dabeno's eyes narrowed, and he barked something I didn't understand at the Lascars, then kindly turned his attention to me again. "And what was that?" he cooed gently.

Even choking as I was, I realised I was in a dilemma. I couldn't refer to the china lady, but if Dabeno really didn't know about her, there was something odd here. It could not have been his mob who was responsible for last night or the china lady his reason for his proposed visit tonight. That meant we were back to Sir Laurence having a finger in the pie, or the Rat Mob, who had no reason for it. Or, I thought with a sinking heart, it could have been at the orders of the Nichols' putter-up. Suppose he were acting independently of the Nichol Gang? Suppose Dinah had discovered his identity?

I took a very big chance. "Some bit of china I was looking after for a pal," was my answer.

Silence as Dabeno stared at me. The Lascars were chattering

on in their own language, and the underling kicked me back to my original place. His name seemed to be Scrapper, which did not inspire me with enthusiasm, as it implied he was ready to fly out with any weapon that came to hand.

"Sit down." When at last he spoke, Dabeno's voice was silky again, so I accepted. "You know my name, Wasp."

"Yes."

"Good. Know what it means?"

"Yes. Bad one."

He nodded slowly. "You'd best remember that, Wasp, because I'm told you're working for the Rat Mob."

"Making enquiries temporarily," I said hastily, wondering just who had given him this information, "over the death of Dinah Johnson." At least I knew why I was here now, which was a relief.

"So why's that? They've got a Prussian in clink for that."

"He could be innocent."

This seemed to be a word unknown to them, because he ignored it. "I'll tell you what you're doing this for, Wasp."

I decided silence was best, and I was right because he went right on: "You're trying to fix this murder on us, ain't you?"

"No," I bleated. "Only to find out the truth."

"Billy Johnson wouldn't hire nobody to find out truth," Dabeno said dismissively. "You've got pigmen friends, ain't you? You're poking your snout into our affairs to peach on us. You can tell your mates in Scotland Yard it's nothing to do with the Nichols and if we find you still poking around, you'll be in the river waiting to be scooped up as dead meat."

I had a wild hope I was about to be released with a warning, but not yet apparently, because Dabeno had thought of something else. "Why do you want to see us if you're only looking for Billy's girl's murderer? Eh?" he roared. "Is Billy thinking we want to get back at him? He's right. But it's him we'd knife, not his daughter. The girl's not to blame. We play things straight in the Nichol Gang."

Here I was thinking that the Rat Mob and the Nichol Gang were the toughest gangs in London, and all the time they were honest men—according to them. I couldn't mention the delicate matter of Dinah possibly having discovered Dabeno's putter-up, for I'd be in the river for sure. I had to play this carefully—which was easy in this case because it was what I believed.

"It's like this, Mr. Dabeno," I began as chattily as I could. "Housemaids often get into awkward situations. There's a footman at the place she worked who didn't like Dinah Johnson associating with this Erich Mayer because he wanted her himself. If, and it's only if, this Prussian fellow didn't kill her, my belief is that it was this footman. He could have let her in the door when she returned after her night out, and killed her. He's a brute of a fellow." I kept my eyes averted from the even nastier one in front of me.

"What's his name?"

"Joseph Belt. He was at the funeral today."

There was a long pause. "Nothing to do with us," he said at last, looking at his underling for confirmation—which was too eagerly given. "Never heard of him. You'd better get out, Wasp."

I was only too thankful to obey, even though it was clear that the name Joseph Belt had rung a bell with Dabeno. And yet if Belt was acting on their behalf, Dabeno would have begun to look shifty as soon as I mentioned the word *footman*. I was not going to get any further on this, however, so I decided to accept his invitation to leave. There was one more point I had to clear up. "You said you were planning to rob me tonight. Are you still going to?"

"None of your business," he roared.

I'd stirred up a hornets' nest, and the veins were standing out on his neck he was so agitated.

In my view it was my business. "The Metropolitan Police are guarding my place now."

Instead of scaring him, he burst into raucous laughter. "Hear that, boys? We're terrified. They couldn't guard a barrel of beer." He paused for thought. "I tell you what, Wasp. My friends here will accompany you back to your place to see whether you're telling the truth about this piece of china of yours. And if you're not, Wasp, you might be very sorry indeed."

All the way back, guarded by the Lascars with Scrapper guarding them, I thought about my being made very sorry. This was not pleasant so instead I thought about the lady whom I left peacefully looking out of the window and whom I'd now placed in danger. Should I appeal to the police guard? When we arrived, there was indeed a constable on duty, for which my neighbours would not thank me. I could feel a knife at my back, however, which persuaded me not to chat to him, and with sinking heart I was escorted upstairs.

The first thing I saw when I opened the door was that the china lady had gone.

I couldn't make the Lascars understand why I was upset, and the thoroughness with which they hunted through my rooms was admirable—Dabeno would be proud of them. Even the chimney brought down a load of soot. When they approached the sailor doll, however, my heart was in my mouth, thinking Ned had put it in the doll again. But as they angrily shook the doll to pieces, nothing fell out. I seized it from them, almost hoping to feel the comfortable weight of the lady, but there was indeed nothing inside it.

I sank down exhausted when they'd gone, the events of the day finally catching up with me. The Lascars had looked wistfully at the jar of pennies under my bed, but oddly enough they didn't take it. Not worth their while perhaps, although to us it was our entire savings. Scrapper saw it too, but even he didn't think it worth his while. This did not cheer me up, however, as it suggested Dabeno was not so named for nothing.

At last they had gone, and I could wrestle with the fact that the lady had indeed vanished this time. Not even Ned was here, and so the faint hope remained that he had for some reason of his own taken the lady with him. Then to my joy I heard his voice behind me.

"I'm back, guvner. Didn't mean to go off like that. I've brought a pie for supper."

"That's mighty kind of you, Ned," I struggled to say, though pies were the last thing on my mind. "Ned, where did you hide the lady? Did you take her with you?"

He looked surprised, then his eyes grew big as saucers as he took in her absence. "I haven't touched her."

"She's gone then," I said heavily. I must have looked very bad because Ned said anxiously, "We'll get her back. Don't be upset, guvner."

"No. She's gone forever."

A pause. "I'm still here," he said.

I managed a smile. "I'm glad of that, lad."

All this while, I hadn't seen a sign of Mr. Chuckwick, but the next morning, as we were setting off with mournful hearts for our daily work, I heard the sound of footsteps on the stairs. Expecting Mr. Chuckwick, I was surprised to find it was Constable Peters.

"I'm on my way to Claremont House, Mr. Wasp. They sent a messenger this morning. It looks as if you might have been right. That footman, Joseph Belt, is missing. His effects have gone, too."

CHAPTER SEVEN

I was torn in two directions. It was most gratifying to hear that Constable Peters and therefore the great Sergeant Williamson were now persuaded that Joseph could be guilty of Dinah's murder. The constable had come to urge me to go to Claremont House to sweep up whatever soot I could find lying around concerning Joseph's movements on the night that Dinah had died. I might, he said, be able to find evidence to charge him with—if he could be found. The post mortem report had found no sign of pregnancy or sexual attack, he told me, but that didn't mean Joseph couldn't have been forcing his attentions on her, leading to murder. If so, Erich Mayer might have been falsely accused, and I could help to prove it.

I'd have been glad to do so, but I had this feeling I was being pushed along by others, and I like to keep the brushes firmly in my own hands. I'd been pushed off to meet the Rat Mob, readily permitted to meet Erich Mayer, pushed off to meet the Nichol Gang. All of them appeared anxious for me to find out where the truth lay over Dinah's death, but they were also anxious to distance themselves from it. Someone else did it, which is a natural reaction, especially if true. But where did truth lie? Pontius Pilate had trouble answering that question, so what hope did I have, a mere chimney sweep?

Joseph Belt was indeed the answer most in accord with my feelings, but I like to be sure I've measured up the whole chimney first, and so far there was nothing to prove his guilt, except his running away. I hadn't taken to the man, a brute who thought himself entitled to any girl he wished; I'd met footmen like him before. As in any other line of work, those with brains make butler, those without have to create their own little empires. Most do it peacefully, hoping for a wife and children one day and a room or two they can call their own, but some— and I thought Joseph was one—want power in their greedy hands immediately and thought power over women was an easy way of getting it.

"You think he's guilty, Mr. Wasp?" Constable Peters asked anxiously.

"Oh, yes. But like a mutton pie from Rag Fair, Constable, it's hard to see the meat for the potatoes."

He looked even more anxious. "The meat being?"

"The same old problem. How did he get the body from the house to the Victoria fountain? It's a fair walk from Claremont Lodge and the gates to the park would be locked."

From the way the constable wouldn't meet my eye I knew this was worrying him too. "It's only a wooden fence along the park and not a high one. He could have broken it down or leapt over it." He looked at me hopefully.

"He could," I agreed. "But put yourself into his livery, constable. You kill the poor girl by mistake, so you either leave her on the spot, running away as fast as you can, or you try to hide the body. Either way you're scared, you didn't mean to do it. Why didn't he run away then, not now? Or if he decided on hiding it, why choose a difficult place? You can't carry or even drag dead bodies very far even if you're as big as he is. There's a canal nice and handy by the side of the park, so why not tip the body into that? As for asking her to go into the park with him at that time of night, and breaking down a fence to do it, well, Dinah sounds a sensible girl, who wouldn't have truck with that. There wouldn't be time anyway. They'd have to be back by eleven o'clock when the butler locks the door."

Even as I spoke, I remembered what Mary had said about Joseph being upset and dishevelled that morning after Dinah's death, and how haggard he still looked when I first met him. Suppose he *didn't* come in? Suppose he'd left her in the park dead, and slept the night in the stables?

Constable Peters frowned. "So you don't think he did it?"

"I do. But I don't know how he got her where he did—or, what's more important, why."

The constable had nothing to add to this, except to suggest I should be on my way to Claremont House the very next morning. That reminded him of something, however. "I thought you were being protected, Mr. Wasp. There's no one outside your place now."

"It's too late," I said sadly, thinking of my lost lady. But she wasn't Scotland Yard's business.

I got up the next morning none the happier. I began to feel I was the only person I could rely on, now both the police and Mr. Chuckwick seemed to have vanished. Ned too had already disappeared, not even making himself a drink. I could tell Jack was still on his mind, but what bothered me was what he might be doing about it. I had this feeling that Young Nipper came into the story somewhere, and that he could be leading Ned astray. There'd be no point in trying to lead him back for a while, not till he had got his thoughts straight, but I was unhappy. It wasn't like Ned to neglect our daily work without a word to me, and I feared he had taken to more instant methods of earning his pies than by cleaning chimneys.

The only way to stop that was to find out for sure who killed Dinah, bring Joseph to justice, and then go to Billy Johnson and tell him the case was finished, and so Young Nipper could take his nippers off my Ned. I had a feeling that the Nipper had plans of his own that didn't fit in with Billy's. I also had a feeling that I was preparing to enter unknown and dark territory.

I collected my brushes, still feeling hard done by, and went to greet Doshie, who at least was pleased to see me, even though there were signs that Ned had given him his breakfast, despite neglecting his own.

When I reached Claremont House I saw a familiar face. The constable who had so briefly guarded Hairbrine Court was now on duty here at the main entrance—a promotion he no doubt appreciated. The tradesmen's entrance was unguarded, and I could hear such a chatter that I was undecided whether to interrupt it. Mindful of the fact that I had a professional job to do here as Sir Laurence's appointed sweep, I went about my work without interruption, but as I expected silence fell when I entered the servants' hall afterward, as it was general knowledge I had some kind of connection to Sir Laurence.

Mr. Longfellow solved this difficulty by greeting me like a long lost cousin. I've never had any sort of cousin that I know of, but I imagine this phrase means a warm welcome—and this one was to my surprise. Tea and muffins were pressed upon me, and I was even permitted a chair reasonably close to the table. After a moment or two the chattering began again, with lurid speculation from the male servants on the probable murderer who had fled their ranks and reasons why, and sobs and shudders from the ladies.

"This Joseph," I asked, when I judged I was able to join the conversation. "I suppose he left of his own accord?"

They all stared at me, astonished. "Of course he did," Mrs. Poole snapped at last.

"He told you he was going, did he?"

"His clothes have gone," Mr. Longfellow announced. "That shows he meant to go. Couldn't stand to be here any longer." I could see by his lugubrious expression that Claremont House was still letting him down, being not what he was used to. Girls being murdered, and now footmen running off without permission from the butler were not part of his private list of duties.

"You're right," I said wisely, although all this proved to me that if Joseph hadn't gone of his own free will, someone in the house had made sure his effects disappeared too.

"I talked to him yesterday at the funeral," I said chattily, and all eyes again fixed on me, as if I were a troublesome fly they didn't know how to swat.

"Poor Dinah," Mary volunteered bravely. "The funeral must have upset Joseph all over again. He said afterwards you had it fixed in your mind that he murdered poor Dinah, and that must have been why he ran away."

Mrs. Poole spotted her opportunity. "He said you were a spy, Wasp. That's why Sir Laurence asked you to be sweep here, so you could spy on Joseph."

A nasty atmosphere began to develop, and even Mr. Longfellow seemed to desert my side, judging by his disapproving silence. It was time to come clean—although this is hard for sweeps.

"I suppose you could call me that," I said cheerily. "But it's not Sir Laurence I'm working for. It's Dinah's parents."

This put the cat among the pigeons all right, and settled the question of whether they knew who Dinah's parents were.

"Bless me," Mrs. Poole moaned. "We'll all be murdered in our beds."

"More likely I will," I observed genially. This caused a laugh, fortunately, even though to me it had the flavour of a grim truth. I decided not to tell them that the Nichol Gang was also interested in Dinah's death.

The atmosphere thawed despite my revelations, and Mr. Longfellow confided, "You mark my words, it was someone else murdered Dinah if it wasn't Mayer. It couldn't be Joseph. No footman of mine would stoop to murder. Anyway, that Prussian's a foreigner. What did he want with a nice English girl?"

No one replied since the answer would seem obvious, since love doesn't depend on language. Instead, Mrs. Poole asked, "Her parents must be thinking Erich's innocent or they wouldn't be asking you to make enquiries."

"That's a very good point, Mrs. Poole," I answered, impressed, "and one I've pondered over myself. It seems to me they must have had their suspicions—perhaps because of something Dinah told them about Joseph. They want to be sure the right person gets his deserts."

Mrs. Poole nodded approvingly, delighted at her intuition, and I breathed a sigh of relief that this explanation, while a simple one, pleased her. There need be no mention of the Nichol Gang. I had to be careful, bearing in mind Joseph would have needed an accomplice to get the body to the park—and if Joseph was not acting for the Nichol gang, then that accomplice was probably present here. It could have been the other footman, the odd-job boy, or the outside staff.

I cleared my throat. "Now I've been thinking, Miss Mary. You said Joseph looked most upset after the murder and hadn't shaved."

"Until I had a word with him," Mr. Longfellow pointed out sternly.

"Yes," Mary whispered. "In a real state, he was."

"Did he have a room of his own here or share one?"

A silence, and my eyes went to the other liveried young man, who was red in the face.

"Michael shared a room with him." The butler's eye fell on the blushing footman, and obviously seeing the guilt there in his face, roared, "Was Joseph missing that night? It wasn't reported to me."

"He threatened me," the young man blurted out. "You know what he's like. He said he got locked out and spent the night with the horses, but if I said anything it would look as if he'd murdered Dinah and not that Prussian, so I didn't."

I could well understand that Joseph could be the intimidating sort, but by the look of him Mr. Longfellow would also be good at intimidating if he so chose.

"Didn't it occur to you, Joseph might have murdered Dinah himself?" I asked gently.

His eyes grew round. "Why would it? Joseph wanted to marry Dinah, he said she was willing and then that Prussian bloke came along."

"Is that true, Mary?" I asked.

"No," she said indignantly. "Joseph was always following her trying to—well, you know. She wouldn't have anything to do with him. Told him she'd tell Lady Mallerby."

"That's not what he told me," Michael said sulkily.

It wouldn't be, of course. I believed Michael over this, but he had a lot of learning to do about life.

"I locked up as usual at eleven o'clock," Mr. Longfellow announced severely. "Nothing untoward occurred."

I wasn't going to challenge him. "Any ideas on where Joseph might have run to?"

There was a general shaking of heads. "The police asked that," Mr. Longfellow replied. "We haven't."

"Home? Parents?"

"Shouldn't think so," Michael volunteered. "They live in Bluegate Fields."

I could see his point, and it was a frightening one. This was one of the worst alleys in Wapping, where the houses held ten or more to a room. If a child left to take up work—or crime—there would be no going back. Another would have filled his place, so it was unlikely Joseph would be found there.

I was still hesitating over whether to ask my last question when a bell rang in the corridor. Mary hurried out to answer it, and came back to tell me that Sir Laurence wished his chimney to be cleaned. I could see the word *spy* on everyone's lips as I picked up my brushes and followed Mary upstairs.

"In the throne room today?" I asked.

"He's always in the desert on a Monday," was her reply.

My question had to be put quickly to her. "It's been suggested," I said tactfully, "that Sir Laurence himself might have had an eye for Dinah. Ever mention that, did she?"

She blushed. "I really couldn't say."

"That's very right of you, Mary, but you see, Dinah's dead so we—" I included myself grandly with the police by this word— "need to look at every possibility, just so we can rule out the nonsense ones."

She looked at me fearfully. "Not very much nonsense, Mr. Wasp. It was Mr. Alfred, Sir Laurence's son, who Dinah had trouble with."

"Not Sir Laurence himself."

"No," she said simply. "That's me."

I didn't like the sound of that. "Is that so? And you don't like it?"

She shook her head violently, and I thought about trying to have a word with Sir Laurence about this. I was getting ideas above my station perhaps. What could a sweep do? And then it struck me that perhaps there was something.

I found Sir Laurence sitting cross-legged in the middle of the tent, and he courteously invited me to sit there with him until I explained that with my bowed legs I found it hard sitting on the floor and I'd rather stand.

"You've heard about footman Joseph disappearing," he then said without preamble, and when I nodded, he continued, "It looks as though the police could have been wrong about Erich Mayer."

I had a mental image of Sergeant Wiley's face if he could

have heard that. "Perhaps," I said cautiously.

He shot a look at me. "You're doubtful. Why's that?" (As if he would take a sweep's opinions into account, but it was flattering to be asked all the same.)

"Until they've found Joseph Belt and proved he was guilty, they won't let Erich Mayer go."

He frowned. "You might be right." In one graceful movement he leapt to his feet, white robes flowing all round him. I wondered how his valet managed to keep up with his duties, laying out Arab dress one day, Chinese the next, and court breeches the next.

"We could keep Erich Mayer's spirits up," I suggested, "if he knows there's a chance he might not be brought to trial after all."

"Excellent, Wasp." Sir Laurence smiled. "The Prussians are a touchy nation, and we have to be diplomatic. Their ambassador is beginning to ask questions about Mayer's detention. The quicker Joseph Belt's guilt is established the better, don't you think?"

"Or Erich Mayer's innocence." I was curious about his priorities.

"Naturally," he agreed. "I suggest you concentrate on the former though—" and when I looked surprised, he added, "I'm sure the embassy is in touch with the police over Mayer's situation."

I agreed with him, but here I was being pushed gently into a chimney again, and so I decided to use a stronger brush to get out.

"About that china statue I mentioned to you, Sir Laurence. It's been stolen."

He didn't even look surprised. "I heard about that," he said easily. "The police told me you'd had another burglary. Unfortunately, the constable could only guard one side of the premises at a time. I gather the burglar came in through the houses at the back of your lodgings and into your yard."

This was news to me, and it was interesting that Sir Laurence was so closely informed about my humble doings. It showed I was on the right track.

"About this china statue, sir. Perhaps it isn't so worthless as you thought. After all, there was the burglary at the Gables where Eliza Hogg worked and two raids on my home. And now they've got what they wanted."

"Who are *they*, Wasp?" he asked politely.

"That's what I don't know, sir. But I shall find out."

He looked pleased with himself. "It is fortunate then that I asked to see you. I have another statue for you."

I was most surprised. This was a turn of events I hadn't expected.

"Here." He swept out of the tent and came back with a white statuette, which he put into my sooty hands. At first it looked similar to the one I had lost, but the feel of it was different, so I looked closer. Then I could see this was nothing like my lady. No purity of expression, no peace about her. Nothing. It was a lump of china, that's all. And what *that* said to me was that there was something very strange going on here. I wasn't going to tell Sir Laurence my thinking though, for he must be involved. I would thank him most gratefully—and do my thinking afterward.

There was something else I could do, however. "You take thought for people, sir," I told him gratefully, "and this statue proves it. Most grateful I am. This must be a good house to work in. There's proper respect between master and servants' hall. There are some places where the master and his sons in particular think they own the servants, particularly the women. And that doesn't make for a happy house. Word soon spreads."

The message got through. He stared at me with narrowed

eyes, and the time for pleasantries was over. "Get out of my house, Wasp. Your job's finished."

"Not quite, sir. I'm answerable to the Rat Mob and now to the Nichol Gang."

I could see him summing me up. Then, surprisingly, he laughed. "Have it your way. I can see you're a bit of a diplomat yourself. Carry on. It always helps to have a happy house."

In high good humour, he even paid me for cleaning a chimney that didn't need my attentions.

I found Ned waiting for me that night, most contrite, but not telling me where he'd been. I showed him the new lady statuette, without commenting on it. I didn't need to. Ned took one look at it, and I thought he was going to smash it to bits with the boot he'd just taken off, but he spared it that. He made no move to put her on the table, however, so I did it myself. He looked at me in horror.

"Just in case we get any more visitors, Ned," I explained.

He saw my point and even managed a grin. "But I'll get our real lady back, guvner," he assured me. He was only boasting of course, for he hadn't a chance of that, but I pretended to be grateful.

My heart was heavy though. Outside these rooms there seemed a blanket of yellowish black fog over the whole of life, not just the usual smoky clouds over London; and for once I could not see my way through to the shining light of our Lord above. Everywhere offered menace, nothing offered hope. Even Ned had secrets of his own, and I lay down that night without even the strength for my usual prayer.

Next day I decided to set out for Joseph's former home, which was yet another place it was best to go alone. As I said, Bluegate Fields is known for its dirt, crime, overcrowding and general stink. As a sweep I can go where no police dare, but no one will touch me. I fit in here. The fishermen, the sailormen and judies all pass me by. Once this was a street of decent houses, now they were lodging places or drinking dens like a hundred other tumbledown hovels. There would be one privy for the whole house, despite the ten or so people to a room, and no water save a pump at the end of the court.

I grew up in a place like Bluegate Fields and count myself fortunate to have escaped its misery. I pity those who can't escape such places through no fault of their own, maybe being crippled after an accident or widows left on their own, or people just too tired to care. Joseph was born in one of these pits of misery, and he'd done well to be a footman. For the first time I wondered how that had come about.

I took a deep breath in the stinking air outside before I knocked on the door to face the interior one, which would be worse. I could hear the noise of screaming children, and the door was opened by a sad-eyed woman with a baby at her breast, and sallow-skinned children in rags pulling at her skirt. As I'd thought, wherever Joseph had run to, it wouldn't have been here.

"I'm looking for Joseph Belt," I said pleasantly to a blank face. "Seen him recently, have you?"

A shake of the head was all she gave, but I don't think she even heard what I said.

"He's left his place of employment," I went on. "Any friends or relations he might have gone to?" I might have been speaking one of Sir Laurence's fancy languages for all the effect my question made on her. The words friends and relations had no place here. "Married sisters?" I asked.

Married didn't mean much here either. These people live in such poverty and squalor, they were too squashed in to appreciate a ring for any other purpose than pawning it. I wondered whether this woman even knew her son might be wanted for murder.

"Joseph?" Her eyes focussed on me for the first time. "Said something about getting a boat."

Would that be now or years back? It could mean anything. I could make all the enquiries I liked, but if Joseph came here last night and it was true about the boat, then he was gone. There'd be no hope of finding him if he was on his way to Indialand or America. The only hope of proving him guilty would be through evidence from his accomplice who helped him move the body or in proving Mayer's innocence, despite Sir Laurence's wishes that I should not concern myself with that. Though for the life of me I couldn't see why Sir Laurence should care so much—either over this or over the china lady.

It occurred to me that the only connection between Dinah's death and the china lady was Sir Laurence himself.

My next task, it seemed to me, was to find out who Joseph's accomplice was—and indeed if Mayer was guilty who this could have been, since he could not have moved the body alone any more than Joseph could.

Where better to begin than to listen to the Prussian band? After making enquiries as to when it might be playing, I arranged to clean the chimney of Claremont House (they must have been the cleanest chimneys in London by that time) on the Saturday and go to listen to the band afterward. Sir Laurence had kept his word and I had not been barred from the house. Indeed I still received twice the usual rate for each chimney I cleaned there, so I could afford to take time to listen to bands, taking into account my income from Billy Johnson.

Being a Saturday, there was a mixed crowd in Victoria Park, for all it was still January. There were families out to take the cold air, sailors who'd managed to lurch their way up from Wapping, together with what seemed most of the population of Bethnal Green and Whitechapel. The band was playing in the pagoda room by the lake, and the pagoda made a lovely sight with its upturned edges and dainty structure and vivid colours. A few people made their way across the bridge to listen, but I was happy to stand by the lakeside, for the music was loud. The lively marches and dance music struck a false note in the dainty building, but they were certainly popular with the crowd, especially when the band played a few English music hall songs to finish on a jolly note. Erich had said that his friend Carl Weber played a trombone. Not being sure I could pick out the latter instrument, I had to ask which one was Carl when the band eventually finished and made its way across the little bridge to ask us all for money. I obliged, thinking one of my chimney threepenny pieces would be a good investment for Carl's goodwill.

"Mr. Weber?" I asked, when this young man had been pointed out by the important-looking bandmaster. All the bandsmen— seven in all, as Erich had already been replaced—were fine, sturdy young men, who looked very grand to me. This Carl looked down on me most superciliously.

"Who are you, please? I have no chimneys to clean."

I told him I was Erich's friend and believed he was innocent, and then he condescended to give me his full attention, especially when I said I'd been to see Erich in Newgate.

He exclaimed in surprise. "*Ja.* He is innocent. I know that. He love Dinah."

"Then you'll help me?" I said firmly. "I work for the girl's parents."

At that he looked suspicious. "Why would they wish Erich innocent?"

The same old question, and I explained as well as I could. I told him about Joseph Belt, at which he looked more hopeful. "Yes, I help you," he told me eagerly, and I began to warm to him.

"Were you there that night when Erich returned? He told me you all shared the same lodgings. She was killed on fourteenth January." Only ten days ago, but it seemed longer, so much had happened since then.

"Yes. We share a room at the lodgings. Erich was back there at not much past eleven of the clock."

"You're sure?"

"*Ja*. Our landlady, Mrs. Pridefoot, say we must be in by eleven-thirty. She go to bed then, and that night I and two others play music to her and her husband downstairs in their parlour, so we all know when Erich come home."

"Did you tell the police this?"

"Of course."

"Then how did they think Erich managed to kill the girl and take the body to the park?"

"They say he lied about taking her to the Eagle and what time they come back," he told me simply.

Now that was something I hadn't thought of. Perhaps Sergeant Wiley had a point. "Didn't the police check at the Eagle to see if they remembered Erich?"

"Yes, but who would remember one girl, one man, out of so many? How would the police describe them?"

I had an idea about this. I remembered when I was at Scotland Yard in the small room with Constable Peters I'd seen a photograph of the policemen, and wondered whether the pig-men ever took photographs of prisoners. If so, the constable could take one of Erich Mayer to show his likeness at the Eagle; perhaps someone would recognise him as being there that night.

Carl was most enthusiastic about the idea, and said he would tell not only the police but his embassy about it. I sensed Sergeant Wiley would not be so enthusiastic, however, and decided to go to Scotland Yard myself, hoping that Billy Johnson would not mind paying for another growler fare.

To my pleasure, Constable Peters took to the idea at once, although he said he'd have to get permission from Sergeant Williamson. That took several days to obtain during which I was most impatient. Every day brought us nearer to Erich's trial, which Constable Peters told me would be in March. There had naturally been no word of Joseph Belt either, who must be sailing far from these shores. In fact, there was no word about anything. Not even of Ned, who seemed to have abandoned me and the chimney sweeping trade. He even stayed out all one night.

I was very glad when the constable eventually arrived at Hairbrine Court, even though he brought bad news. He showed me the photograph of Erich—whose sad, scared eyes stared out at me accusingly for achieving so little. "I've taken it to the Eagle," the constable told me gloomily. "No one remembers him."

This was a blow, but I urged him to try again, as he could not have showed it to everyone there in just one visit. All in all, however, I felt encased in soot. With Joseph on a boat goodness knows where, and my china lady gone, I felt I'd let Billy Johnson down, let alone Ned. Jack's death was my fault.

I decided it was time to report to Billy, and offer to give the job up. When I did so, he listened very keenly, and so I was expecting a death sentence. Instead, he said, "No, Wasp, I don't want you to give up. If there's something to find, find it. Sounds to me as if we were right and this Joseph did murder my Dinah. Tell me more about him."

"His name's Belt—"

"*Belt?* I've heard that name before."

There was a great rustling of crinolines and skirts and Doll hissed something in his ear. Billy's face turned red. "Of all the hell and tommy cheek. We kicked him out."

"Of what?" I asked, not understanding.

"Of the Mob," he bellowed. "Nasty piece of work, he was. He

was only with us a month or two, years ago. Maybe thirteen he was. In the Mob's youth team with Young Nipper. He tried to do the dirty on us. He snitched to the Nichols. Now that's something I don't like. Doll here said knife him, but I'm a reasonable man." Billy smirked, as she grinned. "We kicked him black and blue out of the Mob, and you tell me he ends up a footman. How'd he manage that?"

Another turnabout. Dabeno had known the Belt name too, and no wonder. Was murdering Dinah Joseph's revenge on Billy? No, too much time had gone by. Did the Nichols set Joseph up to murder the poor girl, or did he really love her and kill her out of jealousy? Or, it occurred to me, even more chillingly, had Dinah recognised him or found out about his background, and threatened to lose him his job?

CHAPTER EIGHT

I like the River Thames, especially when I'm troubled. It's freedom for me, particularly in the dawn when lazy old London is shaking its bones and slowly emerging into a day's work. The river flows on by, and I like to think it gives a friendly nod to an ageing chimney sweep sitting on a stone by its muddy banks. I nod back to cheer it on its steady, even journey to the sea. In the dawn light it takes on all sorts of colours, changing with every moment, unlike later in the day when the river settles down and decides to carry out its job of bearing vessels onward.

At dawn most vessels are lazily thinking about moving out of their docks and moorings one by one. At this point where I sit, near the entrance to St. Katherine's Dock, the vessels aren't so thickly moored in ranks as they are farther up, and I can see the river itself. On the opposite bank lies the Borough, which, like the river, provides an escape from London, as through it runs the Dover Road. I've never travelled to Dover, but I imagine it as another great port with another great fortress that guards this old England of ours, as the Tower does London. Here where I like to sit, I'm almost in the shadow of the Tower, and I thought that too gave me some kind of place in this world. And yet my history books told me that both the Tower and Dover Castle were built by invaders, so England can't always have been safe.

That's long past now, and we Londoners can go about our everyday business without fearing that some new warrior might leap off one of these oceangoing ships, telling us he's another

William the Conqueror.

I come to this place when I want to think about a problem, and that day I wanted to think most carefully about the pile of soot I'd been plunged into. Ned was still absent, so I'd carried my sweeping equipment here myself. He'd been out all night again, and I had to think what, if anything, I could do about it. At about twelve or thirteen, we'll never know which, Ned's old enough by Ratcliffe standards to decide his own future, and my dread was that he'd decided to throw in his lot permanently with Young Nipper's crew. Knowing I would frown on this, he had felt he had to leave me. That's what I thought by night, as darkness overtook me and crept into my mind, poisoning my senses, but here in the dawn I could hear the good Lord's voice again, and more clearly than I had for some time. He seemed to be saying: "Nonsense, Thomas Wasp. Use the brains I bestowed on you, and stop feeling sorry for yourself."

"I'll try, Lord," I replied humbly, "but if You could give me a helping hand just at this moment, I would be much obliged."

There didn't seem to be a reply, so I sat there for some time watching the mudlarks and other river people collecting the rubbish thrown up by the tides in the hope of making a penny or two. They are early risers as the pickings are best then, when they've had time to gather from the wash of the tidal waters together with the influx of far less savoury waters down the many sewers that still demand our great river should bear their filth away.

Mudlarks aren't always children; there are people of all ages down here for what they can find to help them live another day. They have no time to watch the river. They are solely intent on surviving. What are poor women to do when their man has left them either to seek another path in life or to join the ranks of Heaven or Hell? What are men to do when there is no work to help them support their families? Or when they grow old and no one will offer them work? The workhouses open their maws to engulf whoever needs them—but their demands are high. *Come to me*, they say, *but bring with you your hopes, your dreams, your loved ones so that I may destroy them.* The workhouse, for all its tempting face, can be a coffin more frightening and final than the ones buried in the churchyards.

So what was Tom Wasp doing here at dawn, when he had an honest trade to ply? I felt guilty then, and wondered whether this was the message that the Lord was sending me. But I thought not. It seemed to me He had some other purpose for me that I couldn't quite grasp. I could see very well that He wanted me to find who killed Dinah Johnson. It can't be often that God sides with the likes of the Rat Mob and the Nichol Gang, but over this it seemed that He was, whether they appreciated His presence or not.

And here lay the second part of my problem. My opinion was that Joseph Belt was the guilty party. After all, I reasoned, as a steamer blew a horn so close I nearly jumped out of my sooty skin, the murderer had to be either Erich or Joseph or some third party who knew it was Dinah's evening off. Although I believed Joseph killed her, I still had to consider the alternatives. If he had an accomplice, then it would probably be someone in the household. Could Sir Laurence's son Alfred be involved? I could surely believe Constable Peters and the postmortem report that Dinah was not in the family way, but I was beginning to wonder just whom else I could believe in. Only myself, I realised sadly—and Jemima.

Thought of her made my heart feel tender. It wasn't so much her pretty hair and eyes, as the way she had of making life's path seem clearer and brighter. But there, I'm a chimney sweep in my middle years and she a girl with her life before her. She'd marry some young footman soon; someone approved by Billy Johnson of course, and have children of her own. I've often wondered what my babes would have grown up like.

Then I brought my mind back to God's purpose for me, since it seemed to be slipping away. Could I imagine Mrs. Poole or Mr. Longfellow, or the footman Michael strangling Dinah? Had one of them spied on her and Erich as they returned? That would have been difficult, given the nature of a servant's duties. What about the coachman or stable lad?

Now, that, I realised, was a line I hadn't yet followed up. Perhaps my mind hadn't been wandering; the Lord had just been leading it gently to just the point He reckoned I should deal with next.

I began to be aware of the coldness of the stone beneath me, and that my limbs were stiff, so I decided to leave. Stones are necessary if you want to sit on the bank, as the mud thrown up by the Thames is most unsavoury. Fortunately, as I stumbled my way toward the steps, I fell in with a gentleman with a bowler hat and white apron, who in the course of conversation told me he owned a hot drinks stall.

He asked me where I was going, and I explained I was about to start calling the streets for trade. Where would I begin? he asked, and I told him I had a mind to go to Wellclose Square.

He seemed to think this was a good idea, and that he would come with me. But first, I should take a cup of warming cocoa with him. I agreed that was also a good idea—especially as closer attention revealed that this was Mr. Chuckwick. His stall turned out to be a Soyer's cooking apparatus, set down beside a hot chestnut seller, an uncouth individual who eyed me suspiciously, even though the smell of the fire and chestnuts must have overpowered my own trade's aroma.

"Mr. Johnson's idea," Mr. Chuckwick explained. "He treats us most generously in return, of course, for good work from us."

I wondered how the good work was measured. One crime

committed a night, or one unfortunate soul despatched from the world per day? On the whole the Rat Mob would prefer the former, I thought, although the latter was undoubtedly on their list of achievements. I decided not to ponder this further but to sip my cocoa with appreciation.

"Mr. Johnson," Mr. Chuckwick informed me in due course, "is of the opinion that there is something going on." He paused and stared at me earnestly.

I remained silent, as this needed explanation. Did it concern Dinah or something nearer home—such as Young Nipper and my Ned?

"You believe," Mr. Chuckwick continued, "that this footman Joseph killed Dinah, and so does Mr. Johnson. He is *concerned*, however. He needs to be reassured there is not more at stake than the rejection of man by a woman. Can you give me that reassurance?"

"No." That was all I could reply.

"Ah." Mr. Chuckwick sighed. "I both regret and rejoice, Mr. Wasp, that our acquaintance cannot yet end if you feel there is another element."

"There has to be. It's what it is that bothers me." I had a silent discussion with my cocoa. If I suggested that Joseph had perhaps worked at any time with the Nichol Gang, as well as snitching on the Rat Mob for them, I might be starting another war between the two gangs. Billy might then still believe that the Nichol Gang had sent Joseph to kill Dinah in revenge for the Rat Mob having encroached on its territory. But if I didn't tell Billy about Joseph's possible past, I would be betraying the terms of my employment.

"Mr. Johnson is a fine man," Mr. Chuckwick said warningly, and I realised I had no choice.

"Indeed." I tried to be wholehearted in my approval and gulped to give me courage. "Suppose, just suppose, this Joseph still had connections with the Nichol Gang—or had them in the years since he left the Mob?"

Mr. Chuckwick could not disguise his alarm at this statement, realising the consequences as clearly as I did. "Oh, I trust *not.*"

"But," I said hastily, "you tell Mr. Johnson that should he go after the Nichol Gang for information in this respect, he could be wasting his time while the real culprits behind Joseph who ordered Dinah's murder escaped." Who these might be, I had no idea as yet. My brush was lodged halfway up the chimney and would not budge.

"Who else could it be?" Mr. Chuckwick pressed me anxiously, almost squeaking in alarm, and glancing at the hot chestnut seller nervously.

"I don't know yet," I said, trying to sound mysterious, like a Scotland Yard detective. "But there's nothing to suggest the Nichol Gang put Joseph up to killing Dinah. Look, Mr. Chuckwick, when you do your impersonations you remain the same person underneath, don't you?"

"I believe I do." He seemed pleased, if bewildered.

"And the Mr. Chuckwick your wife knows is always the same person—you?"

"I trust it is," he vowed, a trifle anxiously.

"Dinah's murder is like that," I concluded grandly. "We believe that Joseph killed her. What we don't know is which of the many faces this case is putting on leads to the truth, the reason that he did it. It could be personal jealousy; it could be more." What that "more" was I did not dare contemplate, but there was no slipping back down the chimney now.

"I believe that I understand you, Mr. Wasp," Mr. Chuckwick said gratefully. "Whether Mr. Johnson will is another matter, however," he added.

"You tell him that I'm working on it."

With that, we drained our cocoa and parted on reasonably friendly terms, although while I went about my duties, I was aware of a horse and cart following me, either to guard me or spy on me. I swept three chimneys that morning in Wellclose Square, and all the while I was thinking of Joseph and how Dinah's murder might have been part of some larger plot—and if so what that plot might have been. Whatever it was, it wasn't yet connecting with the other troubles that were besetting me: the burglaries at my home and the theft of the china lady. These troubles went straight back to Eliza Hogg.

Did that make two problems for me to solve, or only one? The only connection between the two was Sir Laurence Mallerby. Whether that was coincidence, or whether there was a link, I couldn't yet see. I gave my brush in the third Wellclose Square chimney a final push, and managed to get soot in my face as I stared up to check if the flue looked clean—something I never normally do. Perhaps the soot was getting to me in this case too. Unless I cleaned it properly I was going to get a bucket of soot in my face thrown by Billy Johnson for sure, and probably another one from the Nichol Gang—not to mention one from Scotland Yard and Sir Laurence. And it looked as if it might be very black soot indeed. The chimney I had so blithely agreed to climb for Billy and the one Eliza had sent me up might be two flues of the same stack, and I didn't know where they joined up, only that dark passageways were looming ahead of me.

But I've never given up on a chimney yet. I never know where the twists and turns of old chimneys will take me: along, up, slantwise, horizontal. All one can know for sure as one struggles in the dark is that it is the way of chimneys, unlike sewers, to eventually reach the light above.

I only hoped this case would do that too.

★ ★ ★ ★ ★

Coachmen are the proud face of the stables. As this was a town house, Sir Laurence kept only a small stable here, and thus Mr. Silas Rodway doubled as chief groom with only one lad to help him. Fortunately, word had obviously spread from the house that I had to be tolerated while Sir Laurence smiled upon me, and so Mr. Rodway graciously allowed me to sweep the chimney of his lodgings by the stables before speaking to me. These four horses were a far cry from Doshie; if horses could be said to look down their noses, these were certainly doing that at me.

Luckily, the Lord had prompted me to bring Jemima with me, and Sir Laurence had proved surprisingly cooperative in this, by arranging it with Mr. Periwinkle at the Gables. To be truthful, I wasn't sure whether this message had indeed come from above in the interests of finding Dinah's killer or whether it came from my own thoughts that I would like to see Jemima. In vain I reasoned with myself that a pretty girl can achieve more with some people than a dirty sweep, and my guess was that the coachman would be one of them. Also, I tried to tell myself that the more Jemima could help, the more pleased she would be, which would help her grieving.

Only the tip of her nose showed above the scarf Jemima had wrapped around her chin against the cold when Doshie, the cart and I met her outside the Gables the next morning. February was now here, the gloomy month, when even if the sun peeps out, it has no warmth and when cloud and rain bedevil the skies and the spirits. On that Tuesday, however, Jemima sounded cheerful, despite the circumstances, and it struck me that the Gables, unlike Claremont House, seemed a happy sort of place to live, despite the murder that had taken place there the year before. Claremont House went on from day to day but had no soul, or if it had, I was not yet privileged to have seen it. I wondered why that was. Because of Sir Laurence and his family? Despite his attitude to housemaids, Sir Laurence seemed happy enough in his family life. Or did the unease stem from the servants' hall itself? That was very possible, although experience had shown me that generally lack of content spread downward.

"What do you want me to do, Mr. Wasp?" Jemima asked as we trotted along. Doshie seemed to take on a new sprightly air with such a pretty passenger and I felt like a king. I could have been the fabled Prester John himself and wouldn't exchange this moment for a seat next to Her Majesty at her gracious son's wedding next month.

"I want you to make the coachman feel big and important," I said gravely. "That's hard for you, being a sensible girl."

She laughed. "I'll do that, Mr. Wasp. But why?"

"He may talk more that way."

"You're right. Pa thinks I have that effect on his men."

I could imagine how far apart Jemima and the rough element of the Rat Mob and their judies were, and it made me all the more determined to find Dinah's killer.

"Dinah too?" I asked.

Her face saddened. "Yes. I know it seems queer with Pa and Ma doing what they do, but they didn't have no choice themselves, so they wanted Dinah and me to be different."

The name of Silas Rodway suggested a large man to me, but the opposite proved true. He was almost as short as I was, with sharp eyes and a knowing manner, which sized Jemima up before she had even said good morning. She'd have a hard job impressing him, I thought. I was wrong.

"Oh, what splendid horses." She clapped her gloved hands together in delight. "Just look at that filly, Mr. Wasp. You've good stock, there, Mr. Rodway. I can see you're a dab hand."

A nod was all he gave, but I could see my path was eased already. "This must be a sad house at present," I said. "What with the housemaid's death and Joseph Belt going off like this."

His sharp eyes were still assessing me. He would have heard about my being Sir Laurence's spy and maybe even my connection with the Detective Department at Scotland Yard. "Can't see why. They've got the Prussian banged up for that."

"Some think he's innocent," I observed.

"Come to me to prove it, have you? Doing the pigmen's job for them?"

Jemima quickly intervened, hot with anger. "I'll tell you, Mr. Rodway, why we're here. Dinah was my sister and I want to know who killed her. I want to be sure it was Erich Mayer, and now that Joseph Belt has run away—he upset my sister so much—I want to know if he could have been responsible."

"Just because he's gone missing," Rodway grunted, though less aggressively than he had been. I saw his eyes flicker as he looked at her, and would like to have emptied my soot bag over his dirty thoughts, but I forced myself to wait.

"We don't know," I said honestly. "All we *know* is that Joe told Michael he spent all night in the stables. It wasn't his night off, so that seems odd."

A silence while Rodway considered this. "He might have done. Not that I saw him. The lad told me he thought he saw him."

"Is he here?" Jemima asked, deducing that this must be the stable boy.

"No." Rodway grinned.

Time for me to push harder. "Sir Laurence is interested now. He doesn't think Mayer's guilty either. If when they catch Joseph, it turns out some of his servants were lying to protect him, he wouldn't be pleased."

Another silence while Rodway seemed to be debating whether to do away with me here and now. "And you'll be the first to tell him. Fine thing for a sweep to be doing the master's work."

"He isn't a sweep at the moment," Jemima said promptly. "He's my friend, I asked him to find out what happened to my sister, so anything you could tell us . . ." She broke off with a sob, which sounded genuine to me.

Another silence, then Rodway spoke in a different tone. "I'm sorry, miss. I liked Miss Dinah. A great loss."

"Anything you could tell us, Mr. Rodway, I'm sure we'd be much obliged," she said haltingly.

Rodway looked at her. "Joe spent the night here. You're right. I saw him. The lad let him in, and called me. Said he was locked out. Looked scared out of his wits. Mr. Longfellow would have his guts for garters. He'd slipped up the road to the pub for a drink, and left it too late to get back. When he found out next morning about Dinah he came back here and made us swear to keep quiet or they'd think he did it."

This had the ring of truth, but all the same I had to bear in mind that Joseph needed an accomplice and who more likely than Silas Rodway—currently trying to wriggle out of the situation. It was time to be firm, and a little careless over the truth—as I knew it. "Did you know Joseph used to work for the Nichol Gang? Dabeno's lot."

I knew I'd hit a bull's-eye immediately, because Rodway went very pale indeed. "He never said," he muttered.

"The Nichol Gang and the Rat Mob are keen to find Dinah's real killer, so it's as well you're not involved. As I said to Dabeno the other day . . ."

"You?" Rodway looked so amazed at this, it took the fight out of him, and Jemima looked at me a little oddly.

"Me," I said firmly. "Dabeno wants to know what Joseph had been up to. Giving the Gang a bad name." I could see Rodway still didn't believe me.

"He wouldn't use a sweep." But there was doubt in his mind.

"Call me," I said more bravely than I felt, "the advance scout."

That convinced him. "It weren't nothing to do with me," he gabbled.

"Sir Laurence is very keen for the truth to come out, too."

It seemed it couldn't come quickly enough for Silas Rodway now.

"Joseph came in about midnight, so Jamie—he's the lad— said. He called me down. Joe said he'd lost the time. The clock in the pub showed something different, and he'd had a spot too much to drink. The lad showed him a pile of hay he could sleep on."

"And that's it?" I asked when he paused.

"No. He had something in his jacket he didn't want us to see. Didn't think anything of it, but later I did. It was a purse."

"Where is it?"

"Don't know. Not here now. Must have burnt it, I reckon. But the lad and I both saw it." He glanced at Jemima when he'd finished. "You've the look of her," he said awkwardly.

"Thank you, Mr. Rodway."

She said it so sweetly, I knew she meant it.

I realised Constable Peters should know of this as soon as possible, and Jemima said she would like to come with me. I was very agreeable to this, although I wondered whether Billy and Doll would like their daughter to go that far in being "different." Still, she was a witness, and so valuable to their cause. She stood clutching her own little bag in the entrance hall of the Scotland Yard police headquarters, awed by her surroundings, as indeed I still was. For a sweep and a housemaid to be present here showed what a great society England had, despite the terrible difference between the circumstances of rich and poor.

Constable Peters asked for me to be sent up this time, and we were led upstairs by a supercilious individual. Constable

Peters looked taken aback when he saw my pretty companion, and rushed for a seat for her. He remembered her from the Gables, he told her, and was glad to see her again. There was no side room for us this time, I noted.

He listened patiently to our story, and congratulated me, but somehow I sensed he was not quite as impressed as I had expected, despite Miss Jemima telling him how well I'd done. In fact, it was she who charmed Rodway, and I would tell the constable that when I had a chance. He couldn't take his eyes off her. I almost had to remind him of why we were there.

"Would this be enough for you to release Erich Mayer?" I asked.

"He's already been released," Constable Peters said to my astonishment. "I took the photograph round again and he was recognised this time, and then we talked to Carl Weber. I didn't think that that would be enough for Mayer's release, but Sir Laurence got him freed at the request of the Prussian ambassador. He came before the magistrate this morning, and charges have been dropped."

I was still most surprised. "But Joseph Belt is long gone on a boat to goodness knows where, so there'll be no catching him—"

"We already have," Constable Peters said, his eyes on Jemima, not me. She looked most admiringly at him, perhaps thinking how efficient he was. Which he is, of course, but he's also a good-looking young man.

"You've found him?" she gasped, as I imagined sailing ships boarded by troops of foreign policemen at Sergeant Williamson's orders.

"Have you asked him why he did it?" I asked at almost the same time.

"No, we couldn't. He's dead, Mr. Wasp. A body bearing identification of Joseph Belt has been found up north of

London, Hertford way. He's been murdered. Sergeant Wiley is on his way there now."

My head was spinning with these new developments, but Jemima seemed indisposed to discuss them. She was full of Scotland Yard and what a pleasant young man Constable Peters was. At least he had got her eyes shining again, so I said no more as I took her back to the Gables. She took my hand in hers, as she got down from our cart, and thanked me, saying she'd enjoyed the day and it was nice helping the police. I was glad Billy couldn't hear her.

Doshie and I went slowly back to Hairbrine Court. Joseph's murder was a sad state of affairs I thought, as I thanked Doshie and stabled him in the Black Lion yard. Did this affect the question of whether Joseph had killed Dinah or not? I could not work it out. My brain was in a London particular of its own. I had been so sure I was up the right chimney, and now found that Joseph hadn't gone away by boat. Had he taken a railway train, and if so, why?

I wondered whether Ned would be back when I reached our home, but as I walked up the stairs to our room, there was still the same empty heaviness that tells you no one else is around.

"Ned?" I called out hopefully, but there was no reply, and I could see no sign that he had been here during the day. Everything looked as I had left it.

Almost everything. Something *had* changed.

The china lady was back, eyes cast peacefully down, by the window looking on to Hairbrine Court. This was no mere lump of white china. This was our real lady.

CHAPTER NINE

I slowly took off my boots while I thought about the events of the past few hours. My left boot's removal time was spent contemplating Erich's release and Joseph's murder, and wondering how they affected my job for Billy. Could it mean that I had been wrong and that Joseph was innocent of Dinah's murder, but that someone wanted him to stay the chief suspect? Or was he indeed the murderer, as I firmly believed, and someone, such as Billy, had killed him in revenge? Or did his murder have nothing to do with Dinah's death but everything to do with someone finding him before the police? This last thought involved coincidence, which I don't care for, and besides, Hertford, wherever that might be, sounded a long way from Ratcliffe.

And that brought me to my right boot's removal and the other matter that might or might not be coincidence. What was my china lady doing back here? Had Ned hidden her safely and decided to return her? I couldn't believe that. I knew my Ned, and his anger had been genuine when she had been lost. But if Ned had nothing to do with it, then it was highly probable that Sir Laurence—or rather someone on his behalf—had. I wasn't going to believe his apparent generosity to me over the lady was coincidence. But if he was personally concerned in this matter, why return the genuine lady now? This seemed very strange to me and I relinquished my right boot with reluctance, as my thoughts had not yet taken me much further.

Except for one. The lady's reappearance might have something to do with Ned, even if her abduction had not. Then followed another thought. If so, would she be safe here? I could
only answer no to that. She should be hidden somewhere safe
again until I could find out what this was all about. The next
thing I realised, staring at my working boots standing side by
side, was that nowhere in these rooms could now be thought
safe. For a moment my mind was blank, but then the perfect
place presented itself to me.

I speedily put both boots back on, and very tight they felt, as
my feet had looked forward to relaxing after a day's work. I
picked up my soot bag, went over to the china lady—and
hesitated. Could I really do this to her?

"It's for your own good," I assured her anxiously, and it
seemed to me her enigmatic smile was an approving one. Looking at her, I had another thought: I would wrap her up first
before plunging her pale beauty into my bag. I found the bit of
cloth she'd originally been wrapped in when she was hidden
inside the sailor doll, wrapped her up carefully, and placed her
in the bag. Whoever saw me with this would suspect nothing,
since it was routine for me to empty it in the night soil men's
yard most evenings. Not that I was going there this evening.
Mr. Chuckwick might be curious about my journey, but at this
time of the evening he might be off duty.

As I picked my way through the filth of the Black Lion's
stable yard, Doshie looked surprised to see me.

"I've brought an apple, Doshie," I said, for the benefit of the
only person who was around—the publican himself. He's a
surly individual, but I did him a good turn once so he doesn't
object to my comings and goings.

Doshie enjoyed his apple even though it was only one of the
cast-offs from Rag Fair that they throw away at the end of the
day, and he didn't seem to mind while I poked around in his

hay box and put the lady inside.

"You rest there, milady," I told her. "I'll be back for you soon as I've sorted this mess out." Doshie peered over my shoulder to see what was going on, so I stroked his forehead so he could get used to the newcomer. Then I made my way back to our lodgings.

I was hardly back and divested of my boots for the second time when Ned came in. He was whistling in a casual sort of way, and I knew then that he had been involved with the lady's return. His eyes immediately went to the table by the window—and if I needed any more confirmation there it was written in his face: guilt and shock together.

"Where's she gone?" he cried. His face crumpled, his shoulders heaved and I saw tears beginning to run down his face. "They've taken her again—I wanted you to have her back, guvner."

"There, there, boy. Don't fret, Ned." I held him tight as if he were a child again. Only when Ned was a child he would never let me hug him; he was too scared. Now it was different. "I've just hidden her somewhere safe."

He began to relax and the shoulders heaved less violently. "But I wanted us to be able to see her."

"You hid her all this while, Ned?"

A look of dismay. "No, guvner. Oh, no. It was pinched. I just pinched it back for you last night."

To think I'd misjudged him so. All this while he'd been absent, he hadn't been abandoning me, he'd been trying to get the lady back for us. After a while when he'd recovered himself, I braced myself for the questions I must ask. "Who took it, Ned? And how did you know? And how did you get it back?"

I suspected I wasn't going to like the answers to these, and I was right. At first I thought he wasn't going to tell me, because his face went sullen and he kicked a chair leg viciously. I told him it wasn't the chair's fault and now was the time to tell me the truth.

Even then he wavered, but his eye went to the tasty-looking fish I had brought home for supper, and he knew we had to be on good terms if I was to cook it.

"It was Young Nipper," he blurted out, stealing a glance at me to see the effect of this admission. The lack of surprise on my face must have encouraged him, for it all poured out then. "I reckoned he knew something about that Mallerby place that he wouldn't let on about."

I frowned. "So Billy Johnson knew about this?"

"Don't think so, guvner. Young Nipper's a leery one, and plays his own game. He'd been interested in that burglary we had and seemed to know about the china lady, so I told him she'd been pinched. He said he might be able to help, only"— another glance at me "—if I did the same for him. Me being thin, I can get into places where others can't. I said only if he helped me get the lady back."

There was a pleading note in his voice that tugged at my heart, but I couldn't let him see that yet because I needed to know the worst. "So I did a couple of jobs for him," Ned continued, trying to sound casual about this, and I kept my peace. First get the truth on the table and I could reform Ned later. "Then he said we'd do over Claremont House," Ned went on miserably, "as that was where the lady might be."

"How did he know that?" I frowned. This was getting mysterious indeed. Was the Rat Mob involved after all?

"Don't know, but he did. I guessed it would be in the Chinese room."

I supposed this was natural enough to hide it where it would least be noticed, but even so, it worried me.

"Nipper said I could go after that, while he picked up the other stuff."

"And what was that? The Crown Jewels?"

"I don't think so, guvner." Ned hasn't learned irony yet, so he took me seriously. "I don't think the Queen would like that. I didn't ask Nipper what he was after—I thought it best not to."

"So you did it. Anyone see you?"

"Don't think so, but I didn't like it. There was a larder window left open, so it was easy. I wriggled in, opened the door and in comes Nipper and his pal." A pause. "It was funny being there at night."

"It would be," I agreed. "What happened then?"

"I got out quick once I'd found the lady. But then the trouble began," Ned added dolefully.

"The pigmen heard you?" I asked sharply. "Someone in the house?"

"No. We all got clean away. But Young Nipper took the lady off me."

"*What?*" I knew then my misgivings about that young man were more than justified.

"I think it was her he wanted all along," Ned said. "Wanted me to get it for him. That was all."

"Nipper wanted her, or the Rat Mob?" I asked. "And what's it doing back here?" I didn't like the way this was shaping up at all.

"Nipper dosses down in Cable Street, or says he does. I wanted to cut back along the Highway so the pigmen wouldn't see us."

I nodded, understanding his reasoning. The Highway is the only place where even on a February night there are so many folk rolling out of the pubs, gin palaces and penny gaffs in the small hours, well plied with drink to keep them warm, that a couple of lads wandering along with a bag wouldn't be noticed. Not by pigmen anyway, who don't care to be out at that time of night on the Highway. The old Charlies, the night watchmen, had an understanding with the boozers, but the new blues don't have this skill.

"Nipper had the lady in his swag bag," Ned explained, "so I . . ." His voice faltered.

"You dipped it?" I asked gently.

"Not exactly."

"What then?"

"I squeaked on him to a couple of Billy's men we ran into. After all, he works for the Mob, so I told them what a lot of swag we had that night."

"And?" It sounded as if the worst of the news was on its way now.

"Nipper couldn't say nothing, but they took the bag and had a look inside and there was a bit of a scuffle."

I could imagine it—except that "a bit" was probably an understatement. "What happened then?"

"I dipped it again while they were hammering each other, and ran." Ned looked at me hopefully, not knowing whether to expect praise or blame, and indeed I did not know which to provide.

"Ned," I said at last, "I'm lucky to have you to protect me. You've got brains and a heart. They don't always go together."

He looked most pleased at this. "Can we have that fish now, guvner?"

We could. To Ned the matter was already forgotten, I realised. But for me I couldn't see where this was leading, save that there were still dark places ahead. This case was like a warren of Wapping alleys: you set off down one only to find yourself blocked at the end, so you turn around and twist a bit only to realise you're lost. I read a story once about a foreign man in an underground tangle of caves and passages who had to find his way to the centre to kill a big monster. He was lucky as his lady friend had given him a ball of string to help him find the way. I didn't have such a ball of string in this affair—unless the china lady was one. Everything seemed to come back to her, but could "everything" include Dinah Johnson's death? That still didn't seem possible to me.

How, for instance, did Young Nipper know about the china lady? I could have sworn that Billy Johnson didn't know about her, but then I remembered I'd had a feeling he and Mr. Chuckwick might know more than they were letting on. Even so, Nipper was a nasty piece of work, I decided, and it wouldn't surprise me if he had fingers in more mutton pies than the Rat Mob. Was he, as Joseph too might have been, working for the Nichols? It was the Nichols handling the job of stealing her from George Hogg and then from me—although, if Dabeno was to be believed, someone else got there first. That someone could only have been working for Sir Laurence or Young Nipper himself. And none of that made any sense at all, although February was not a month when fresh night air leads to larder windows being left open by chance.

"Did you know they're having a ball?" Ned said, spluttering through his fish, a while later. I'd cooked it on the fire, together with an onion or two. This question came out of the blue as for the duration of our meal I'd let the matter of the burglary drop.

"Who?" I asked, bewildered. We don't have many balls in this part of London.

"At Claremont House," Ned explained patiently.

"No, I didn't." I couldn't see it would greatly affect me.

"All the swells are coming."

"How does Nipper know that?" I was getting very curious now.

Ned looked a little guilty. "His sister's the new housemaid."

So that was it! Questions were being answered now, and I felt relieved. Not for long, as a new concern presented itself. Why would Young Nipper plant a sister in the house if it was just for one burglary? Such a thing was not unknown of course, but even so it was yet another coincidence. If Ned was right and my china lady had been the main object of the exercise, the outlook for me, as Nipper would realise that Ned had pinched her back again, looked as murky as an unswept chimney. All in all, Claremont House was beginning to look as if it was the centre of this case. Or was the centre my china lady? Either way, I was back to the beginning again: where did Dinah's death fit in?

What would Billy do if he knew Young Nipper was busy creating his own little empire? I couldn't ask him because he was the sort who keeps things bottled up ready to pull the cork as and when *he* liked, not at a time of my choosing. Then I thought of the one matter that was slipping by me. Dabeno ran the Nichols, but because he was a larger setup than Billy, he got at least some, probably most, of his jobs from the putter-up. And he wasn't going to be Young Nipper. With foreboding, I realised I wouldn't get anywhere by questioning Billy or Dabeno; there was only one place I could go, and that was Claremont House itself.

I presented myself there nice and early on Wednesday. I had some difficulty tracking Mr. Chuckwick down, as it turned out he was impersonating a muffin man and his tray got in the way of my view of his face. The still half-full tray accompanied us—to Ned's delight—in the growler that Mr. Chuckwick agreed to hire on behalf of Mr. Johnson to reach Claremont House. The first person I saw upon my arrival was a pigman on duty outside the main entrance and another at the tradesmen's door. The third was Mrs. Poole.

"Any chimneys needing cleaning today?" I asked her.

"You'd best come in," she said, none too friendly. "We need them clean for the ball on Saturday, but there's trouble in the house again, and plenty of it." She glared at me as though it was all my doing—as indeed it could be said was true.

The servants were just coming out of the hall after breakfast, and I noticed there was a new footman already, as well as the new housemaid. She was fair-haired, fair of face and sharp of eye—just like Young Nipper. I wouldn't trust her an inch if I were Mrs. Poole or Lady Mallerby. Footman Michael was coming out with Miss Twinkle, who predictably sniffed at seeing the *ramoneur* here once again.

"You seem very fond of the chimneys here, Wasp," she said in her superior voice.

"We're both workers in the same cause, Miss Twinkle," I told her gravely. "No doubt you're here to sew dresses and shirts for the ball, and I'm here to make the fires go well."

Another sniff, but I could see Michael wanted a word and so I didn't vanish up the nearest flue as she would no doubt be wishing.

"Have you heard the news about Joseph, Mr. Wasp?" he asked me.

"I have, and very sad to hear of it if you counted him as a friend. But not if he murdered Dinah."

"No friend," Michael said. "But it's the shock. Knowing he must have done it, and yet now someone's murdered him."

Mr. Longfellow joined us at that moment to inform us that God moved in mysterious ways, and this was undoubtedly His way of avenging Dinah.

I did not agree, my opinion being that man's hand played much more part in this than our Lord had, but Miss Twinkle looked consoled at the thought. "May that be the end of the troubles to this house. A murder, and now a burglary," she lamented.

"Ah yes, Mrs. Poole mentioned you'd had a problem here," I murmured.

There was a sudden interruption in the form of my old friend

Sergeant Wiley, who was marching down the corridor toward us, snarling, "You here again, Wasp? Make a habit of turning up after burglaries, do you?"

"I'm sorry to hear about it," I said, not being a fish to rise to his bait.

"We know who did it," he said proudly. "No call for your nose to be poked in."

I sensed Ned cowering beside me. "Who?" I enquired.

"Not your business."

I could hardly tell him it was very much my business, and luckily Mr. Longfellow had something to observe on the matter of burglaries. "This would not have happened in my previous position," he told us. "And to think Sir Laurence is a friend of the Prince of Wales."

"Sir Laurence is the victim," I reminded him. "And hardly responsible for the deaths of Dinah Johnson and Joseph."

Mr. Longfellow shuddered. "I had expected to find myself in a better disciplined household where none of this could have happened."

"I agree," Miss Twinkle said promptly. "As for myself, I expect to be working on good English cotton shirts, not white flowing robes."

"Clockwinder," came another voice, and a man with an elegant bag of tools touched his cap to us all.

"You're not our regular," Mr. Longfellow said suspiciously.

"For the ball, Sir Laurence said. Don't want cuckoos cucking and cooing at the wrong moment, do we?" the clockwinder said cheerily.

I watched as Mr. Longfellow escorted Mr. Chuckwick, who had abandoned his muffin tray for this new occupation, to the upper floors of the house, wondering whether he was working in the capacity of Billy Johnson's spy or my guardian. No one would notice him today. Despite the police presence, it seemed like an ants' nest.

The next ant I rang into was Constable Peters, here to see Sir Laurence. He at least was pleased to see me, and I asked him cautiously if he were here about the burglary or Joseph's death.

"Sir Laurence thinks it's about the burglary, and I'll keep it that way," he told me, looking mysterious and somewhat flushed with importance.

"Any more news about Belt?" I asked.

"Garrotted he was, like Dinah Johnson," he told me in a whisper. "Found in a field."

"Is Hertford anywhere near the sea?" I asked, wondering if Joseph had taken a boat round the coast to avoid the expense of the railway.

"Nowhere near it. We're also here because Sir Laurence wants us on guard on Saturday evening, what with the burglary and so forth. There's a lot of important people coming here, including—" he lowered his voice, as if the house were full of potential assassins—"the Prince of Wales himself." He hesitated. "What about you coming, Mr. Wasp? Sir Laurence mentioned it would be a good idea."

I was taken aback. What did he have in mind? If Sir Laurence had been responsible for the burglary at my lodgings, did he want to have another go and so had to ensure I was elsewhere? It was possible, and I was doubly glad I had hidden the lady so safely. Or did Sir Laurence suspect I knew about the disappearance of the lady from his Chinese room? My head began to swim with possibilities. Nevertheless, I don't often get invitations such as this, and I could see no reason to say no.

I wandered outside once I had done the chimneys, leaving a somewhat nervous Ned in the servants' hall. I walked out of the door down to Bonner Bridge, which runs over the Regent's Canal and is the main entrance to Victoria Park. Once again I wondered how Joseph and his accomplice managed to pull

Dinah's body all that way. Or had she still been alive at the time, which raised more questions?

The fence surrounding the park was not very high, but there was no sign, the gatekeeper told me, of its being broken down that night. It was quite a long walk over to the fountain where Dinah was found, but I took it, in respect. I looked up at the imposing structure. The cherubs inside the colonnades had not watched over Dinah that night, and it was a lonely place for her to lie. I walked over to the Royal Hotel entrance, and thought of the lamplighter and gatekeeper strolling in early the next morning and finding her. It was nearly three weeks since her death and I was no clearer as to why Joseph had killed her, even though the case could be said to be over now that Joseph was dead. I should have to report to Billy Johnson, and yet there was still a niggle in my mind that I didn't know the full story.

I walked back toward the towpath and the canal, pondering this, and realised that by mistake I had come not back to the Regent's Canal but to the one they call Duckett's. This has only been working as a proper canal again for the last few years, and joins the Regent's Canal at the Old Ford Locks to link it to the River Lea Navigation canal going up north of London.

It was then I remembered that Duckett's Canal is more properly called the *Hertford* Union Canal—and I knew at last how Joseph and his accomplice might have got the body to the fountain. I grew excited at this idea. Suppose they had put the body on a barge moored in the Regent's Canal, at the nearest point to Claremont House? They could have hidden it in the cargo hold, and then taken the barge through the locks to Duckett's Canal; this also borders the park, but is much nearer to the fountain. Dinah might even have been alive when she was taken on board. At that time of night there wouldn't be many people about. Easy enough to support Dinah, dead or alive, between two hefty men. They'd just look like drunken boatmen returning to their bunks.

And that, too, must have been how Joseph had reached Hert-ford when he ran away. The sailing ship I had imagined he had taken to foreign parts was in fact a different kind of boat, a nar-row boat, as barges are called.

Full of excitement I went to find Constable Peters again, who was most interested in what I had to say, as it might lead them to Joseph's killer. He would be making enquiries about the barges that had registered through the Old Ford Locks both on the night Dinah died, and on the day that Joseph disappeared. We then went to inspect Duckett's canal together, and found a point where the fence looked as though it could have been climbed or broken down. I became so interested in this, that I quite forgot I was a sweep and fancied myself a real detective.

As the constable left me, he asked me casually how Miss Jemima was. Apparently Mr. and Mrs. Periwinkle were coming to the ball on Saturday and had suggested, he mentioned with a slight blush, that Miss Jemima could come to "help out" for the evening. It seemed everyone would be at the ball, and so I was highly pleased that I too was included, even though I was no Prince Charming to greet my Cinderella. It seemed, however, that Jemima had another one ready waiting for her.

As regards her sister's murder, I was now left with only one question: why take Dinah as far as the fountain? To get away from any suspicion that might attach itself to the barge? I remembered that it was only by chance that she had been recognised as soon as she was, as her purse had been taken away from her. Eventually she would have been identified, but time would have passed by then. To whose advantage would that be? To give Joseph time to run away? But if so, why didn't he leave in the narrow boat that evening?

And how, if at all, did my china lady fit in?

I still had no answers. It seemed to me I should give up being a detective and stick to my brushes.

CHAPTER TEN

It's not often that sweeps attend balls, and properly speaking I wasn't invited to this one. Nevertheless, I scrubbed my face, thanking the fact that Saturday, 8 February, was one of the days that water flowed in Hairbrine Court, which had reduced its grime to a pale shade of grey.

I tried to encourage Ned to do the same, but although he agreed to spit on a rag and have a go at his face and hands, he wouldn't go near the running water. No pie in the world would be strong enough inducement for that. I daresay one of these days he'll take a fancy to a girl and then it might be a different story. Knowing Ned, he'll probably find himself a young lady chimney sweep, just to avoid the problem. There are quite a lot of them in the trade these days.

We took a growler to Claremont House that Saturday evening. It had been a cold day with fresh winds, and that had not helped my gloom. I hadn't told Ned where I had hidden the Chinese lady, but I think he might have suspected, and I preferred to leave Doshie guarding our treasure rather than risk a curious publican finding her. I was getting used to this grand way of life of taking growlers everywhere, and had to remind myself that it would only last while Billy was paying. I only hoped I'd be able to satisfy him I'd done my best, and indeed I supposed I was progressing, with Erich's release and Joseph now believed to be guilty of Dinah's murder. I even knew how the murder had been done. But I did not feel happy about the "why."

"Pigmen," remarked Ned tersely when we arrived at Claremont House—and he was right. I've never seen so many pigmen together, save at Scotland Yard. There were pigmen guarding the gates, pigmen guarding every entrance from what I could see, and no doubt pigmen hiding in the bushes front and rear. The Prince of Wales has his own special pigman, so I've heard, so there must have been extra guards for him. I thought about his grand coach no doubt making its way along Bethnal Green Road at this very moment and wondered what the local population there made of it. I found much the same situation in the usually decorous servants' hall and kitchens. I had had some difficulty reaching them, owing to the pigmen guarding the tradesmen's door, who had to call Mr. Longfellow for reassurance that I wasn't an assassin after the Prince of Wales' blood.

There were footmen and serving maids and cooks rushing everywhere like an anthill tipped out its normal routine. Liveried footmen sped to and fro with dishes for the banquet supper tables, which made a glorious spectacle of colour and appetising delights. I gaped at what still remained laid out on the kitchen tables and Ned's face was a picture as he tried to take in all the glories of what looked like ducks and other game adorned with all manner of vegetables moulded into decorative shapes, not to mention the hams and rolls of beef. Fish twinkled at us, proudly ornamented with jelly and shellfish, and strange shapes of food I did not recognise bore witness to the grandeur of the occasion.

"Better than Rag Fair, eh?" I joked to Ned.

He nodded vigorously, his eyes fixed on his great love, the pies; these were huge, luscious-looking creations, so shiny with glaze that they made you want to bite into them right away. I made sure that Ned didn't, however. Instead, I drew his attention to the swan in the middle of puddings. This was not a real live bird, but a confection of what looked like cake, cream, and a hard white substance. A web of fine white threads surrounded its base together with coloured sweetmeats.

"Out of 'ere, Wasp." I heard Mrs. Poole's stentorian tones behind me and Ned and I were sent back to the servants' hall. I feared we might be there all evening, so I knew I must assert myself. "I'll need a word with Mr. Longfellow, Mrs. Poole."

"He's busy, and so am I," she snapped.

I believed that. The servants' hall was full of young housemaids in black and wearing mob caps. I recognised Mary, but she had no time to stop to chat, and then to my pleasure I saw Jemima in the corridor, who winked at me as she hurried by with a plateful of cheese.

"Well, Mrs. Poole," I answered, standing at the doorway so that she could not pass out. "I'm here at Sir Laurence's request, so I'd like to see what's going on."

Mrs. Poole was clearly weighing up her chances of getting into trouble if she didn't help me against her natural instincts to ignore me. I'm glad to say the former consideration won, and she became quite amiable—for her. "Follow me then. Mr. Longfellow has his own special watching place at the end of the passageway. It's the footmen's livery room, but there are a couple of spy windows on to the main hall, so that Mr. Longfellow can keep an eye on the situation to see when he's needed."

Although I wasn't sure what I should be looking for, this sounded a good place to begin—especially if Mr. Longfellow was there. The butler always knows everything, or thinks he does. I left Ned to his own devices—usually a bad plan, but sometimes it works. I think he was glad, because once having established his credentials with the pigmen on the door, Ned mentioned airily that he'd keep an eye on the outside. Did he suspect that Young Nipper was waiting in the bushes to dip the Prince of Wales' pocket as he descended from his golden coach? If so, I could be of no help, and he would indeed be better alone. I could mop up any disasters afterward.

I walked up the passageway, keeping to one side so that I was not bowled over by the constant traffic up and down. I gathered from Mrs. Poole that the guests would start to arrive at any time now, with the Prince of Wales making a grand entrance after all the others had assembled. I was as nervous as though I were waiting to meet him myself. I found Mr. Longfellow in charge of this small room, which he was sharing with at least six footmen, and a cloud of white violet powder. This was obviously where the wigs were freshly powdered by the footmen before they hurried on duty. The six men, spick and span in their livery, pushed past me to the hall where I saw through the spy window they were lining up like toy soldiers ready for the guests' arrival.

Mr. Longfellow was his usual dour and disappointed self. The mere fact that the Prince of Wales was about to arrive seemed not to impress him at all, in comparison with the grandeur of his previous position. Fortunately, other fellow observers joined us. The clockwinder was present—for some reason that Mr. Chuckwick must have explained to the butler. His muffin man days seemed to be over. I sighed, wondering whether Mr. Chuckwick would be accompanying me for the rest of my life. Perhaps he would be marching me up to the Pearly Gates in due course, to ensure that St. Peter treated me properly.

There were also several ladies in the room, perhaps the governess or lady's maids, and even Miss Twinkle was at hand to attend to emergencies over the ladies' dress, as she informed me. Today, she was clad in a modest black crinoline, the skirts of which she whisked away from me in case my black rubbed off on hers.

Nevertheless, she treated me to a good evening, as though I were a real person to her, worthy of acknowledgment. This was a rare privilege, and I duly responded. To the guests I could now see arriving in the hall, Miss Twinkle herself would not count as a real person, just as no doubt to the Prince of Wales many of those guests wouldn't be real people themselves. To our social superiors anyone less superior risks being seen by them as a sort of waxwork. The difference is that we are moving waxworks, specially designed to adorn the scene. I reflected that only the poor people at the bottom of this pyramid never have any waxworks of their own to look down on, but then most of them are so food- and hope-deprived that they haven't the energy to care whether they are real people themselves. It's left to God to sort out this injustice, and luckily He doesn't go in for waxworks.

"That," Miss Twinkle informed me breathlessly, "is the Dowager Duchess of Blessington."

I had never heard of the lady, but it was a pleasure to look at the beautiful silks and satins worn by Lady Mallerby and her guests. As I watched Sir Laurence and his wife receiving their guests, I felt I was both part of this colourful stirring scene and yet separated from it. I daresay my companions in this room felt the same. I'd no objection to this, as I thought of it as I do a lovely tree in blossom in the spring; it raises the heart, but I don't want to be a tree myself.

From what I've seen of London society as I clean its chimneys, I wouldn't want to be part of that either, although such lovely scenes of jewels and silks and satins lift my heart. I daresay that when their wearers return home, they face their problems too. There's a dark side to life everywhere you go, and I doubt if the Prince of Wales himself is always happy. They say he had differences with his father, and his mother is very strict. Of course she has to be; she's our Queen, and yet a woman too. Her mourning for the Prince Consort is as real as that of any East End widow. I remember how I mourned my Maria, and no doubt the Queen has felt much the same since Prince Albert died a year or so ago.

"The Prince will arrive last," twittered Miss Twinkle importantly, as though she were privy to royalty's closest secrets. "These are merely ambassadors arriving now."

An odd remark—merely an ambassador. I smiled to myself, reflecting that waxworks are only waxworks if they so think of themselves that way, and Miss Twinkle obviously saw herself at a royal level. Nevertheless, it reminded me of my task. Sir Laurence had mentioned ambassadors in connection with Erich Mayer, and I wondered if the Prussian ambassador would be coming here. Tonight Sir Laurence was in formal dress coat, silk waistcoat and white bow tie, not in flowing white robes, although one or two guests so clad arrived. I heard Mr. Longfellow sniff at yet another departure from what in his view was proper. I was lost in admiration at the sight, however, and recollecting why I was here was difficult with this colourful display before me. Indeed, why was I here? I had forgotten that question. Were my rooms being ransacked yet again? It was hard to think with all this going on and the band's music in the background.

"Handel," said Miss Twinkle, which I did not understand. She explained that he was a composer who had been born in Saxony but lived in London some while ago and had composed music for our king. This piece of music being played now was known as "the Arrival of the Queen of Sheba" and from this I deduced that the Prince of Wales must have arrived.

"The French ambassador," she breathed in my ear, and I could see a dapper, smart-looking gentleman with a most at-

tractive lady on his arm. "The Prussian ambassador." Her voice
rose in a crescendo of excitement.

I was excited too. This was the man who had so earnestly
sought the release of Erich Mayer—and had succeeded. I felt
proud of my small role in this, and wondered if he knew a
chimney sweep had helped. His face reminded me of someone,
but I could not think who and put it down to the excitement of
the occasion. I decided I should compliment Miss Twinkle, as I
needed all the friends I could get in this house.

"You're well informed, Miss Twinkle."

"Miss Twinkle," Mr. Longfellow announced, as if this was
new to me, "is known at all the best houses in London, including my *own* previous abode."

That was an honour for Miss Twinkle, I thought, most
amused. Mr. Chuckwick must have thought so too, for he voiced
a suitable reminiscence about the clocks he had wound in
Windsor Castle. Appropriately, the music rose to a fine crescendo.

"He is coming," Miss Twinkle cried, and we all stood to attention. Not that the Prince would know that, as we were not
within his sight, but it seemed right to do so.

Miss Twinkle monopolised one spy window, and I had the
other, as Mr. Longfellow had promptly left to join his line of
footmen outside. Mr. Chuckwick was peering over my shoulder.
Through the ranks of the footmen, I saw a young man in
evening attire, with a moustache, dressed most correctly. So
that was the Prince of Wales, and I felt privileged to be here. I
had read in the newspaper that his marriage next month would
take place amid much state and pomp, and it is rumoured that
the Danish princess Alexandra is a lovely lady. The wedding will
be at Windsor Castle, but in order that the people of London
may see their future queen, there will be a procession in state
when the Princess lands in England with her parents.

After the Prince of Wales had entered the ballroom to meet
the guests, the excitement in the footmen's room ended, and we
returned, regretfully, to our own jobs. Only I could not do so.
Mr. Chuckwick's job was to guard me, but I had no job that I
was aware of. That was soon to change.

"Sir Laurence's instructions," Mr. Longfellow told me later that
evening. "He would be obliged if you would stay overnight, Mr.
Wasp. He wishes to see you in the morning."

This plan did not suit me at all, even though Ned was
enthusiastic about it. I'm not sure of his reasoning, but I felt it
might have something to do with leftovers from that banquet. It
was going to take more than a piece of decorated duck to soothe
my unease, however. There was an odd atmosphere in Claremont
House, as though its real life were going on elsewhere and that
even this ball had been planned to this end, not just as a social
occasion. Now I was being moved around like a brush in the
chimney and I didn't like it. Apart from anything else, who
would feed Doshie? Would Mr. Chuckwick? No, I could not risk
that. I was going to have to insist on returning home.

This was made easier for me by a summons to the drawing
room after the Prince and most of the guests had left. Here I
met Mr. and Mrs. Periwinkle, to my pleasure. Lady Mallerby
and Sir Laurence were also present, however, hovering in the
background, as though politely remaining at a distance from
their friends' conversation. By the look on Lady Mallerby's face
she was not pleased at seeing me, but I understood this attitude. "We want to thank you, Mr. Wasp, for—" Mr. Periwinkle
beamed.

"Being such a friend to Jemima," Mrs. Periwinkle finished for
him. She was looking very bonny in a low-cut pink silk dress
with no waistline, which Miss Twinkle said was a Princess line.
My word, Mrs. Periwinkle looked one tonight.

"When I last called at the Gables," I said, "you had had the misfortune of a burglary. No more trouble, I trust?" There were far too many burglaries around at present for my liking.

"Fortunately no," Mr. Periwinkle assured me.

"Of course we often wondered what it was—" Mrs. Periwinkle began, but this time it was her husband who broke in, although not to finish her sentence.

"You were a good friend to Eliza Hogg." He looked at me very keenly. "You saw her in prison."

Here we go up the chimney again, I thought.

"Indeed he did," Sir Laurence called out. "And Eliza gave him a present. Unfortunately, it's been stolen."

Mr. Periwinkle frowned. "So I understand. It seems, Laurence, if you'll forgive me—"

"Rather a coincidence," Mrs. Periwinkle finished timidly, "that both our houses have been robbed."

"I'm a chimney sweep," I said mildly. "Not a robber."

An exclamation of horror. "Oh, Mr. Wasp, of course not. I trust we did not imply that," quoth Mrs. Periwinkle. "We merely hoped you might have some thoughts on the matter, as you knew Eliza well."

"Jemima's father suggested at poor Dinah's funeral that we should speak to you. We knew Dinah, of course," Mr. Periwinkle said.

So they were bringing Billy Johnson into this obviously by design, which did not please me. I did not want the Rat Mob involved in the matter of the china lady, but now it was beginning to seem as if Billy might well have known about her. I realised I had been underestimating Billy. He knew about the burglary at my lodgings, and what it was about. Was that through Mr. Chuckwick or through Young Nipper? And who, I wondered, was Young Nipper working for?

"The burglaries at your homes must be mere coincidence," I

said, looking as puzzled as I could manage. "Eliza's gift to me was only a sailor doll."

Sir Laurence sighed. "We'll speak in the morning, Wasp."

Oh, would we, indeed. "I'm agreeable to that, sir, but I'll be returning home this evening."

He frowned. "I want you here."

"I have my responsibilities, and I have my lad with me."

"Ah yes, Ned." Then came a silence that I didn't care for, but finally he shrugged. "Have it your own way, Wasp. I'll send my carriage for you in the morning. How about that?"

"Most kind, sir." I avoided Lady Mallerby's eyes. What she would make of a chimney sweep sitting on her nice carriage cushions, I didn't care to think. I thanked Mr. and Mrs. Periwinkle, who were looking bemused. I suspected they had been talked into this appeal to my finer nature by Sir Laurence and had little idea why. I did. Sir Laurence wanted the china lady back.

As I left the drawing room, I saw that the band was leaving, and with a jolt of surprise I saw a familiar face. It was Erich Mayer. Why this should take me so much aback, I don't know. Why shouldn't he rejoin his band? I could see Carl Weber too, and it was then I realised who the Prussian ambassador had reminded me of. Yet another imponderable coincidence. I could no longer trust my head, owing to the late hour and this series of inexplicable circumstances. Everyone, it seemed, had something to demand of Tom Wasp, but I was totally unable to work out why.

Next morning, my head was clearer, but I was not looking forward to my appointment with Sir Laurence. If he had wanted me to stay overnight at Claremont House in order that my humble rooms could be turned over yet again, my insistence on returning home had deterred him. Nor had the china lady's hiding place been discovered. Doshie was still guarding his trophy, and even Ned had not yet discovered it, or at least he had not commented on it.

I was growing tired of my position in Claremont House, halfway between the Mallerby family and its servants. I felt at home with neither, and preferred the Rat Mob, since I felt on securer ground. It is said that there is honour among thieves, but I never yet heard of a saying that there is honour among diplomats.

Sir Laurence's carriage did indeed arrive as promised, and so I had no choice but to take it to Claremont House. Mr. Silas Rodway was driving it, and did not look impressed at his mission. I decided to travel alone, and entrusted Ned with looking after Doshie for the day. After all, if he found the china lady, he would not dare remove her.

This summons by Sir Laurence still had the air of a plan to me, and one over which I had little control. There were too many of these coincidences: the Prussian ambassador at the ball and the Prussian band were one example. I told myself that the Prince of Wales was more than half German, and the Prince Consort had been German, and so the choice of the band had been a compliment to the Prince. But despite the joyful sound of Sunday morning church bells, my unease did not lift. After all, that's what I understood diplomacy to be: something that looked rational, but underneath represented something quite different.

I was not permitted the front entrance, but once inside the tradesmen's door I was led by Mr. Longfellow straight to the morning room, as though I were a real guest. Sir Laurence was certainly treating me well. One would think I was a diplomat myself, in view of the chair he waved me to; we were facing each other across the writing desk man to man, not diplomat to sweep.

"I owe you an explanation, Wasp. You seem a trustworthy person, and Mr. and Mrs. Periwinkle have a high opinion of you."

"Thank you, sir." Watch out, I told myself. There's something coming your way, and it's not going to be good.

"Enjoy the ball, did you? It's not often one can see England's royal family, peerage and diplomatic service all at once, eh?"

"No, sir," I agreed. It was going to be worse than I thought. Last evening's invitation to me had been in order to impress me; this meeting was to make me into his puppet.

"You'd like to serve your country?"

I could be a diplomat myself. "I like to serve Her Majesty, sir." So it was going to be *very* bad.

"That Chinese statue . . ." he began casually.

"The one you kindly gave me, sir?" I relied equally casually.

He eyed me sharply. "No, Wasp. The one you lost, but now have back in your possession."

He thought he'd trick me, but I was there before him. I wrinkled my brow—not that he would see that amid the grime. "Why should you think that, sir? It was stolen, as I told you." I'd been right. He *had* planned another raid.

He sighed, as if with the heaviest of burdens upon him. "Have you ever seen a juggler, Tom? Ever wondered how they keep all those balls in the air at once without dropping them?"

"I've never tried it myself."

"You are fortunate. It's a diplomat's job to do that all the time. But sometimes the balls crash to the ground out of control. What does one do then, eh?"

"Pick them up, sir?"

Another keen glance, as if he sensed I was mocking him. I wasn't. I was playing for time till he made his point. "I try to, Wasp, but sometimes I need help." He leaned purposefully across the desk. "I need *yours*. Are you willing to give it?"

"It depends what's needed," I said practically. Sir Laurence wasn't the sort of man I took easily to, but that didn't mean he was a villain.

"My job is to keep all the balls of the world, especially European ones, in the air together, catching them and tossing them up again one by one, and *not* letting them go. Understand? England, which is me, for the sake of this argument, has to be constantly juggling. It's our role."

There was nothing I could add to this, so I let him continue. I would do better listening to what he said than thinking about what I could reply.

"If we're not careful," he continued, "all the balls are going to crash rather soon, in fact very soon in my opinion, and that Chinese statue is the reason. Yours, I mean, not the one I gave you. Although the word *yours* must, I regret, be disputed."

Now this annoyed me. "The one you told me was worthless, sir?"

He had the grace to look shamefaced. "It's a statue of the goddess Kwan-yin, made by the great Chinese potter Ho Ch'ao-tsung three to four hundred years ago. It's called blanc de Chine ware here, but more correctly it's Te-hua porcelain. It's valuable of course, but its importance far outshines that. It belongs, or belonged, to the emperors of China. To them, including the current emperor, she is priceless. Kwan-yin is the Chinese goddess of mercy, and is believed to give protection against adversity. There is a story that she appeared as a vision to the Chinese army in a recent battle, to give the soldiers courage; they won the battle, and her prestige was enhanced even further. The emperor will make no move without her presence, since over the years emperors have become superstitious; good fortune will only come in battle with the blessing of Kwan-yin, which for the emperor—who for our purposes represents the whole leadership of China—means his porcelain image of her."

Whatever role I thought the statue played in this affair, I wasn't prepared for this. I found it hard to believe that my china lady (as I shall always think of her, even if she is made of porcelain) had belonged to an emperor of the great China. But when I thought of my lady's calm, lovely features and the way she looked so peacefully out on mankind's frailties, I could believe in what Sir Laurence was telling me. And to think she was currently living in Doshie's hay box.

"What is she doing here then?" I asked, sticking to what seemed the central point.

Sir Laurence smiled. "A good question, which we have all been asking ourselves. We believe the answer is this. There was an unfortunate incident in sixty-one, when we were still at war with the Chinese, and when I was once again in China with Lord Elgin. The Chinese saw fit to ignore the rules of war, and took twenty or so of our men prisoner while they were under a flag of truce. They tortured them abominably and most of them died. We were thus compelled to burn the emperor's summer palace to show our displeasure, and during that unfortunately essential operation, looting took place—not, I assure you, by the highly disciplined British soldiers, but by French troops.

"We believe," he continued, "that part of the French loot was the statue of Kwan-yin and that George Hogg bought it from its temporary possessor, in the hope that it had some small value. In fact, it now holds the balance of war and peace in Europe, although naturally George Hogg could not have guessed that. Something may have made him realise that he had more than he had bargained for, for he did not sell it, but hinted to Mr. Periwinkle that he had something of value. Unfortunately, before Mr. Periwinkle passed this news to me, George was dead and—well, our only conclusion could be that Eliza had stolen it for herself. The rest I think you know. The balance of peace and war, Wasp."

All I could think of was Doshie in his stable, or perhaps even out with Ned at this very moment, leaving the lady unguarded. "Just a statue, sir?" I found myself squeaking, in my effort to work out how this applied to what had been happening to Dinah, Joseph—and me.

"A symbol of China's potential power, and a particularly dangerous one at present. After the summer palace episode the Chinese signed a treaty to give Britain what we wanted, namely the ability to trade freely at some of their major ports. Since then an uneasy peace has prevailed between our two nations—not least because the Emperor now has other political troubles. For many years the Taiping rebels in the south of the country have caused him many problems, seeking to break away from Peking. They are currently threatening our interests at ports, especially at Shanghai. Our interests and the Emperor's therefore—unusually—coincide. Regrettably, last September the commander of our forces in Shanghai was killed and there has been, and still is, argument over his successor, which means there is a weakness there, though we trust that shortly General Gordon will be appointed.

"At the moment, therefore," he continued, speaking in a low voice to indicate how serious and secret this all was, "we are in a position where China is forced to accept us as allies in order to fight off the Taiping challenge while we ourselves are weak. The emperor desperately wants his statue back in order that the Taipings can be defeated and, he hopes, we can then be evicted. We need to prevent him from getting the statue back at least until we ourselves are stronger. Unfortunately, as you will recall, there was a burglary at the home of Mr. and Mrs. Periwinkle, and Oriental thieves were involved, knowing the statue was, or had been, there."

"It was fortunate Eliza gave it to me, sir." I remembered the attempted burglaries and the sailors Sergeant Wiley had been after, and wondered whether this was how the Nichol Gang had become involved. Whether through the putter-up or not, they had been asked by the Chinese to track down George and his statue.

"Indeed it was," Sir Laurence replied dryly. "However, I need to find it urgently, Wasp, but as you know—" was there an emphasis on the *know?* "—Claremont House is not safe either. I had mistakenly thought that it would be safer with you in Hairbrine Court as no one would assume a chimney sweep possessed it."

"Then why steal it back, sir?" I asked him flatly.

"Ah." He hesitated, then saw my expression, which I like to think was relentless, and he gave in. "It ceased to be safe to leave it with you. There's another ball I'm juggling with, you see. Prussia. Its new chancellor von Bismarck is flexing his wings, trying to make Prussia predominant over all the other German states and then unite them into one."

"But this Kwan-yin isn't a German goddess."

"That is true, but diplomacy is a complicated matter. There are two duchies that Bismarck wishes to join a united Germany, Schleswig and Holstein." This meant nothing to me, and he explained that these were currently under the protection of Denmark, but Denmark's claim was disputed by Bismarck; Bismarck foresaw a battle coming up over this matter and was eager that England should stay out of the way. "The more he sees we are occupied with China fighting the Taipings and arguing over goddesses," Sir Laurence said, "the more he will be pleased."

There seemed to be so many balls to juggle in diplomacy that chimneys began to look very simply planned in comparison. "Denmark, sir?" This seemed a name much nearer the top of the chimney so far as I was concerned, and I seized on it. "But the Prince of Wales is about to marry the Danish princess.

Denmark wouldn't like it if England kept out of the way if there was war."

According to what the patterer and newspapers told me about the doings of the world, all these countries seemed to behave like sailors turning out of Paddy's Goose on docking night. One starts a brawl and all the others pile in.

"We'll have you in the Foreign Office yet, Wasp," Sir Laurence laughed, though I privately thought that if reasoning as simple as this was the only qualification for governing one's country, it couldn't be as complicated as I thought.

"The Prince of Wales who graced us with his presence last night, and whom you no doubt glimpsed," he continued, "is to marry the daughter of the heir to the Danish throne, and the current King of Denmark is in fast failing health. When he dies, the future of Schleswig and Holstein will immediately arise and there could be war between Prussia and Denmark. Bismarck is determined we should not take Denmark's side, and equally the Prince of Wales would be concerned that we *should*. All our attention needs to be on Europe, not on China if war is to be averted."

I could see this was a most difficult situation. "So you want to keep the statue here but the Prussians want to return it to the emperor of China?"

"Well done, Wasp, although I fear it is worse than that. I suspect that von Bismarck wants the statue, because his aim is not to return it to the Emperor but to the Taipings—which would cause civil war in China, and mean Britain's undoubted intervention if our valuable trade is to be protected. Any local squabble between Denmark and Prussia would go unnoticed, so Bismarck would reason. Do you understand my position?"

I told him I did, but both my head and my heart were heavy. "What you want is to keep the statue under your personal protection."

A flicker of his eyes. "Yes."

"Pardon me, sir, but she's not safe with you. You had a burglary, just like I did."

His face grew as black as mine, as he realised we were at checkmate. If I admitted I had her at present, then I would be admitting on Ned's behalf that he had done the burglary. If he admitted he had stolen her from me in the first place, he was admitting to the burglary from my home.

I felt some sympathy with his dilemma. "I'm sure she's in a safe place, sir, wherever she is." Neither Prussia nor China would be invading Doshie's stable.

He lost his temper then, and crashed his fist on the table. "By God, Wasp, I'm ordering you to surrender that statue. I'll have you taken away in chains—"

"And have the story made public, sir?"

A silence while he glared at me. "It's safe?"

"I'm sure it must be, sir, wherever it is."

"Would you hand it over to Sergeant Williamson?"

"When I've finished my job, sir."

Another crash on the table. "And what, Chimney Sweep Wasp, do you blasted well consider to be your job?"

This was easy to answer. "Finding out the whole truth about Dinah Johnson's death, sir."

Diplomats may come and diplomats may go, but Dinah's life had been taken from her through no fault of hers. This is a dark enough world without making it one in which an individual life counted for nothing. Dinah's mattered to me—and it did to her sister and her parents. I still had to find out the connection between that and Eliza Hogg's gift to me. I was getting closer, but I wasn't there yet.

And I had to find it without the watchful eye of the spies that Sir Laurence would doubtless be setting on me. What was one chimney sweep's life once they had followed me and found where I had hidden her? Nothing. And therefore, I reasoned, I needed the cooperation of Mr. Chuckwick.

CHAPTER ELEVEN

No sooner had this fear become lodged in my mind than I realised I'd left Ned alone at Hairbrine Court, and I decided that my energy would be better spent in returning there as quickly as possible than in blaming myself for that. My next step would be to find Mr. Chuckwick, not for my own protection but because of this new information from Sir Laurence. For once, there was no sign of him, however. I scoured the empty forecourt, and on enquiring from Mr. Longfellow, I discovered there had been no sign of the clockwinder that morning. I had grown to have some faith in Mr. Chuckwick's constant ability to present himself like the genie in the tale of Aladdin, so his absence was a surprise—and today not a welcome one.

I considered using some of my money to hire a growler but thought better of it. Sir Laurence was a cunning man and could easily have a growler in his pay waiting round the corner. I told myself I was not thinking rationally, but as it seemed unlikely that Sir Laurence would have a whole omnibus company in his pay, I chose that means of transport, only to be frustrated in that none seemed to be passing my way. By the time I found one that would take me to Commercial Road, my legs were sore and my mind confused over what to worry about first.

Climbing upstairs to the top of omnibuses, although it provides me with a dose of London air, is difficult for me, but going inside even with my newly scrubbed face would not be popular with other passengers. I took a careful look at the omnibus driver and as he took no such careful look back, I presumed I was safe from spies. All the same, I was much relieved when I reached Commercial Road and was able to hurry toward Hairbrine Court. There still had been so sign of Mr. Chuckwick, and I was almost sure he was not the omnibus driver. Had I been abandoned by Billy Johnson? Had he heard about Young Nipper—and Ned?

"Ned?" I called out as soon as I reached the stairs to our lodgings, but there was no reply. Full of fear, I opened the door to our rooms—and to my relief, although there was no Ned to be seen, there was no sign of the lodgings having been ransacked yet again. Then I heard laughter coming from the yard below. Peering through the window I saw a different Ned to the one I knew. He was almost clean! He seemed to be in the company of a pigman, so I hurried down to the yard to find out what the reason for this phantasmagoria might be.

"Good morning to you, Mr. Wasp." The pigman's hat was lifted to reveal Mr. Chuckwick.

Ned looked shamefaced. "It wasn't so bad, guvner," he told me, referring to his changed appearance. "Once I got used to it."

"One begins with the face and hands, and the rest will follow, Ned," Mr. Chuckwick assured him.

"You've done a good job there," I praised him. "He's quite a handsome lad when some of the grime comes off. Next week you can come to the baths with me, Ned, and see if it comes off the rest of you." He did not look delighted at this prospect, and muttered something I could not hear but closely resembled language that our Lord would not countenance.

"I trust you do not object, Mr. Wasp. It seemed to me," Mr. Chuckwick said gravely, "that my time was better spent this morning in guarding Ned and your premises than yourself. Fortunately, Mr. Johnson keeps a few blues' uniforms. They come in handy."

I began to like Mr. Chuckwick even more. "It's time for talking," I told him, and he agreed, only considering his chosen garb of the day, he suggested that we move from Hairbrine Court to an area where it did not matter if he was seen chatting with me for some time. Such an association could otherwise affect both our reputations. Ned could accompany us, however.

We settled on a green spot we both knew on Tower Hill, both having our reasons for liking it. Mr. Chuckwick thought it appropriate with his current disguise that he should frequent a place so connected with law and order—in view of the many cruel executions carried out here in former times. I liked it just because, despite the way that houses and shops have fought over its land for many a long year now, there still remains this bit of green grass, rare enough in our part of London.

Mr. Chuckwick gave his professional opinion that we were not being followed and so I gave Ned a whole sixpence to make himself scarce for a while, in order that Mr. Chuckwick and I could talk alone. He scampered off toward the Tower again, which fascinates us both, as it has been as much a prison as a palace over the centuries. They must be much the same in effect, though the living conditions vary. Kingship must be a sort of prison in that the risk of death lurks in the wings and robs one of peace of mind, and its duties steal one's freedom. Her poor Majesty must find that.

Mr. Chuckwick and I bought ourselves a mug of beer from the Bull, a public house nearby, and sat down to discuss our situation. It was hard to talk to him at first, he being in a pigman's uniform, but his earnest eyes soon reassured me.

"Is the real Mr. Chuckwick sitting here with me," I joked, "or are you thinking as a pigman?"

Mr. Chuckwick considered this question seriously. "Let us agree that he is," he said at last, a trifle reluctantly, or so it seemed to me, "within the confines of my duty to Mr. Johnson."

This seemed reasonable, if chilling, in view of my fear for Ned. "Mr. Johnson hired me to find out the truth behind his daughter's death," I began. "It's my belief, as you know, that it was Joseph Belt who killed her. All clear so far?"

"It is." Mr. Chuckwick nodded gravely.

"Joseph Belt is now dead, murdered for whatever reason. I can see there might be a case for someone wanting to kill me for knowing that Joseph, not Erich, killed Dinah, but why does your job still extend to guarding me? And do I even have a job anymore?"

"That isn't for me to say, Mr. Wasp," Mr. Chuckwick said immediately. "Those are my orders."

"But you'd agree it looks very strange."

"I do."

"Should I be having a chat with Mr. Johnson?"

"I believe you should, and—" he hesitated, "urgently."

"There might be a difficulty there. Can I trust him?"

A pink glow of indignation suffused Mr. Chuckwick's face. "Of course."

"And all of you, Giant George, Young Nipper and the rest, work only under his instructions?"

Mr. Chuckwick answered cautiously, I thought. "We are all devoted to Mr. Johnson."

I sighed. "It's a funny thing about devotion. Easy to think because we're devoted to someone that everyone else is too. Maybe some people start off devoted, and then something else steps in the way. Money perhaps, a woman, or fear. It's all too easy then to forget we're so devoted to someone, and get devoted to someone else, normally oneself. Suppose someone was not as loyal as you, and suppose that someone's disloyalty affected your job looking after me. Wouldn't there be a clash?"

Mr. Chuckwick looked grave. "If so, I would consider it my

duty to assign my task to another. Might I suggest, Mr. Wasp, that you take your concern to Mr. Johnson as soon as possible?"

I had to bear in mind that the Rat Mob was the second biggest gang in east London, and that Mr. Chuckwick, for all his rosy Mr. Pickwick face, was a member of it.

And I was not.

"You've got faith in Mr. Johnson," I replied. "Maybe you know everything, maybe you don't, which is where the faith must come in. Question is, if I go to see him, can I have faith? Or, not to mince my words, would Ned and I come out again in one piece?"

Mr. Chuckwick looked very upset. "You are a philosopher, Mr. Wasp. We are all mortal, and thus fallible to changing circumstances. We have but feeble minds that often choose to see what is around us only and what we want. Pray do visit Mr. Johnson. We *must* have faith, Mr. Wasp."

It was as far as I would get, so I changed course. "And what's your faith in, Mr. Chuckwick? Mr. Johnson or our Lord above? Or both?"

I received a beatific smile, which sat oddly with his pigman's uniform. "Mine is in Mrs. Chuckwick. I have so many jobs, Bug Destroyer to Her Majesty or captain of one of her ships, for instance, that it is hard to find my own self at times. Fortunately, Mrs. Chuckwick has no such difficulty. She tells me who I am and to trust Mr. Johnson. I do so."

"Even in this affair of his daughter's death?"

"She believes there is something amiss. Not with Mr. Johnson," he added hastily, "but something that is escaping the attention of all of us."

"That might cover a wide field," I observed.

"Mrs. Chuckwick said to me only yesterday that crime isn't what it used to be. Of course, as a pigman myself . . ." He broke off apologetically. "My apologies. I quite forgot myself. Crime used to be a simple matter of dipping, prigging, safe-cracking or slumming, but now——." He paused to draw a sombre breath. "There are wider dimensions, Mr. Wasp. *Foreigners* to deal with."

To hear this from Mr. Chuckwick's lips was chilling. It brought a reality to Sir Laurence's words that all his talk of diplomacy and other countries had failed to do. War between nations sounds a mighty thing, but it all comes down to bullets, bayonets and bodies—and they can lurk in every dark alley as well as on a battlefield.

"Mrs. Chuckwick," her husband continued, "is of the opinion that Mr. Johnson might be getting in over his head, and not even be aware of this situation."

"In what way?" I asked carefully, knowing not to rush him or he would take fright. Did he mean over Young Nipper or with Dinah's death or his daily work?

He took his time in answering, looking at the great Tower beneath us, and what remained of the green hill around us. "Many heads were lost here, not foreign ones for the most part, but traitors to our country and its way of life. It was a simpler age, Mr. Wasp. Other means have to be found to dispose of them now."

I nodded slowly, though I could not understand where this was taking us. What I did understand was that he was right. I needed to see Billy urgently.

The next evening, I received the summons I had been told to expect, although the choice of messenger was pleasantly unexpected. It was Miss Jemima, on her evening off from the Gables. She was clad in a dark cloak against the chill, and apart from Mr. Chuckwick waiting patiently for us in a growler, I could see no one else taking an undue interest in my movements. I had checked the previous evening that the china lady was still in Doshie's hay box, finding it hard to believe that something so lovely could cause such trouble between the nations. I had also checked most carefully to see that no one was following me or that so far as I could tell no one was watching my lodgings.

We were going to her parents' home, so Jemima told me, and hardly to my surprise, this was not at the rear of Paddy's Goose. We were passing the London Docks on the road to Wapping High Street, not that far from where I had been taken to meet Dabeno and his gang. The growler stopped at a house that was by no means that of a swell, but equally this was not Bluegate Fields standard either. It was a clear choice on Billy's part, I realised, as this house would hardly cause attention from passing pigmen, although the River Police's and Metropolitan Police's stations were so near.

Jemima knocked at the door, which was opened by Giant George. He filled the entire doorway, looking me up and down most carefully, as if sizing me up for his dinner. Fortunately, Jemima whisked me past him unscathed. Mr. Chuckwick anxiously explained he would return to Ned immediately, which caused me a moment's alarm—but I told myself I had faith in Mr. Chuckwick, and even if he had orders to hurt Ned, he would not do so.

Jemima took me into a most pleasant room in which Billy and Doll were sitting by a fire, once again looking like any other middle-aged couple taking a rest in the evenings after a day's toil, save for Giant George guarding the doorway. This was no ordinary house inside, and there was a lot to guard. It was packed with old china and silver and gold objects, giving it a grandeur I had only seen matched in the best of the swell houses I had worked in.

Billy and Doll rose to their feet as if I were royalty, but nevertheless we greeted each other cautiously. I felt as if Billy and Doll were mentally circling round me and growling like lions at Jamrach's Menagerie.

Billy opened the proceedings. "So Joseph Belt's dead."

"He is. It's my belief that he killed your poor daughter with the help of someone on one of those narrow boats moored on the Regent's Canal, took her on the barge to Duckett's, and then into the park from there. When Joseph ran away, he probably took the same barge. So, what I'm here to ask you," I said plainly, "is whether my job for you is over or whether it goes on."

"On," said Billy menacingly, although Doll did her best to look friendly.

"Over why Joseph killed her or why he was murdered?" I asked, puzzled.

"Both." Billy's fist had a crash that could rival Sir Laurence's, given a big desk rather than the arm rest at hand.

"I'm glad I asked, Billy. That means it can't have been you ordered his killing."

His eyes bulged. *"Me?"*

"In revenge, Billy. That's what he means," Doll grunted. "Fair enough. You were talking about it."

"I'm not sure revenge was the reason he was killed," I said hastily.

"That's good," Billy replied unemotionally. "Wish we had done it, but this one can't be laid at our door. You told us he'd taken a boat, so I had my men down all the docks checking out what boats left that night. Now you tell us it was a barge. Who did him in then?"

"Most likely the boatman or the barge owner. The pigmen are looking into it."

"Then it can't have been because of Dinah's death that he was killed," Doll said, doing her best to seem as tough as Billy, but having a hard job. This was her daughter we were talking about.

"Why not?" Billy snapped. "Forgotten *them*, have you?"

Doll shook her head, and I hadn't forgotten them either. We were back with the Nichol Gang.

"They set Belt on to murder my girl," Billy said flatly, "and then made sure he couldn't squeal on them."

This twist hadn't occurred to me, but then I saw the flaw. "Even if he did once, Belt didn't work for Dabeno anymore."

His eyes narrowed. "And how do you know that, Wasp?" he asked softly, and I could see his body tense.

Truth makes a good weapon sometimes. "Dabeno used his methods of persuasion to have a chat with me, and then kicked me out. He told me they had nothing to do with Dinah's death—"

"And you believed them?" A snort from Billy.

"Why should they bother to get hold of me if they were involved? No, I reckon he used to work for them once—like he did for you, but they threw him out."

He slowly took this in. Then he grunted. "They could have hired him again, just to kill my girl."

"They said not, and why should they lie to *me?*" I asked. "They could have wiped me out at any moment."

"Wrong," Billy decided. "Not if Dabeno knew you'd come crawling back to me. Sure you ain't been double-dealing, Wasp?"

Now was my chance. "I'm sure. What about your side?"

Doll gave a gasp, and Billy looked as if he'd explode. "A snitch in the *Rat Mob?*"

"Most pipes get leaks."

"Are you telling me I've got a squealer on the books?"

"You know you have," I said simply. "Young Nipper."

He studied me for a moment. "And what's that to you?" he asked mildly.

"Ned. Young Nipper led him astray."

"Strikes me he didn't need much leading," Billy retorted.

"Ned took back what had been pinched from us already. Nothing more."

"And what was that?"

Time to speak out now. "A piece given to me by Eliza Hogg."

"The Newgate Knocker herself, eh?" Billy looked interested, but I sensed this was not new information for him. I'd been right about that. "You got it now, have you?"

Careful, Tom, I warned myself. "If you think you've a right to it, Mr. Johnson, owing to Young Nipper being *sometimes* part of the Rat Mob, you're welcome to try. Why not? The whole of the Metropolitan Police Force, and the Nichol Gang, and maybe the putter-up are all in the queue first though."

Billy looked a bit strange. "Are they?"

"While they're occupied with me," I pointed out, "you could be fruitfully employed elsewhere."

He looked blank at that, but then he took my meaning. He might pick up some good jobs elsewhere. He laughed aloud. "I don't know what your game is, Wasp, but you mean well. So tell me, you being such a knowledgeable cove over how I should run the Mob, what would *you* do about Nipper? I've been taking my time deciding. Doll says to chop him, but I've a tenderer heart than she has."

A nervous giggle from Doll, while I thought it over.

"If it were me," I told him, "I'd get Mr. Chuckwick to give him a talk about the advantages of loyalty."

"And then what?" Billy asked with mild interest.

"I'd point out the dangers of disloyalty in a friendly way to him myself. Tell him Mr. Dabeno sees things the same way as you. And doubtless, just to be on the safe side, tell him the putter-up sees things that way too."

"Him?" Billy did react now. He looked both terrified and somewhat impressed. "You know who he is?"

"No idea," I said truthfully. "I'd be dead if I did." It was a sobering thought.

"You think *he's* mixed up in this caper?"

I hadn't given this angle much consideration, being too concerned with more pressing issues, but now I did. "Yes," I said. "And you do too, don't you?"

"You tell me," he grunted. "You're the one having long chats with the swells."

For a moment our eyes met and it seemed to me that we were working in the same flue. "If jealousy was the reason Joseph killed Dinah, he wouldn't have had time to find someone handily moored in the canal *after* he'd killed her. It must have been arranged in advance, which is unusual in a crime of passion. And even more unusual for the barge to take him away later, when it looked as if he might be under suspicion."

"You mean someone was looking after him very well," Billy said slowly.

"Not if they murdered him later. And would someone go to all that trouble to help him out if he only had his own private reasons for killing your daughter?"

Doll's face was a picture of misery, and no wonder, but Billy was tougher. He wanted the truth behind this puzzle. Or did he? When I heard his reply, I rather doubted it. "That proves it's the Nichol Gang, don't it?" he said eagerly. "He did it as a warning to me."

Here we were again, round and round the Mulberry bush. The Nichol Gang and his pet theory, although the word *putter-up* was staring me in the face.

"Not my thinking, Mr. Johnson. I think Dinah found out who the putter-up was."

To me this was far more likely, especially if he had some connection with Claremont House. I didn't have Sir Laurence in mind, or even Mr. Alfred, but there were others, such as Silas Rodway or even Mr. Longfellow, although I couldn't see how it would fit in with their daily duties. So perhaps I was sweeping the wrong flue.

"Nah." Billy was desperately thinking of alternatives, apparently still nervous of the very mention of the putter-up. "It's Dabeno's lot. They got hold of Belt to do their dirty work and then killed him when he'd done it. They've got some big job on, and maybe Dinah got in the way."

"Big job?" I queried uneasily, suspecting my china lady was involved in this. "How do you know? Young Nipper?"

Billy gave me a sideways look. "You leave Young Nipper to me, Wasp."

"Who then?" There was something strange about this Young Nipper affair, but I wasn't going to get anything more from him.

"From the pigmen." There was a touch of defiance in his voice.

"You've got a snout?"

He sighed. "It's come to a pretty pass, Wasp, to find my daughter's walking out with a pigman. And not even with her old dad in mind. Says she *likes* him."

With a sad heart, I realised he meant Constable Peters and Jemima. They'd suit, of course, both shiny and young with the world at their feet—in their dreams at least. And who can live without dreams?

Mr. Chuckwick returned in a growler to take Jemima and me back to our homes, so my protection was continuing. There was still a job for me to do, although I couldn't see my way through the gloom to where it lay. The growler stopped at the Gables first with St. George's in the East looming above us, and I climbed down to see Jemima safely inside the door. This was at Billy's request, but I would have done it anyway.

Jemima took my hand as we reached the door. "I hate going in late at night," she said, echoing my thoughts about her sister.

Dinah had thought she was safely home, but she wasn't.

She looked so sad, I took her hand in its little black glove and held it close to me. "We're coming to the end," I said, "when we can all be at peace over Dinah."

She smiled faintly, then leaned forward and kissed me on the cheek. "You're a dear man, Tom Wasp," she said.

I watched her as Mr. Tomm opened the door and led her into safety, then I turned back to the growler and Mr. Chuckwick. I still felt her lips upon my cheek. It was stinging, but not with the cold of the frost now forming, but with sadness that she could never be mine.

Chapter Twelve

I was in a sombre mood that night, and sensing this, Ned seemed to catch it from me. I bade goodnight to Mr. Chuckwick, who had insisted on following me up to our rooms, but anxiously tried to persuade me that in the circumstances his duty was to remain with us all night too. I said that he also had a duty to Mrs. Chuckwick and all the little Chuckwicks, and, admitting this to be true, he reluctantly departed. I had noticed as we entered the court, however, that there was a gentleman loitering under a gas lamp trying his best to indicate he was merely a drunken sailorman. He needed a few lessons from Mr. Chuckwick, and I hoped this plain-clothes policeman was better at guarding than impersonation.

It was not only Jemima who had left me under this pall of gloom. I didn't want to burden Ned with my worries, but as usual I need not have concerned myself over that. He brought the subject up himself, having wrapped his blanket round him for warmth. The fire had gone out by the time I returned home, and so it was clear that Ned had also been out on some mission. I was too tired to enquire what that might have been.

"Where's all this going, guvner?" he piped up.

"I wish I knew."

"But who's doing it?"

"I don't know that either." But I supposed I owed it to Ned to try to come to terms with this question, which was harder than it might seem. A conundrum of philosophy: who begins a

Amy Myers

crime? The person who makes it necessary or he who thinks of committing it? Or further back still perhaps—those who have let our country come to such a pass that crime is the easiest, sometimes the only, choice to make for some. If a labourer out of work through no fault of his own sees his child dying for want of a loaf of bread, what is he to do? I sighed, glad that I didn't have St. Peter's job.

Nevertheless, I had to give Ned some answer. "It seems to me it's like this, Ned. Dabeno's lot are after something, probably the china lady because of a job they've got on. Johnson's mob *seems* only to be after the Nichol Gang and are only interested in our humble dwelling because the Nichols are. Are you understanding me so far, Ned?"

A doubtful nod spurred me on. "There's another lot interested in this place, but we don't know who they are, although they could be something to do with the rulers of Prussia. Then there's the putter-up of the Nichols—he could be interested too. And lastly there's Sir Laurence, who's interested in all of them, and may have his own fish to fry."

That unfortunately reminded Ned he hadn't had supper, and he pulled a face. I took the hint and said I'd go out and buy us something. The time was getting on for midnight, but there's always somewhere open if you've the means to pay. And thanks to Billy, I had for once. Ned shook his head vigorously at this offer, and then I really did worry. All the same, I took heart that there was a pigman opposite who would guard the place.

"Do they all want the china lady, guvner?"

"Yes, Ned." After all, what else was there here for them?

A pause, and then he let fly with: "Which of them killed Jack?"

"I don't know." I was thinking how much I'd love to get my hands on whoever did. I don't count myself a violent man, but it struck me that perhaps most men could turn to violence if

190

those they love are attacked. And Jack's killer had dealt a most grievous blow to Ned.

Ned glared at me accusingly. "It's time we did know."

I felt I'd let him down. In going about things in my own way, and dabbling in high politics, I had been sidetracked from what was important: finding Jack's killer. The answer to both riddles might be the same, but in my station in life, Jack's killer should mean more than all the china ladies in the world. And it seemed to me, thinking of our lady's gentle face, that she would be quietly nodding her approval of this priority. It was time for a plan, I decided. And tomorrow I would make one.

Meanwhile I must force myself to go out to buy some supper, late though it was. I decided I would bring back a plate or two of mutton stew from the Black Lion and at the same time I could check that the china lady was safe and that Doshie hadn't tried to eat her. Telling Ned to keep quiet and keep the candles burning, I crept out of the house, looking carefully about me both ways. In Blue Anchor Yard the pigman was looking the other way, which was good, because I wanted him to guard the house, not me. I needed no curious eyes on my visit to the Black Lion.

Blue Anchor Yard was especially lively at midnight. As it is on the way from Rosemary Lane to Ratcliffe Highway, the liveliness was due to drunken sailors who were mostly merchantmen from St. Katherine's Dock where the high-value cargoes are unloaded. They were lurching back to their ships or to far from salubrious rooms with judies. All these pubs around here are much the same, out to fleece men from their money in the quickest way to their favours—or disfavours, if you could see the painted harlots who usually hold sway over these pubs. Laughter, paint and sheer brazen greed rule the roost, and bawdy songs and rum are constant companions. During the day it's different, as then the real people take over from the creatures of the night. The night life of the street is always changing. The darkness can be a velvety black, which nurses you as a friend, or it can be a menacing blanket to hide the evil that can so easily overtake you. Is it in one's mind that the two faces are born, or can evil be imprinted on a street such as this from violent deeds of ages past?

Tonight I thought it was the second of the two. It seemed to me that every sailor I passed had it in mind to garrotte a chimney sweep for fun—or were they Dabeno's men disguised? How could I tell? I know one kind of soot from another, but not how to tell a dipper from a killer. I reached the Black Lion thankfully and was about to go inside when I thought I should check on the china lady first. I could not easily carry my mutton stew into the yard, and so it was best done now to set my mind at rest.

I smelled the usual damp and black muck on the entry walls where the sun does not reach—the sun is a sensible old planet and does not delve into evil spots where he is not welcome. It was quite a wide entry for several horses were stabled here, and carts must have room to pass. Once perhaps carriages came through too, but not now, for prosperity had abandoned all hope for this place. I knew that Doshie was happy enough here, however, and indeed I could hear his whinny. He must have heard me coming. My feet squelched through the usual muck and mire in the passageway and then into the yard of muddy detritus where all of life's waste seemed to be thrown.

It was lit only by a couple of oil lamps provided courtesy of the Black Lion for those few of their customers who left horses here, generally like Doshie, so old and bony that they were no temptation even to knackers. There was a restless feeling abroad tonight amongst them, they were pawing the ground and giving the occasional neigh or whinny. Was that because of my appearance here? I did not think so, and I was anxious to get this business over and done with.

I could see Doshie's rump in the gloom and it comforted me, a sure point in an uncertain world. Even as I hurried toward him, however, I was aware of black shapes looming up at my side from behind. I had a moment to see two glaring eyes in a face that pushed itself so close to mine that I was aware of its smallpox scars. Then everything moved too fast to be conscious of anything else. There must have been four of them, to attack one chimney sweep of middle years. I was suffocating from the press of their arms, my head pulled back and something tight and then tighter round my throat. I glimpsed stars above me, or were they caused by my eyes as the scarf or rope bit deeper? Was I on the ground or only halfway there? I could not tell. There seemed no ground and no heaven, only pain and the smell of drink and smoke.

"Where is it, sweep?" a hoarse voice grunted in my ear. I could not answer, for now I was being kicked and beaten too. I choked and the pressure slackened on my neck as they waited to see if I would answer.

But I didn't.

"Where is it?" the voice grunted again.

"Kill the bastard," seemed to be his pals' suggestion.

In easier circumstances I might have thought that if they followed this advice they would never find what they were looking for, but my only thought then was I would be dead very shortly, if I did not do something about this situation. But what *could* I do? If I fought, I'd be dead; if I misled them, I'd be dead.

I am no hero. I wanted to serve my queen, as much as any man, but I didn't want to die for her. And I did want to watch over Ned for a few years yet. He needed me.

So I told them where the china lady was.

"In the manger," I croaked, even in my pain thinking that this sounded like the angels guiding the shepherds to the infant

Jesus. This comforting image ran through and through my head as I was hauled to my feet like a sack of soot, only soot can't feel bruises or lose blood, as I was doing.

"There," I whispered, pointing to the hay box. I was set loose and promptly fell down. I was hauled up again, and one of them supported me this time as we pushed past Doshie, who turned his head and looked at me reproachfully. "Beg pardon, Doshie," I added, even in my pain.

He must have looked even more reproachful as I stood by his hay box and let them throw all his precious food onto the floor. I closed my eyes, unable to bear the sight of the china lady whom I had betrayed in the greater interests of Ned.

"Where is it?" the voice yelled in fury.

"In there."

But she wasn't. When I managed to open my eyes again, even I could see that the hay was all scattered on the ground but the manger was empty.

I closed my eyes again and prepared for St. Peter. I'd be able to see firsthand how he carried out his job.

I never thought of angels having white uniforms and caps, but that's what I saw as I opened my eyes. Two seemed to be dancing on the ceiling, but after a minute or two they resumed the more usual upright position at my side. Convinced of their beatific status, I timidly asked the whereabouts of St. Peter, since I could see no pearly gates.

They both looked surprised, but seeing I was serious, one of them said in the gentlest voice I'd ever heard (except perhaps Jemima's):

"We're the Nightingales."

Not being in good health, I thought they were something to do with birds, as they sang so sweet a song, but the other nightingale added: "You're in hospital, Mr. Wasp. We're nursing sisters trained by Miss Florence Nightingale. You're in the London Hospital."

That brought me partly to my senses. This hospital on Whitechapel Road, a mile or two from where I live, is a great and noble institution over a hundred years old now, and built originally for the sick poor of our part of the world. I qualified under both headings, but it was the heading of sick that occupied me at present.

"I'm not dead?" I asked, still doubtful about my good luck.

"Badly hurt, but no bones broken."

I began to remember how it had happened and put a hand to my throat. I quickly took it away again for the instant pain was very bad.

"You've been here nearly two days now," the younger of the two told me.

I was about to ask how I had arrived, but then thought of a more important question. What about Ned? He'd be worried about me not coming home. He'd had no supper. He could survive, I told myself. We had our jar of pennies for emergencies. A new worry, though. Would he know where it was? Had it been stolen? And what about Mr. Chuckwick? Was he here under my bed guarding me? I began to move to check this, but it was too painful and so I quickly stopped.

"There've been several people here to see you," my angel added.

"A young lad? Twelve or so?"

She told me there was, and thus reassured, I drifted back to sleep.

When I woke up next time there was a bowl of broth before me, them thinking—rightly—that my throat was too sore to take stronger fare. With each sip I felt a little better, but I was told I needed to be in here a few days yet. So the trail of visitors continued.

First of them was Constable Peters, who looked most concerned. I hadn't had the pleasure of seeing myself in a mirror, but what I could see beyond the nightshirt they'd given me didn't make me any handsomer. My skin was blacker than soot could make it in most places, with interesting shades of purple breaking it up. I had heard the operation bell ringing once or twice and thought at first that heaven's trump was summoning some poor soul, and next time it would be for me. It turned out that it was to call surgeons for operations and I dreaded that one might ring for me. I did not fancy the chloroform or the fact that I knew more died from infections during the surgery than from the original cause itself. I sent a silent thank you to my attackers for being so considerate as not to break my bones, except a rib or two.

"You were found by one of our men," Constable Peters told me. "Young Ned ran out and told him you hadn't come home and where he thought you might have gone. When they reached that pub, Ned found you in the yard."

"But not those who attacked me too?" I asked, alarmed in case he too had been harmed.

"No. We don't know who they were."

These words were getting very familiar now, I agreed with Ned. It was time we did know.

"There's one thing I have to ask, Mr. Wasp." Constable Peters looked awkward about doing so. "The sergeant needs to know."

"Sergeant Wiley?" My mind wasn't right yet. Of course this affair had gone beyond Wiley.

"Sergeant Williamson," Constable Peters said with a touch of pride. "And what he wants to know is where the statue of the Chinese goddess is. Mean anything to you?"

"I'd like to know that too, Constable."

Before I could tell him, my prime candidate for settling the answer to my question arrived hot on the heels of Constable

Peters, and immediately burst into tears. "I thought you were dead, guvner."

"So you're crying because I'm not," I tried to joke. Stupidly, because Ned took me seriously.

"I didn't *want* you dead."

From the look on his face, it was an understatement. "Well, Ned, you and I can continue sweeping on together for a few years yet, eh?"

"Yes, guvner."

That established, it was time to move on. "What did you do with the china lady?" I asked him sternly.

He looked startled. "The real one? Nothing."

"You found out where it was, didn't you, and moved it again. Now that was good because whoever attacked me didn't find it. But I need to know where it is now."

"But I never took it, guvner." He sounded most indignant. "I couldn't find it, and I looked everywhere."

I can tell when Ned is telling the truth and when he isn't. And I knew that he was now. But if he didn't have the china lady, who did? And where did I have to start looking for her this time?

The angels said I could go home when my throat and ribs were healed, but they seemed to be taking their time. It was nice having Nightingales around me, but I fretted as to what Ned might be doing—or what Young Nipper might be doing to him. I didn't know whether Billy had had his chat with Young Nipper or not, and Ned could be at risk if he hadn't.

Ned came in to see me, but never said much about his doings, except that he'd done a few sweeping jobs on his own. I applauded this, as it showed strength of character. Apart from Ned and my other regular calls, Jemima came with Mr. and Mrs. Periwinkle's permission and was so sweet I was sad all over again. Then I rejoiced for her, for she blushed so prettily when I said what a fine couple she and the constable would make.

I had one more significant visitor in this affair. I woke up one day to find a villainous face next to mine, which I recognised. At first, being still a mite confused, I thought it was Dabeno come to see me, but then I realised it was Billy Johnson and he'd brought Doll with him. She'd kindly brought me a gift of two bottles of gin, which wasn't exactly what my throat was craving, but was a kind thought.

"A bad do, Wasp," he grunted, having inspected my throat at such close quarters. "Glad they didn't finish you off."

"I am too," I said mildly.

He grinned, and his face suddenly seemed less villainous. Doll, catching the spirit of the moment, let out a hearty cackle. We were all pals together, it seemed.

"What's all this about then?" Billy got down to business. "Who done it?"

"I wish I knew." Not again, I thought.

"I've heard," he said, putting his face even closer to mine, as if he suspected the Nightingales of having evil intent, "that there's a certain something that the Nichols think you've got. It must have been them done it to you, eh?"

"What something?" I asked guardedly, intending to skirt round this idea of his that the Nichol Gang was responsible for everything bad that happened in East London, especially anything bad to Billy Johnson.

Seeing I wasn't going to spill any beans, he added, "That Chinese bird."

I took this to mean my china lady, and told him the truth. "I don't have her."

"That's what they're after. The big job. So, I've been think-ing," Billy said proudly. "The Nichols done you over—and got what they came for. Right?"

"Wrong." I decided to come clean—difficult for a sweep even with the daily ministrations of two Nightingales, who seemed to have a mission to scrub me clean enough to meet St. Peter in good shape next time. "But it's gone anyway."

"Then they've got it some other way," he said darkly. "The way I see it is this. They set up the burglary at the Gables looking for this Chinese bird. Doing a job for some Oriental blokes, so I heard."

"Yes," I agreed warily.

"But they didn't get her, you got her, and now they've got her." He sat back, waiting for my approval of this intellectual deduction.

This time I remained silent, as there seemed no changing his belief that Dabeno now had the china lady.

"They must have thought straight off," Billy continued triumphantly, despite my lack of cooperation, "that Jemima pinched her from George Hogg and gave her to Dinah. So Dabeno's lot killed Dinah, but you had this lump of china all the time."

This was a theory that had some merit, I admitted, and one that had never occurred to me. All the same, it didn't bode well for me if the final responsibility was to be mine for being the innocent recipient of Eliza's gift. Luckily Billy didn't seem to be bearing malice.

"Belt was our man," he assured me.

"He killed our Dinah, because the Nichols hired him to," Doll continued the theory tearfully, "although our darling didn't have the statue like he thought. So Belt had to run because the Nichols were after him for slipping up on the job. They caught up with him, and a bloody good job too."

It could have been a brilliant solution, but I still thought it was the wrong one. It was almost as if Billy was too scared to entertain the idea of the putter-up being involved. And who could blame him for that?

I needed to know where I was—other than in hospital, thanks to my unknown assailants. "Have you spoken to Nipper yet?"

Billy looked grim. "I told you, Wasp, leave Young Nipper to me."

"I can't," I pointed out. "I don't pour water into leaky cans."

His eyes bulged and for a moment it looked as if my other ribs might be joining the busted ones. Luckily, Doll intervened.

"He's right, chuck."

At this marital intimacy, he calmed down. "Young Nipper's all right, Wasp. How d'yer think I'd get by without a snout in every trough, eh? I heard about this Chinese bird job as soon as they took it on."

I sighed. It seemed everybody knew everything, except for me. "What about Dabeno? Does he know about Young Nipper?"

Billy sighed. " 'Course he does. I've got his snout amongst my lads. We all know what's what, and where the lines are drawn, so we don't step over them. Well, not too far," he muttered, slightly red in the face.

"You said *every* trough," I reminded him.

Billy glared at me. "Had to keep a watch over you, Wasp. For your own good," he added hastily. "Told Young Nipper to plant his sister in Mallerby's place in case you made a hash of it. Then I got Nipper to do the place over when he told me about this Chinese bird being pinched."

"Did I make a hash of it?"

"Not yet." A glint came into his eye.

"So what comes next?" I asked carefully. I didn't like that glint.

"I'll tell you what comes next," Billy said grimly. "You and me, we've both got scores to settle now with them Nichols, me over Dinah, you over this—" he waved a hand toward my bruises "—and that Chinese bird of yours. It's time to fight it out."

I didn't like the sound of this at all, but Billy swept on:

"We're going to fix a meeting with the Nichols to sort it out. And you're coming."

"I'm much obliged, but—"

"When you're better," Billy added thoughtfully.

"That won't be yet," I said quickly, seeing a chink of hope here. "Why don't you have your meeting and tell me what happens?"

"No. You're coming with us," Doll informed me lovingly. "You and that kid of yours."

"Where?" I yelped, glancing round in the hope that Constable Peters might be coming in to rescue me.

"Don't worry," Doll said fondly. "Mrs. Chuckwick's taking you and Ned in until we give it to them Nichols hot and strong."

I closed my eyes. If I was to see my way through this pickle, I needed some more broth.

CHAPTER THIRTEEN

Fortunately, the Nightingales had different ideas to Billy Johnson, and insisted on my remaining under their care for another few days. At the end of three, however, Billy grew impatient, and lo and behold, on Tuesday, 18 February, a real carriage turned up at the doors with orders to deliver their patient to Mrs. Chuckwick. Even then I might have baulked at this, had it not been for Ned's happy face peering out of the carriage at me. I think he was overjoyed to be in a real one, not just a growler. Once a growler would have seemed a luxury to him, far beyond our means—but thus are our expectations of life adjusted.

I was helped out by the nurses and tenderly lifted into the carriage. By whom? By Mr. Chuckwick of course, with Ned shoving from behind. Mr. Chuckwick was doing such an excellent impersonation of what he claimed was a personal physician to Her Majesty that the Nightingales made no objection to my leaving.

I bade farewell to the London hospital with great regret, however, not only because I was leaving my singing Nightingales behind me but because I was none too happy about where I was going. True, staying with Mrs. Chuckwick and all the little Chuckwicks had a merry sound to it, and I could see little harm coming to me there. But it was the thought of what was looming beyond that that didn't please me. I like getting on with things in my own way, and all I could see coming from a battle between the Nichols and the Rats was a sorry mess—of which I might be part.

Would such a fight take me any further in the matter of Dinah's death and Joseph Belt? Unwillingly, I supposed it might, and since I had little choice in the matter, I decided to look on the bright side—and stay firmly on one side while the "negotiations" were in progress between Nichols and Rats.

"Look, guvner," Ned said breathlessly, after we reached the other side of the river and were driven into a maze of back streets.

I looked. Mr. Chuckwick was beaming, as we got to the other side of the river. The carriage was depositing us at a most neat little brick house of two storeys, with a tiny front garden.

"Designed by Prince Albert," Mr. Chuckwick explained gravely, "for the poor of London."

It would have been most obliging of Her Majesty's late husband to have thought of us, but this time I knew Mr. Chuckwick was wrong. There was talk of some cottages being built to Prince Albert's designs here, but none had yet been finished. Mr. Chuckwick's cottage had the air of an established home—and a most welcoming one too.

It was a small house inside, with but two rooms downstairs and two upstairs. It seemed that the little Chuckwicks had been deprived of theirs and were to sleep on the floor downstairs so that I could have their room and Ned could either share with me or with the little Chuckwicks. These consisted of two lads of about seven and eight and a little girl about five.

"The apple of her mother's eye," Mr. Chuckwick informed me and the lady of the house promptly appeared. I was curious to see what Mrs. Chuckwick might be like, imagining a pink-cheeked rounded version of Mr. Chuckwick, but to my surprise a slender, vivacious lady appeared, with dancing eyes and curls. She won my heart immediately with her gentle embrace; the embrace, she said, was to show me "How welcome you are, Mr. Wasp" and the gentle because "of your misfortunes."

She then won Ned's heart by a mention of newly baked cake waiting for us, and put the cap on both these triumphs by introducing the little Chuckwicks one by one.

"Good morning, Mr. Wasp. Good morning, Ned," the eldest, Arthur, dutifully said. He seemed the serious one, and eyed us with curiosity rather than resentment through being deprived of his sleeping room.

"And this is Timothy," said his mother proudly. Timothy seemed the shy one of the family, and slunk behind his mother.

"And I'm Matilda," crowed the little girl. "I can dance. Shall I show you?"

I said I would be much obliged. Ned pretended he was too grown up for that stuff, but all the same I think he was captivated by her, as she held out her skirts and danced for us. The dance was "ring-a-ring o'roses," and concluded with the other two little Chuckwicks joining in the song and "all falling down" as the words dictate.

As the days passed, I enjoyed myself so much at the Chuckwicks that I almost forgot the reason I was there. I was under no illusions, however. I was being guarded lest I try to make my escape before the big meeting. I suspected that I was Billy Johnson's evidence for a legitimate reason for a pitched battle.

Mr. Chuckwick disappeared at odd times of day and night, as elusive at home as he was in his working life. When I saw him depart from the house with a briefcase and lifting his hat to his wife, I could almost have thought him a governor of the Bank of England, had I not known his true calling. Then I realised that's exactly the impersonation he wished me to have in mind. To impersonate Mr. Dickens's Fagin would not inspire confidence in me. Ned too disappeared during the day, which he said was necessary for looking after Doshie. That was true, and I tried not to think what other mischief he might be up to. Instead I attempted to forget my worries in my pleasure at the Chuckwick residence.

But then this idyll came to an end as all idylls must.

Billy Johnson arrived one evening when it was already dark, with Doll close behind him. I knew this was a business meeting, because Mr. Chuckwick was present but his wife and the little ones had made themselves scarce. My heart sank, and I promptly sent Ned away with them too, as I didn't want him to know when the battle was to take place.

"It's fixed." Billy was looking very pleased with himself.

My doom was settled. "What's to happen?"

"Dabeno, me, you and the mobs is what's going to happen."

It almost sounded cosy. "Wouldn't you get further if it was just you and Dabeno?" I asked in a last-ditch plea.

He looked at me as if I were still out of my mind. "I'd be dead meat in minutes. You can't trust that lot. I have my chaps, he has his. We carry a white flag of truce." He looked very satisfied with this solution. "That way the pigmen won't be interested."

Knowing Sergeant Wiley, it seemed to me he'd be most interested if he saw upward of a hundred or so of London's criminal world all making their way toward one rendezvous, white flag or not. However, Billy knew his own business best, although from what little I had seen of Dabeno, I'd put my money on him. I wondered if I could get word via Ned to Constable Peters, but decided my own neck had taken a lot of beating recently and I didn't want to be put in the firing line again. Better to play my own game, find out what was what and then see Constable Peters.

I felt happier now that I had my plan, "So when's it to be?" I asked cheerily.

Billy smirked, as if he could read my mind quite well,

although I hoped he hadn't picked up on my decision. "Now."

The word froze me. Surely he couldn't mean *now?* Leave this cosy fireside for Paddy's Goose or a similar hole?

"We had to toss for ends," Billy said brightly, and, as I looked at him blankly, added, "We lost. That macer Dabeno loaded his dice. We're this end. See?"

I didn't.

"His mob chose Wapping end. Easier getaway."

A terrible suspicion came to me, and I hoped I was wrong. "It's a pub?" I asked, hoping against hope.

He snorted. "No pub would have us."

I didn't blame them.

"And it's blooming February," Billy added. "No prancing around outside for our lads."

My terrible suspicion was getting stronger. "Not the tunnel?" I asked weakly.

Billy looked pleased at my powers of detection. "Spot on, Wasp. Know it, do you?"

Of course I did. I nearly lost my life there last year, so this was an ill omen indeed for what was to come.

Sir Isambard Brunel's tunnel under the river Thames running between Wapping and Rotherhithe has been open for twenty years for those who don't mind walking, but no arrangements have yet been made for its development for carriage traffic, though it is rumoured that a railway company might be interested. Meanwhile, only those who don't mind descending steep steps to the ill-lit tunnel beneath use it—which means chiefly visitors who've heard about this curiosity. In the evenings there are few of these, and a nastier place Billy and Dabeno couldn't have chosen. Once down there, the fight could be bitter, and no patrolling pigmen were going to hear. In any case, there wouldn't be any around, as none of them sees this no man's land as their duty to cover. So far as they were concerned, the two gangs could march toward each other, approaching from opposite ends like two great armies, and proceed to slaughter each other at will.

Worse, there are in fact two tunnels running side by side with arches at intervals to give access to the other one. Oh yes, there were plenty of places for assassins to lurk, which would give an extra spice to the slaughter.

Billy was grinning his head off. "We're going to have quite an evening, Wasp. You, me and Dabeno."

I swallowed. "Aren't you coming, Mrs. Johnson?" I asked Doll.

"Put my head in that place? No thanks." She looked very cheerful about it.

So, it was Billy, Mr. Chuckwick, the Rat Mob, the Nichol Gang—and me. Up there somewhere St. Peter must be getting ready for a busy evening.

The Chuckwicks' home seemed a long way behind me, as Billy's growler drove down Swan Lane in Rotherhithe. The entrance to the tunnel was very close now. The south side of the river has many places that rival Ratcliffe Highway for squalor, and Jacob's Ditch near London Bridge is a worse rookery than the Nichol where I was born. The twisting lanes and byways of Rotherhithe are far better than them, but that doesn't mean that Her Majesty would ever choose to live here.

I could see the Rat Mob gathering at the tunnel entrance, even without Billy's telling me proudly who they were. I've never seen a more villainous-looking crowd. Perhaps it was just the effect of the evening light, but their suspicious eyes and belligerent stance made me almost pity the Nichols, who were probably already marching to their fate along the tunnel from the Wapping end.

I can't see into their hearts, I told myself. What drove these men to become villains? Then I decided to stop being so compassionate when one of them aimed his spit at me as I got down from the growler. Billy looked unconcerned. He simply told Giant George to lay the offender out—and so he did. The Mob left one short as we prepared for the descent into hell.

Even in my fright, it amused me to see the Mob lining up so meekly to pay their pennies to go down into the tunnel. Mr. Chuckwick graciously paid for me, however. I saw the clerk didn't look too happy, and I wouldn't have been surprised to learn that he shut his booth rather quickly that evening.

I was last down the stairs, owing to my legs still being bad. Billy wasn't taking any chances that I'd turn tail and scamper off though; Mr. Chuckwick escorted me down. Billy and Giant George were in front, and I thought I could see Young Nipper behind them. I wondered what part he would be playing this evening or whether he might disappear without a trace as an acknowledged snout. We were about fifty in all, and the Mob spread out between the two tunnels—a good plan, as they could check that none of the Nichols had got as far as this in order to ambush us.

Even though I was at the back of the Mob, I could feel the tension as we marched. A whisper passed down from the front that the Nichols could be seen coming toward us. I could not see them, owing to my being shorter than anyone else, but briefly the crowd in front of me parted and I had a glimpse of them—or rather I had the impression of a black mass of men coming straight for us. There are few lights in this tunnel, but they were enough to reveal this scary sight. Belatedly I began to wonder what weapons this fight was going to be based on. I feared that this was going to be more than a war of words, and I croaked out my fears to Mr. Chuckwick.

He was most encouraging. "All agreed. No chivs." Chivs being knives, this was a relief.

208

This should have made me feel better, but my body was still pointing out to me that I had nearly died from an overdose of fists and boots. Furthermore, Billy himself said the Nichols couldn't be trusted. Not like the Rat Mob.

"Don't worry, Mr. Wasp," Mr. Chuckwick added to comfort me, "we've all got our chivs with us. It's Dabeno's lot that won't have them."

At that moment, there was a roar and I could see the black mass ahead beginning to form into individual heads, all shouting their loyalty to the Nichols.

"Dear me," Mr. Chuckwick gasped. "This isn't what I usually encounter in my profession of gardener to the Duke of Timbuctoo."

I was shaking in my boots, trying to convince myself that if the situation really got bad I could always scuttle back to Rotherhithe. No one except Mr. Chuckwick might notice, and he, I hoped, might be lenient. I thought wrongly, because he saw me glancing longingly behind me, and said mildly: "Remember my trade of bug destroyer, Mr. Wasp."

I took the hint. Irritating bugs or sweeps had to be eradicated. No more jobs for Billy Johnson, I told myself, then realised that I could well be right. My services might be terminated here and now in this tunnel.

Our steps sounded like the trump of doom as we marched on, more slowly now that Armageddon was in sight. I thought of that story about the Light Brigade in the recent war in the Crimea, and how the cavalry had charged on their horses along the valley to their certain death, all in the name of England. It was thought to be a glorious thing, but I wondered if the same would apply to sweeps caught up on the battlefield of the Rat Mob and the Nichols.

The noise was growing, as voices rose in anger. Insults were already flying, if not bullets.

And then the two front lines stopped. I could see Billy and Dabeno, with their two henchmen, Giant George and Scrapper, talking in the middle of the two armies. The mobs were closing in on one another now, and yelling so loudly there was no hope of hearing what the chiefs were saying to each other. Sticks and much less savoury weapons were being brandished—no chivs that I could see *yet*—and the armies were spread across both tunnels to give a wider front of attack.

"Quiet the lot of you!" I recognised Dabeno's roar, hastily followed by one from Billy, who added:

"We're here to do business, not to listen to you lot."

Having finished his first roar, Billy sent up another one, and I heard what I had dreaded: "Wasp! Where's Wasp? Come 'ere."

I was forced forward by Mr. Chuckwick into accepting this invitation. I noticed that he was still smiling. I wondered savagely whether he thought he was impersonating the goddess of mercy, or even Jack Ketch the hangman.

He pushed me up to the quartet, and then left me. There was a deathly hush while Giant George and Scrapper awaited their bosses' order to squash me flat, and Dabeno and Billy considered what came next.

"So," Dabeno sneered at last, "someone did you over as well as your lodgings. Weren't us, but they did a good job, I heard."

No harm in agreeing. "They did."

"Learn your lesson, did you?"

"None to learn," I said bravely.

Dabeno took a pace forward, and showed me a giant fist. "Oh you have, Wasp, you have. Are you going to tell us where it is, or are you, Billy Johnson?" So far, in my pain, I had not given much thought to *who* had been responsible, only why it had happened. Dabeno was claiming it hadn't been the Nichols, but just at that moment I was not inclined to believe him.

Billy looked taken aback. "Me? I've got nothing to do with

this job. It's Dinah I'm here about. You banged Wasp up, so you must have this Chinese bird."

"Look, pal, I never did him over, and if I had the china pot of yours, I wouldn't be here, would I?" Dabeno roared in return. "Think I want to spend my time with you Rats?"

"Think we would come to meet you gonophs, if we *did* have this pot you're after?"

"Yeah." Dabeno replied softly in reply to this insult to his professionalism—gonophs being only minor thieves. "Because that way it makes you look good. You're clever, Billy. I'll say that for you."

"Can't say that of you, Dabeno."

Dabeno took his time over this one, and decided it was time to up the stakes. "We had a pact: no prigging on each other's jobs. Right?"

"Right," Billy agreed warily. I began to inch myself backward, while still keeping my eyes in rapt attention on the two leaders.

"We got this job," Dabeno growled, "to do with a couple of Orients. Easy enough. Break into this house and pinch an old bit of china. The owner was dead, they said. It was *our* job, see? What's it got to do with you?"

"Nothing," Billy said promptly. "Like I said."

I inched back a little further.

"Then why you got that sweep with you, then? He's got the china judy."

"Nothing to do with china," Billy said. "He's been finding out who killed my daughter."

"Then he's mine first. I'm going to do him over here and now till I know where the china is."

My inching backward came to a sudden end as two arms reached out to grab me. Scrapper's and Giant George's.

"He's doing my job, Dabeno," Billy roared. "Keep off him till I say so."

"Five minutes. Now what this about your daughter?" Dabeno snarled. "We had nothing to do with her death."

"Oh, yes? Joseph Belt killed her. And that's where you come in, *pal.*"

I thought Billy was going to jab Dabeno in the chest, but luckily he thought better of it, as Scrapper and Giant George both forgot me and moved in to protect their chiefs. Dabeno, I saw to my relief, was getting worried.

"Look, Billy, we were getting paid for burglary, not a murder. Where's the business sense in that? I tell you, Billy, Belt wasn't working for us. We threw him out years ago."

"You wanted revenge on me, Dabeno. You thought I'd been pinching your jobs."

"You *did,*" he howled. "You're mucking in on this bit of old china."

Not surprisingly, Billy howled back. "And I've told you I'm not."

"Then who is? And I thought you killed Belt!"

"No, I bloody well didn't," Billy shot back at him.

"Then who did?"

A silence while they both stared at me. I was in trouble. I was going to have to work very fast indeed. I thought of Ned all alone and prayed to the good Lord to make my wits go faster. He obliged, to my relief.

"You're neither of you talking to the right person," I said, trying my best to sound calm. "It's the putter-up you both want. *Your* putter-up, Dabeno. You did this china job as a bit of independent enterprise, didn't you? Didn't it occur to you he'd found out?"

I'd hit a bull's-eye. His face went white. "How did you know?"

"Stands to reason. You say you haven't got the china lady, Billy hasn't and I haven't. So who has? Did it never occur to you the putter-up might have a plan of his own?" I thought I'd leave Sir Laurence out of this.

Billy looked impressed, but Dabeno was fighting back. "Maybe at first the job was my idea. Then I got orders from above to do your place over, Wasp."

A snarl from Billy. "Who is your putter-up?"

Dabeno was quick off the mark now. "Can't say."

"Then we'll make you," Billy roared. "He did for my Dinah too, I reckon. Put Belt up to it. Belt was working for him." Giant George jerked into life at the thought of action.

"I don't know who he is," Dabeno roared. "I get orders through another party."

"Who's that then?" Billy had been doing well but he jumped in too soon. "He told you to kill my Dinah, didn't he?"

My head began to spin at this revolution of approach. My whole body was aching, the mood was getting ugly again and I couldn't see where the argument would go now. I clung on to one hopeful thought: suppose the putter-up was indeed playing his own game, trying to get the china lady for this Bismarck, while Sir Laurence was trying to get her on behalf of England, and the Nichols on behalf of China. Didn't that mean—I felt a surge of hope that I could break out of this spiders' web—that my china lady had nothing to do with Dinah's death after all? And if so—

But Billy was yelling again. "Belt was your third party, Dabeno, wasn't he? The putter-up employed him to go between you and him."

"No he wasn't. Nothing to do with us," Dabeno was shaking with rage now.

Billy swept on though. "Then this putter-up murdered her and you know who he is. You going to tell me, Dabeno? Or am I going to make you?"

"How are you going to make me, Billy?" Dabeno jeered.

I had taken my eye off the ball for too long.

213

"*Like this.*" Billy's powerful fist came out, and Dabeno promptly retaliated—which brought Giant George into play, and Scrapper too. Which brought both gangs into play as well. Billy seemed deliberately to have brought this on, but at least it gave me an opportunity to get into the other tunnel and out of the fray so that they could fight in peace. I couldn't follow the arguments at all, and I couldn't work out why Billy had wanted me here in view of the way things were working out. What part did I play?

It seemed I played none. Everyone seemed to be righting wrongs except for me. There was almost a grim silence reigning as every man concentrated on trying to kill his neighbour in close combat. It was chilling, and I wondered if hell was like this: continuous fighting and no hope of a solution. I could hear the crunch of fists against bone, stifled yells and the thud of bodies tumbling to lie squirming on the ground. What was being achieved? Was there any goal? Perhaps there was none, like most wars. Words start it, fists finish it, for no other reason than that fists are considered to need an airing every now and then.

Or was there some other purpose to all this that I hadn't yet realised, being in the thick of it? Then it occurred to me that I might be able to make my escape while everyone was occupied. I crept to the inner edge of the tunnel where I was less likely to be spotted and began to creep along it toward the Wapping stairs and safety. I might be able to climb those steps before anyone realised I was missing. Heart in my mouth, I was about halfway there, when a cry went up that sent a further chill through me.

"Murder!"

The crowds scattered—and I stood still, wondering whether to stay or go. Nichols and Rats seemed alike now, for there was silence. Murder is still murder, and has to be taken account of. I joined the Mob unnoticed, as the Rats, their caps removed, stood around their dead man, who was lying outstretched on the ground. Blood streamed from his chest, his face was pale, and his body even to my eye was lifeless. A knife covered in blood lay at his side. My heart seemed frozen, for I recognised who it was.

It was Mr. Chuckwick.

Letting out a cry of distress, I made my way to him. No one tried to stop me, and Billy Johnson joined me as I knelt down at Mr. Chuckwick's side, hoping that life might still be there. Billy checked, then looked up at Dabeno, his face white with fury.

"He's gone, Dabeno. Dead."

I was only listening with half an ear, because my heart was too full as I thought of his companionship and loyalty. He had become part of my life. What was I going to tell Mrs. Chuckwick, and what about the little Chuckwicks? I was too heartbroken even to weep.

Dabeno's face was ashen. "Not meant, Billy. Accident. Against the rules."

"You killed my best friend, Dabeno," Billy said menacingly as he got to his feet. "What are you going to do about it?"

"What you want, Billy?" was the stumbling reply.

"Your putter-up, Dabeno. He's going to pay for it."

"I'll put the word round, Billy. Ask the third party. But I don't know who the putter-up is. Honest. I'd tell you if I did."

"Tell me what you do know. Who's this third party?"

"I dunno." Dabeno was almost weeping himself now. "We just pick up messages left in the pub. Honest. The putter-up wants the best jobs for himself, see? We reckoned there was more going on with the old bit of china than we was being told. It was my job, but news must have got to the putter-up because we got orders to pull out. You know how the putter-up works with more than one mob sometimes, so I thought at first they were putting you in the way of the job instead of us."

"And what do you think now?" Billy asked grimly.

"He was working for himself—at least none of my lads are in on it. We thought we'd do over your place, sweep—" Dabeno kindly turned to me "—to find the china bird, but when you was done over by someone else I knew either you were playing us up or he had his own game. And as for this going over"—he looked me up and down—"that's a real professional job. Jimmy Hayes, most likely."

Billy wasn't interested in Jimmy Hayes. "What about my daughter, Dabeno?"

"Nothing, Billy. We don't do jobs like that. If it wasn't the German, then it was Belt killed her at the orders of the putter-up. That's what we think."

"So do we," Billy said slowly. "But I don't see why you're so sure, Dabeno."

Dabeno looked at us in anguish. "Because he wasn't working for us. You got to believe that."

I only half took in his words at the time, as all I could see was poor Mr. Chuckwick's body lying on the floor.

Billy cleared his throat as he saw me looking. "And this is the result. Clear off, Dabeno. Leave this one to my lot. We've a lot of mourning to do."

Dabeno and his men shrank away toward the Wapping exit and we waited until they had done so. Then Billy roared at his own mob. "Me and George and Young Nipper will deal with this. You all clear off too." The Rats slunk off the same way, no doubt to enjoy a few more fist fights outside. As I watched the last of them go, I didn't care, and I don't think Billy did either.

Not with Mr. Chuckwick lying there.

But he wasn't. I turned back—and he had vanished.

"One of my better impersonations, don't you think?" he said, from behind my head.

Billy looked contrite, as he saw the look on my face, and the tears of relief springing up. "Sorry, Tom. Had to do it. Only way to get Dabeno to cough up the truth. That's if it *is* the truth."

The shock was too great for me. I don't remember anything more, until I woke up the next day safely back in the Southwark cottage, with Mrs. Chuckwick bending over me anxiously and Ned peering over her shoulder.

CHAPTER FOURTEEN

Although Ned and I were able to bask in the warmth of Mrs. Chuckwick's care a while longer, which was good for my battered body, my mind had no such consolation. My job was not finished, even though Billy was taking such a bulldog approach himself. That was the trouble. Bulldogs go for anything that upsets them; they are not ones for thinking things through.

It had been ten days since the confrontation in the Rother-hithe tunnel. Every time I attempted to return home, however, Mr. Chuckwick informed me that there was no need to worry. But worry I did. I noticed that Mr. Chuckwick himself was out nearly all the time and could not help wondering if the cosy nest was provided for me so that he need not spend time in guarding me. Consequently I decided that the sooner I was on my feet and back sweeping the chimneys of this case the better. My chance came on Friday, 6 March.

All London was busy, so Mrs. Chuckwick told me, with the arrangements for the grand procession to take place on the morrow. Excitement had flared up like a chimney on fire, especially here in the Borough, which she'd never seen so packed full of people.

Princess Alexandra and her parents would be arriving by ship at Gravesend on the morrow, where the Prince of Wales would be meeting them. The royal party would then travel by train to what we call the Royal West Station—Bricklayers' Arms in the Borough, which is the closest terminus for Buckingham Palace and west London—though it is shortly to be outdated when they finish the new one across the River Thames at Charing Cross. I miss the old Hungerford market, which was torn down for the purpose, but we must progress, I suppose. Although I doubt if those who lost their homes or market stalls see it that way.

The procession would begin at the Bricklayers' Arms amid gaily decked streets; then the princess would travel to Paddington railway station and then by train to Windsor Castle, where the marriage ceremony would take place next Tuesday, the tenth. The little Chuckwicks had talked of little else but the wonderful decorations on the parapets of London Bridge and the Danish flags flying everywhere for the Princess to appreciate as her carriage crossed the river into our city. There had been a struggle to put them up, owing to all the crowds already gathering for the wedding, but now they were nearly ready.

There was a huge arch on the north side of the bridge, and here at the Borough end were splendid medallions of the prince and princess, and, as the little Chuckwicks informed me breathlessly, there was a picture of the queen prancing around with horses. I felt this was unlikely to be her gracious majesty Queen Victoria and therefore took this prancing lady to be Britannia, symbol of this country. Another lady depicted in the middle medallion described to me as dressed all in black seemed far more likely to be Her Majesty.

"We can all go out and cheer as they pass," Mrs. Chuckwick said delightedly. "You'd be well enough for that, won't you, Tom? They'll be passing quite close here." Although it would forever be difficult for me to think of her husband as anything but dear Mr. Chuckwick, his wife was increasingly Dorinda to me, just as I was Tom. The little Chuckwicks—Tim, Arthur and Matilda—were delightful company and a good influence on Ned, because whereas older lads would lead him astray, these happy youngsters looked up to him, believing him a man of the world—and this made him reluctant to spoil this image.

"Princess Alexandra will be queen after Her Gracious Majesty's gone. Not that I want her to go," Dorinda chattered on, while she steamed up the boiler for the washing. "She shows the world that women can rule as well as men."

I privately agreed with this, but I enjoyed having an argument with Dorinda so I raised a few objections. I laughed when she declared that women would be sitting in parliament before long. She grew indignant.

"Who's the head of our country, Tom?"

"Her Majesty Queen Victoria," I said solemnly.

"Then if a woman is able to lead the country, why shouldn't she be in parliament too? Why not prime minister?"

I pretended she had won the argument, and indeed perhaps she had. Nevertheless, I pointed out, "Politics can be a dirty business. Too dirty for women."

She snorted. "Women can play at politics too. Look at Florence Nightingale. She got what she wanted, didn't she, and that didn't happen without a fight with parliament."

I admitted again that she was right. Dorinda was highly pleased, and brought me a freshly baked muffin, which I took to be a political success of my own.

All this talk of politics, however, made me realise that I needed to be active again, both on chimneys and regarding Billy's job. Furthermore, I wanted to know what had happened to my china lady. This week all London seemed to be surging up and down like a bubbling saucepan of water, and I didn't want to be left out. Ned, rather reluctantly, agreed with me about our return to real life.

"You know where we have to go, don't you, Ned?"

He nodded gloomily. "Claremont House." He was no doubt remembering his nighttime excursion there.

I was glad we saw eye to eye on this. Somewhere in that place were the answers we needed. They might lie in the top half of the house with Sir Laurence or at the bottom with the servants' hall, or in the stables—but they were undoubtedly hiding somewhere.

"Think they've got our lady, guvner?" Ned asked. I noticed that it was now *our* lady, not just mine, and was pleased that he thought of her that way. After all, it had been through everyone looking for her that his beloved Jack had been killed.

Mr. Chuckwick, to my relief, had already left for the day, apparently clad as himself, and so I wondered whether he also kept a choice of impersonation clothes at Paddy's Goose. I was on my own now, although my valuable team member Ned was here. If nothing else, he helped to make my arrival anywhere look innocent. We looked like the sweeps we were, the best impersonation of all.

I whispered to Ned that we were going to take a growler and not to let Dorinda see. I gave him a sixpence so that the cabbie would know Ned wasn't having a joke at his expense, and told him to find one and stay with it a little way up the street until I joined him. As soon as Dorinda reappeared, I told her casually that Ned and I were taking a bit of a walk. Well, it seemed as if the cat were well and truly among the pigeons. Feathers flew.

"You can't do that, Tom," she shrieked.

"I have to, Dorinda," I said gently. "It's for Her Majesty's sake."

I hoped this sounded important enough that she wouldn't question me further, for it would be hard to explain just how Her Majesty was involved. She didn't ask anymore; she was too distressed, as it turned out that Mr. Chuckwick was depending on her to make sure I was safe. I told her that I would square matters with Mr. Chuckwick, and then she confessed she didn't want me to go in case I got attacked again. I felt a funny choking feeling at the back of my throat as I told her I too would prefer not to be attacked again, but I would be very careful.

She was not convinced and tried hard to dissuade me. I was lucky that the little Chuckwicks were at their schooling or no doubt she would insist on their coming with us. Instead:

"I could come," she offered eagerly. "No one would attack you then."

I had to turn down this sweet suggestion of hers. "I'm a sweep, Dorinda. No one would really think I'm a danger to them," I comforted her.

"Where are you going?" she asked shyly.

No harm in telling her that. "Claremont House." That was the one thing I knew for sure.

What I was going to do when I got there, I still had to determine.

Nothing there seemed to have changed. The long-case clock ticked on in the servants' hall and the painted moon on its face seemed to be scowling at me as though defying me to prove anything was amiss in this household. As I waited there to see Mr. Longfellow, the other servants continued their daily tasks as though all was right within their world, and indeed it was hard to believe otherwise. Michael nipped in and out, resplendent in his new livery as chief footman, the odd-job boy winked at me in between the frequent calls for his attention, Mrs. Poole gave me a scathing look as she passed by but said nothing about chimneys to be swept. Miss Twinkle sat by the warm stove stitching hems, Mary and Young Nipper's sister scuttled past the door every so often, and I could hear the everyday sounds of a kitchen in full action across the passageway.

Tick-tock, tick-tock . . . whoever invented clocks did a wise thing, for they remind us that life is slipping away whether we want it to or not. For me it was a reminder that time might be running out, and I didn't even know for what! For my china lady? With foreign royalty gathering for the wedding, this would be an ideal opportunity for whoever now held her to slip the package to the next owner. And yet that answer did not fully satisfy me. Any ship at any time could have taken her away for ever. There would be no need to wait for a public event.

The daily life of the house seemed a spectacle spread out before me, from which I had to pick the one patch of soot that was causing the problem. Where was the blockage in this chimney? If in doubt about such a problem, some master sweeps have a habit of dropping a goose or large duck down a chimney to see where it rests, but for my conundrum there was no goose available. Except, I thought sadly, myself.

Had Dinah felt this way? Did she know something was wrong but was not able to drop her goose to pinpoint the reason? My reasoning had got so far as to realise that this third party Dabeno spoke of was indeed connected to Claremont House, but was unlikely to have been Joseph, as junior servants have precious little time off to play messengers for extra work, such as go-between for the putter-up and the Nichol Gang. Only Silas Rodway or Mr. Longfellow himself could have sufficient excuse and seniority to leave the portals of Claremont House for long enough.

Ned sat silently at my side. I like to think he was contemplating good and evil, but more probably it was only his chances of a muffin or pie. If so, he was disappointed. There was no sign of Mrs. Poole or Mary returning—but Mr. Longfellow at last arrived. I asked him if I might be permitted to see Sir Laurence. I could see this idea shocked him in its suddenness, not having been entered on his bill of duties for the day. All the same I persisted, and he could hardly refuse me.

Five minutes later he reappeared, looking his stiffest and most disapproving, to tell me in tones of awe that it was my lucky day. Sir Laurence would see me in the Oriental Room. I decided to take Ned with me, although this too met Mr. Longfellow's displeasure. Perhaps they didn't have sweeps in China. I needed witnesses, however. Suppose Sir Laurence was deeply involved in this matter on the wrong side? As I mounted the stairs, I began to feel I was about to have an audience with Satan himself, but I told myself I was getting stirred up over nothing. Just because every passageway ahead sometimes *looks* black, that does not mean the one you are taking does.

When we entered the Chinese room, I saw Sir Laurence sitting in one of the small temple structures, which blended in with the painted flowers, mountains and bridges on the walls. He looked most impressive, and perhaps he used this procedure for very important occasions. He certainly looked very important, being clad in a silk coat and cap, embroidered with dragons.

"Tom Wasp," he called out. "You have news for me, I take it."

As I walked toward him, with Ned shivering in my wake, I felt like Marco Polo struggling along the Silk Road to bring news from the West to the mysterious Orient, but then I concentrated on how to put my case to Sir Laurence. I decided to speak out. If he were involved himself, he would appreciate this, and there was no sense beating around the bush. I could be disposed of whether I stated my real views or not. He might think it safer to part me from this world just in case.

"There's something bad going on in this house, Sir Laurence," I told him firmly, and waited for a heart-stopping moment.

"I agree," he replied amiably. "Any idea what it is?"

If he expected this to perplex me, he was right. He was being diplomatic and so must I be. I failed miserably. "Something to do with the Nichol Gang."

I saw his eyes react immediately. He wasn't going to beat around the bush, either, by pretending he had never heard of it.

"Which part of it?" he asked politely.

"Perhaps the putter-up, but more likely his go-between with Dabeno, the Nichols' leader." I was impressed that he obviously knew who putters-up were, for all he said was: "Tell me more, Tom Wasp. Do you think *I* hold the honourable position of putter-up?"

For a moment I thought he actually was. His eyes were glittering, but his expression unreadable. I gulped, and told him the truth. "I hadn't thought of that, sir."

I had, of course, but had believed it impossible. With him before me, I was not so sure. Was this the element I had been missing?

He laughed aloud. "Your life's safe with me, Tom. I'm not. Unfortunately, I don't know who is, and I agree with you that it's important. More," he said, dropping his mask of amiability, "it's vital for me to know, both as an employer and as a servant of the Crown. Who is it?"

"Your coachman or Mr. Longfellow," I ventured, giving him my reasons.

"You're wrong about Rodway," he said crisply. "His only sin is the bottle. The putter-up wouldn't touch him. Too loose a tongue."

"Mr. Longfellow then? He only joined your household recently." I knew pigmen were always interested in new arrivals to a servants' hall in houses where a crime had taken place.

Sir Laurence was still impassive and it occurred to me that this is what politicians and spies do. They decide issues, leaving the human side out of it. Was that good or bad? It could be either, but at the moment it was helping me. "Do you have any proof?"

"No, sir, only elimination. There's no one else."

"He came highly recommended,"—he frowned, clearly annoyed with himself for having to make this admission—"though it is true only by one previous employer, and he, I recently learned, has just left the country in unfortunate circumstances. There was a burglary here, Wasp. You know all about that, don't you?"

This sudden attack was unnerving, and I could sense Ned cowering at my side.

"That was not Longfellow's doing," Sir Laurence continued. "Have you considered why not, if he is the villain you believe him to be? The figure was on display for all to see—including the thief. Why should Longfellow not removed it then?"

I knew the answer to that one. "Because he would not know which one it was amongst so many, Sir Laurence." We were surrounded by many Chinese statues, and only Ned would recognise our china lady.

"And the thief did?" Sir Laurence asked none too gently. "I discovered the new maid Susan had left the window open for our thief to enter." He was not looking at Ned, but there was a whimper at my side. "You were attacked in the street later, weren't you, Wasp?" His eyes seemed to be boring into me, as I wondered why Susan was still working here. Could it be Sir Laurence was not above suspicion after all? I had to take a firm line.

"It's all over that Chinese goddess, sir. First it's here, then it's there—"

"And where is it now, Wasp?" he barked at me.

"Here," I had the courage to say. "You took it back again."

No laugh now. "It is indeed here. The police guarding you were actually watching your every step on my behalf, although I regret that they arrived a little late at the Black Lion. It was they who removed the figure, at my urging, from your hiding place. I need hardly say I am working in the interests of our country, not against, Wasp. If Longfellow's our man, it won't be staying here long—or do you still suspect I'm also involved in some shady plan against Britain's interests?"

"No, sir." I had to gamble and assume that was the truth.

"Good. Who do you believe owns Kwan-yin?"

I had no doubts over this. "She should be back where she belongs. With the Chinese emperor. She's too peaceful to be fought over."

His answer surprised me. "I'm inclined to agree with you. She could do least harm there. Would you like to say goodbye to her?"

Without even waiting for my answer, he came out of his little temple and proceeded to remove one of its small turrets; he put out his hand to take the contents—and I saw his expression change. The turret was empty.

White-faced, he whirled round and turned on Ned. "Have you been up to your tricks again?" he roared.

Ned looked terrified and so was I. It was obvious Sir Laurence had known full well who had been responsible for the china lady's earlier disappearance from his house, but where was she now? Was Susan responsible? Mr. Longfellow? Young Nipper?

"No sir," Ned squeaked.

"By God, you'll never see the light of day again if you have," he said so quietly that it scared me even more. I received a special glare of my own. "Is he lying, Wasp?" he asked.

I spoke to Ned quietly, trying not to scare him more. "Men's lives depend on this, Ned, not only the china lady. You'll not get into trouble if you tell me you did it. I'll see to that. We just have to know where she is."

"I don't know. I didn't do it," he howled.

But I didn't let him off that easily. "What about Young Nipper—has he had another go?"

"I don't know," came the wail. "I ain't seen him. Anyway, he didn't ask me to nab the china lady back. I went off on my own

227

while he did over the rest of the stuff."

"Leave Young Nipper out of it," Sir Laurence roared. "He's working for me now. He *and* his pretty sister." A sideways glance at me in revenge for my hints about Mary.

My mind whirled with this new arrangement of loyalties. Did Billy know about this latest enterprise of Nipper's? Was this another example of his "snout" duties?

"How did you know where Kwan-yin was?" Sir Laurence continued to bark at poor Ned.

Ned looked shame-faced. "I reckoned she'd be in this room because you like foreign things. You'd hide her where she'd be happy."

Sir Laurence's face softened a little, so I stepped in smartly. "This is all part of getting the chimney clean, Sir Laurence. We've got four flues here: the china lady, Dinah Johnson's murderer, the putter-up and his messenger." Young Nipper could wait, I thought. "All leading somewhere," I continued, "but we haven't seen the light yet."

"What the hell do you mean?" he snapped.

"It's all part of a plan, sir. Like you said, the emperor, this Bismarck in Prussia, the king of Denmark—that's your plan to keep everyone in the world happy. But what about theirs?"

I saw him take the point immediately. "Longfellow then," he said softly. "Let's deal with him first."

He scribbled a note, folded it up with his seal and then turned to Ned. "I'm giving you another chance, young man." He handed him the letter and a guinea, and Ned's eyes nearly popped out of his head. "Take a cab *now* and get this to Sergeant Williamson at Scotland Yard. And Wasp, show him my garden door. I don't want him seen leaving by the tradesmen's entrance, or the front one. Then make yourself scarce for a while. When you see the police arrive, you can get back here through the same door. *Go.*"

I had to admire the speed at which diplomacy is carried out—although an easy flow of guineas assists such speed, of course. We were instantly on our way, and managed to avoid all curious eyes. I saw Ned safely up into a hansom—a rather shabby one, but he looked proud to be raised so high.

I had my own ideas about how I was going to spend this time. Constable Peters had told me the name of the narrow boat that had taken Belt along the Hertford Union Canal. *Gypsy Prince* was registered in Hertford to an Elias George, a local grain farmer. The lockkeeper at the Old Ford Locks had given evidence of having seen the barge moored near there that evening, then pass through.

I wanted to speak to him myself, however, even though I realised that Constable Peters might already have asked these questions. I had not heard the answers, though, and I needed them urgently. Sir Laurence would be probing Mr. Longfellow as to whether he was the Nichol Gang's messenger, but I, Tom Wasp, was after bigger game (even though I was quaking in my hunting boots at the thought).

Unfortunately, the lockkeeper proved to be a surly gentleman, but an offer to clean his chimneys free of charge next week if he told me what he'd told the police about *Gypsy Prince* seemed to be very acceptable.

"What do you want to know for?" he asked suspiciously.

"Matters of state to do with Sir Laurence at Claremont House."

He guffawed so loudly at the idea of a chimney sweep being involved in matters of state that he cheered up and decided to oblige willingly.

"Anything unusual about *Gypsy Prince*?" I asked.

"No. And if you're going to ask me whether I saw a body being hauled on board, the answer's no. It went through the lock, paid over the toll, then moored again. Dunno what happened then. The only comings and goings I'm paid to watch are those through my locks. After that, I loses interest," he said with heavy sarcasm, " 'specially as it was carrying manure." (Only manure wasn't the word the lockkeeper used.)

"You saw who was on it, though, if it went through the lock."

"Usual team; man and wife, and a boatman. He was a brute of a chap, she was skinny and the boatman a moody sort of chap. Nice horse, though."

So that was it. He'd told me little more than that there were three on board plus, presumably, Joseph Belt, unless he was the boathand. If he'd just murdered Dinah, he might well have been silent. This brute of a chap was interesting. Was it the owner, Elias George, this Jimmy Hayes or the putter-up himself? Or were they the same?

I went for a brief walk in the park over to the Burdett-Coutts fountain. I suppose I did this to apologise to Dinah in a way. I knew Joseph Belt had killed her, but that wasn't the whole story. I was still sure of that, but even if Longfellow was indeed the third party, I seemed no nearer to finding out what that was. Or was I? I had a feeling I'd heard something important today, but blessed if I knew what.

When I returned to Claremont House, Ned was hopping up and down outside the rear entrance to the gardens, and having seen two police carriages drawn up outside the front entrance, I knew it was time for me to walk on stage again. I saw Silas Rodway as we walked through the stables, and casually asked him what was going on.

"Still after that burglar," he grunted. "Why bother? He can afford it."

So that must be Sir Laurence's plan; the "burglary" was again to be the excuse for the pigmen's presence. The minute Ned and I walked into the house, Mary ran up to us. Far from questioning why we came through this entrance, she was gazing at us in awe. "You're wanted upstairs in Sir Laurence's study *immediately*," she told us. "He has been asking for you."

Ned and I quickly hurried to obey this imperial command. The first person I saw as we entered the study was Mr. Longfellow, but it was a different Mr. Longfellow from the one I knew— the stooped and subservient butler, there to obey. This Longfellow lived up to his name, upright, furious and with as evil an expression as ever I have seen on a man's face.

"Where is it, Longfellow?" Sir Laurence was saying. I was surprised they were alone, with no police here, but Sir Laurence broke off to acknowledge our presence with the briefest of nods and an explanation. "The house is being searched, Wasp."

"Of what am I being accused?" Mr. Longfellow asked calmly. His eyes swivelled to me. "And who is my accuser?" he added with a sneer in my direction.

"Theft, and I'm accusing you," Sir Laurence replied promptly. That was a clever move, I thought, for theft would be easier to prove than his role of go-between. He seemed to have absolved Longfellow from knowing about Ned's little escapade, but this time he was easier prey.

"Theft of what?"

"A valuable porcelain figure," Sir Laurence replied.

A supercilious shrug greeted this, and Mr. Longfellow failed to look terrified. This was ominous, I thought. Had he already passed the china lady on, or was it hidden so securely that he knew it would be safe? And if the latter, where would that be?

"Another burglary as you suffered before," he commented dismissively. "Here are your culprits." He indicated myself and Ned.

Sir Laurence did not respond to this point, to my relief, and we waited in silence until Constable Peters returned, with an older gentleman with moustache and beard, whom I thought must be Sergeant Williamson. I took to him at once, even though he did look at me with some surprise until Constable Peters whispered a few words in his ear.

"Nothing found, Sir Laurence," the sergeant reported. "Not in his rooms, nor the rest of the house."

"Have you tried Pug's Parlour?" I enquired, that being the name given to the butler's official sanctum, where he reigns alone.

"No, Mr. Wasp," the sergeant told me politely.

"The wine cellar?" I asked. Not even Sir Laurence would have a key to this; only the butler, and the look of rage on Longfellow's face suggested I might be on the right track.

"Searched," the sergeant said briefly, but he gave me a kindly look. "I did it myself."

The look of instant relief on Longfellow's face was unmistakable. The sergeant must have noticed it too. "Worried, were you?" he asked conversationally. "I'll take another look, and you," he said to Longfellow, "can come with me."

Mr. Longfellow's terror was easy to see. "Belt was done in. I'm not going the same way."

If anything was needed to confirm his guilt, this was it. But where was it leading? And where was the china lady?

Constable Peters pointed out to Mr. Longfellow that he would be quite safe inside one of Her Majesty's prisons, probably Newgate, at which Mr. Longfellow grew thoughtful and reluctantly agreed to accompany the sergeant. I looked at Sir Laurence and he nodded slightly, so I too joined the party, and for good measure the constable and Sir Laurence came too, not to mention Ned. When we reached the cellar the door was open—which Sergeant Williamson said was as he found it. I didn't like the sound of that. Something was going on here, and Mr. Longfellow knew it. He was grinning all over his ugly face.

I could see there was a policeman on duty at the tradesmen's door, and so hurried to have a word with Mary, whom I saw going into the kitchen. "Has anyone called or gone since the police arrived?"

She looked as scared as if I'd accused her of some crime. "No, the policeman said no one could come in or go out."

That meant that whoever unlocked the cellar door was probably still in the house. Which meant if the china lady was no longer in the cellar, as I assumed from Mr. Longfellow's reactions it originally must have been, it had now been moved.

But who by? A feeling of mixed excitement and fear came to me as I realised the truth. The putter-up must be amongst us at this very moment.

I quickly sought out Constable Peters to voice this worry to him, and he looked alarmed. "But everyone's just been given permission to leave if they're not part of the household, Mr. Wasp."

"The putter-up," I cried. "He'll have the china lady."

Constable Peters doesn't believe in wasting time, and so back we both went to the corridor leading to the tradesmen's entrance. We could see ahead of us that the servants' hall must have emptied, as six or seven people were leaving the house through the tradesmen's door. We could see only their backs, but I could recognise most by acquaintance or trade: Miss Twinkle, her day's work packed away in a sewing bag; the butcher's boy swathed in aprons and still carrying his delivery basket; the gardener with his empty trug; Silas Rodway carrying a saddle bag; a baker with a box—and Young Nipper. He was carrying nothing. I was in despair, which made it easier to act.

"Stop there!" I cried, hurrying through the door to see them all disappearing through the grounds.

"Which one?" Constable Peters had caught me up, eager to help but the half dozen or so were going in different directions. I thought of Dinah, I thought of Jemima; I couldn't let them down by being wrong. I thought of Young Nipper, perhaps whistling his way to freedom, then I thought of Susan his sister—and then of Dorinda and her impassioned plea for women. And then of what the lockkeeper had told me: man, wife and a boatman. *Why had I assumed the putter-up was a man?*

"Miss Twinkle," I gasped.

One look at me, a moment's hesitation, and then the constable plunged forward, catching the seamstress up at the gates. As I hobbled up as fast as I could, I could see her fighting like a tigress, arms flailing, claws out, wrestling on the ground with him. Two pigmen and Young Nipper came running to hold her down, and a third pigman to put handcuffs on her, after Constable Peters had seized her needlework bag from her arm. She had to watch impotently as I opened the bag and lifted my china lady out. I felt tears of relief in my eyes. There she was, sending out her usual message of peace and calm, while Miss Twinkle spat out triumphant venom at her captors and myself.

"You're too late," she cried. "Too late."

CHAPTER FIFTEEN

"Too late," Sir Laurence muttered, looking less like an Oriental potentate and more like a diplomat worried out of his mind. "She's playing hell and tommy with us. What did she mean? Is she trying to get us to run around like headless chickens over nothing at all?"

"I doubt that, sir." Sergeant Williamson put into words what I imagine we were all thinking. We feared the worst. My eyes were drawn to the china lady, who now sat peacefully on Sir Laurence's desk, smiling as though she knew the answer to what troubled us, and if only we waited patiently and had sufficient faith in our Lord, we would know it too. But time was not on our side today. Or rather tonight, for it was late in the evening, after that woman had been interrogated but had refused to say anything more. I could no longer even think of her as "Miss Twinkle"; she had taken on a new and horrific aspect now, and the evening would be a long one. Fortunately, Sir Laurence had agreed to send Michael to feed Doshie, who must be wondering what was going on.

Someone had to speak out on what was in all our minds, and I knew it had to be me. Even Sergeant Williamson and Constable Peters dared not voice the terrible fear that the woman had planted within us. We must have made an odd sight, a diplomat in Oriental robes, two plain-clothes detectives, a chimney sweep and a boy of twelve or thirteen. It did not feel odd, however. Fear breaks through barriers that no other emo-

235

tion can even dent.

I plucked up my courage. "This business is nothing to do with the china lady. She was only part of the plan. It's the next stage that the woman taunted us with. And that's happening tomorrow."

As soon as Sergeant Williamson had clapped eyes on the woman, he knew immediately who she was: Eva Grünfeld. He called them dormice, he told us. Twenty years ago there had been a tide of Germanic people settling in our country, mostly peacefully and quietly. German bands were only one sign of them. But occasionally they came for a purpose: to lie dormant until they passed muster as English born and bred. Eva Grünfeld was one of those, born with the added advantage of an English mother. Her father had turned to crime, and ended his days in Clerkenwell on deceiving charges. Eva was devoted to him and when her mother died in poverty, decided England was going to pay for their deaths. She had slipped through the sergeant's clutches after her early criminal successes, and quietly melted into the background. She was reborn as Miss Eve Twinkle, with access to the richest houses in Britain, confidante of every chattering servant and mistress.

Sir Laurence did not agree with me as to when her plan was set for. "More likely the wedding itself on Tuesday," he said heavily.

Sergeant Williamson agreed with him. Tom Wasp did not. "Tomorrow," I repeated. "Windsor will be easier to guard." I had seen pictures of St. George's Chapel where the wedding was to take place, and knew this to be the case.

The sergeant gave me his full attention. "You're right, Wasp. The chapel is inside the grounds; there are benches being erected from the gates to the chapel door for spectators—all of whom will be invited guests. We can guard that more easily than the whole of London."

Sir Laurence went very pale. "Then it's during tomorrow's procession."

We were all silent. Its route was from the Bricklayers' Arms railway terminus to London Bridge, then Mansion House, Guildhall, Temple Bar and then all the way to Paddington. At every moment the procession would be vulnerable to whatever mischief Eva Grünfeld had planned. That means it was more likely to be here in the east of the city, where more people would be watching if the past week had been anything to judge by.

Again Sergeant Williamson agreed. "We can put every policeman in London on to guard it but it won't be enough, whatever the Chief Commissioner says. Every man jack in London who can read a newspaper knows where the procession route is, and the points where it will stop."

"Temple Bar," Sir Laurence said. "It will stop where the City authority gives way to the West London authorities. And there's a stop at Guildhall too."

"And the Mansion House," said I. "There'll be a stop there, so the newspapers say, for the lady mayoress to give flowers to the princess."

Sergeant Williamson looked grave, and studied the map Sir Laurence had laid open on his desk. He bent over it, then straightened up, his fingers tracing a line across the map, which, being quite a small, one I could not see. "Here," he said. "Assuming the crowds are going to be thickest from outside the Bricklayers' Arms, across London Bridge and up to the Guildhall, somewhere *there* is the most likely. So you're right again, Mr. Wasp. Mansion House is the obvious point."

"How?" Sir Laurence's voice was strained, and little wonder.

"A gun from a window?" the constable volunteered.

Sergeant Williamson considered his subordinate's suggestion carefully. "Unlikely. Too uncertain, if the carriages are moving, and probably too far for accuracy to be possible. On the other hand, if the procession is stationary at the agreed stopping points, it could be too risky to shoot. The assassin could be spotted too easily."

"A dagger?" the constable tried again.

"Perhaps. Or a gun at close quarters."

Sir Laurence frowned. "That's even riskier."

"No, sir," the sergeant said. "Not necessarily. With dense crowds, he could wait till opportunity presented itself, perhaps if the police guard became separated from the carriages. With the shock of an explosion close at hand, the crowd's attention would be diverted momentarily, and the man could make his escape."

"But who will the target be?" Sir Laurence asked. "The Prince of Wales or the bride?"

They all began speaking at once as to whether Eva Grünfeld had the Prince in mind or the princess. What was strange to me was that none of them mentioned what was so obvious to me. But I was a short man, and by now there were three large backs in front of me as they pored over the map. Ned was obviously longing to have a peep too, but try as I would, I could not get their attention.

Ned glanced back at me, and saw my dilemma. Brave lad that he is, he took matters into his own hands and yelled out our street cry at the top of his voice:

"*Swee-ee-ep, ho! Swee-ee-ep.*"

The three gentlemen studying the map nearly jumped out of their skins, but I didn't care. I had my opportunity. "It's not Eva Grünfeld behind this, Sir Laurence. It's whoever paid her to do the job. It could be the Chinese emperor, or those rebels you told me about, but if it's Mr. Bismarck, then it's certainly—"

"Yes, yes," he broke in impatiently. "It could be any of them."

Still they did not understand. "Prince Christian, sir, *that's* who they'll try to kill," I almost shouted. "He's the heir to the Danish throne, and the newspapers say he'll be in the same carriage as the Prince of Wales and his bride."

Sir Laurence smote his forehead in a manner that would have been most satisfactory if I'd had time to think that way in such a crisis. "By God, it takes a chimney sweep to tell me my job. Of course, it's Prince Christian they're after. Williamson, the carriages must be closed ones, not open; the order must be changed . . ."

"That would need Her Majesty's permission, sir, even if there were time," came the despairing reply.

Sir Laurence groaned in a disrespectful way that no doubt he would never otherwise have done. "You don't need to tell me, Sergeant. She would never believe it of her German relations. Her husband was Prince of Saxe-Coburg, her daughter's married to the heir to the Prussian crown . . ."

Constable Peters is a brave young man. "I could try to warn Her Majesty, guvner," he said in a trembly voice.

"No, lad," Williamson replied in kindly tones. "She'd eat you for breakfast. Besides, the villains will have time to follow the carriage wherever it goes. *And* to work out what to do if the type or order of the carriages is switched."

"We could tell Her Majesty the truth—that we don't know who's behind it for sure. The emperor of China maybe," I suggested.

"Have you ever tried to tell the Queen anything, Wasp?" Sir Laurence said despondently.

"No, sir." I had swept her chimneys, but I didn't think that would count.

"She is a brave lady, who has withstood assassination attempts herself. She had a carriage accident in Scotland once, thanks to her driver being drunk, and she was suspended upside down by her crinoline in the wreckage for an hour or two. When they cut her down, all she wanted to know was whether Prince Albert was safe. Believe me, whatever one tells her, she wants to know more. And more and more before she makes up her mind. And the more she knows about Miss Eva Grünfeld, the more we're all likely to end up in the Tower."

"I understand, sir."

Discussions continued without me, and I could see that Ned was almost propping his eyes open with his fingers, but I was too nervous to feel sleepy. I ought to be able to do something. It was just what that had to be settled. At last an idea came to me. The police and even the cavalry escorting the procession would only be able to do so much, but I could call on another army. Whether it would reply was a different matter, but I'd do my best.

Sir Laurence was too weary even to ask what the hell I was planning when I demanded his second best carriage and Silas Rodway to take me to Wapping High Street right away, and then take Ned back to the Chuckwicks.

Poor Billy Johnson. He and Doll had gone to bed early that evening in plenty of time to greet the big day with enthusiasm, and now he was hauled downstairs, still wearing his nightcap. Doll did not appear, but Billy was all attention when I told him about the identity of the putter-up.

"So that's it." Billy said heavily. "She gave the orders for my Dinah's death."

"Yes, Billy—" I felt in view of the coming emergency that we were on those terms now. "Your Dinah died at Belt's hands not because he was jealous, but because he was working for the putter-up, not Dabeno after all. Dinah must have guessed who she was and perhaps even that she had some big job on." I thought it was the former, but I needed Billy's help for tomorrow.

"What big job? Not that china pot again?" Billy asked dispassionately, looking as if he was getting ready to throw me out with his own bare hands now he knew the truth.

"Assassination tomorrow. Could cause war in Europe."

Billy looked suspicious, which was not surprising. These were grand words that meant little by the scale of Rat Mob operations.

"There'll probably be an attempt on someone's life in the procession tomorrow." I didn't go into how I knew this, in order to spare his sensibilities over pigmen. "The Prince of Wales or the bride or her father or all of them. *That's* the big job."

Billy stared at me and fastened on the one thing that seemed relevant to him. Tears began to run down his face. "My Dinah got wind of it, did she? She was a chip off the old block, that one, and always was one for royalty. And here's my Jemima all set to marry a pigman. I don't know what the world's coming to. What have I done to deserve this?" he wailed.

"It's what you *can* do, Billy." I cut to the quick of it. "You can avenge Dinah."

"How?" Billy was on my side now.

"Call your mob out for tomorrow."

I had his full attention right away. "What the hell for? I gave them the day off for private dipping."

"Put them at intervals all along the route from Bricklayers to Temple Bar, guarding the procession. It ain't going to be travelling fast, so one of your men can follow the carriage to the next man posted. Two, maybe; have one each side, covering the royal carriages."

"They have pigmen for that," he frowned. "You ask Jemima. She knows all about it."

"They'll be in uniform," I said urgently. "Your lot won't be. They can get closer while the blues are pushed out of the way by the crowds. Besides, your chaps are clever—they'll spot their own sort. Takes one to know one."

Billy's eyes narrowed, but he let this pass. "Maybe. Problem though, Tom. I've got fifty or so lads. Even if I get them all at short notice, that's not enough."

Now for it. I'd already thought of this hitch.

I tried to sound casual. "If Dabeno's lot joins in with you, it will."

He jumped up so quickly I thought his nightcap was going to fly off his head and hit the ceiling. Eyes bulging with fury, he could hardly speak. "Join up with that lot?" he squeaked. "They murdered poor old Chuckwick."

"No, they didn't," I reminded him patiently. "And this is for your country, Billy." And when that left him unimpressed, I added, "And for Dinah."

He subsided. "Dabeno . . ." He groaned, looking at me with pleading eyes.

"*Do it*, Billy."

"*You* do it."

"I can't," I replied. "You know how to contact him quickly."

"How do you know that?" Billy roared aghast. "That's for emergencies only."

"This *is* an emergency," I roared back.

"It's *secret*," he howled.

I took a wild guess—if I proved wrong, I'd lost the game.

"It's pigeons," I said—picking the only method I could think of for spreading news far and wide quickly.

Billy heaved a disgusted sigh. "Chuckwick told you."

"He didn't," I said honestly. "It was the amount of bird shite in your yard—and his—that made me guess." It wasn't, but now I came to think of it, it could have been.

Billy looked at me menacingly. "All right, I'll do it. Mind you, I've never got hold of Dabeno this way before. Doll's not going to like it. The pigeons are her job."

When I at last reached "home," as I was beginning to regard

the Chuckwicks' house, Mr. Chuckwick was waiting in the hallway. The little Chuckwicks—and Ned, I was relieved to see—were fast asleep on the living room floor. The pigeon had arrived quicker than I had, despite Silas Rodway's fast driving.

Mr. Chuckwick looked very excited. "We're gathering at six tomorrow morning, Mr. Wasp, to arrange our positions along the line. Fancy, the Rats working with the Nichols. The message states that the Rats are to wear a Union Jack in their caps and the Nichols a Danish flag so that we can be distinguished along the lines. My word, Mr. Wasp, I'm looking forward to tomorrow. A new chapter in the book of my life."

I didn't share his enthusiasm, but tried to do my best to look pleased at my forthcoming role in this. "Where will you stand?" I asked him.

He looked shocked. "Naturally I shall be guarding you, Mr. Wasp. After all, so far as the Nichols are concerned, I am dead already, so there's no danger to me."

The day of the grand procession was as fine as can be expected of this time of year, early March. A fresh wind brought drops of rain, but I was too agitated to feel the chill or even the usual showers that had bedevilled this long winter.

"Ned," I said, as Mrs. Chuckwick bustled about getting the little Chuckwicks ready for the great day, "I've decided to see the lie of the land for myself today. It's not safe for you."

This was not acceptable, it appeared, as when I tried to tell Ned he should stay with Mrs. Chuckwick, he refused. I said he was my apprentice, and as I was master sweep I should be obeyed. He said he wasn't leaving me.

There was a bit of an altercation, which Mr. Chuckwick stepped in to solve. He would guard Ned, he told me. I must have looked suspicious, because he added, "And Giant George is guarding you."

This was generous of Billy, provided of course that George didn't have a mind of his own on this issue. Fortunately, when he lumbered up to the Chuckwicks' front door, he was quite amenable to the idea. It turned out he had a soft spot for Queen Victoria, and didn't want her son hurt.

The difficulty was that none of us knew who we were looking for. The only person who did know that was Eva Grünfeld, alias Miss Twinkle, and she wasn't talking. Nevertheless, I was in charge of this little group of would-be saviours of their country, and I led the way through the back streets in order to avoid the route of the procession along Borough High Street, Great Dover Road and Old Kent Road, which would already be crowded. When we reached Bricklayers' Arms, however, all I could see was a sea of faces, not only blocking the area all around the railway station, but on roofs and balconies and at every window. Everyone was waiting for the big moment when the Prince would arrive at eleven o'clock by carriage to take the train to Gravesend.

There had been a big storm last night, so I wondered how rough it had been for the princess and her family on the high seas, and whether the poor bride-to-be felt up to what was to face her today. All the way long we had run into crowds making their way to the processional route, and the noise of their singing and shouting came at us from every direction.

I had no clear plan in my head, save that I too would need to follow the procession. As we stood at the rear of the crowd outside Bricklayers' Arms terminus, I felt near to despair. How could I hope to prevent the tragedy likely to happen today? People were standing on the housetops ready for the big moment, peering out of the windows, and there was a happy tension in the air. If I were Eva Grünfeld and responsible for organising this job, where would I position the attack in this impenetrable mob?

Not, I reasoned, *where the pigmen would expect it to be.*

But where was that? Mr. Chuckwick could vouchsafe no authoritative opinion of what pigmen might be thinking on the matter, and Giant George just grunted when I put the question to him.

Ned at least tried to help. "Here where the carriages start or Paddington where they stop."

Normally I'd have agreed with this, but yesterday evening Sir Laurence, Sergeant Williamson and I had decided Mansion House was more probable. Eva Grünfeld, however, would have had time to judge the size of the crowds that might be gathering here today, based on those that had come during the week. She might rightly assume that the carriages and horses would be slow to move anywhere. London would be so densely packed that every time the police moved the crowds back, they would surge forward again and overwhelm them. Similarly the procession's mounted escorts of Guards might get surrounded by people, especially at the official stops. So where would she pick? My mind scrabbled desperately for an answer, but it failed to come.

At last we saw the black smoke billowing up into the sky as the train bearing the royal party approached Bricklayers. We then had a long, tense wait while the official welcome took place on the platform, and then a luncheon was served. For the royal party of course, not for us. As regards our own food, Ned took care of that, though I daresay it was not in the style in which the princess was dining. We were standing by the Swan pub and Ned had the happy thought of acquiring a pie or two to nibble. My stomach was in no mood for pies, but Giant George and Mr. Chuckwick kindly helped Ned out.

At two o'clock exactly, a cry went up as the royal party appeared, and made its way to the waiting carriages. I could not see them, of course, but as the crowd pressed forward and the carriages prepared to depart, I caught a glimpse of the princess sitting next to a lady who must be her mother; they were in the last of the six carriages, and in the back seat facing the horses in front. Opposite her with their backs to the horses were the Prince of Wales on the far side from where I was standing, and next to him sat the gentleman I took to be Prince Christian.

I felt a tremble as I looked at him. It was all very well to have theories about his being the probable victim, but to see the real gentleman sitting there brought it home to me how great the danger was, and how little I might be able to do about it, even with the Rat Mob and the Nichols working their utmost to prevent it too. The princess looked so sweet, she reminded me of Jemima in her spoon bonnet, and a murmur of appreciation was running through the crowd.

I was so spellbound I almost forgot what I was there for, and when I remembered, a kind of panic seized me. What chance did any of us have of stopping this assassin? Then I took hold of myself and told myself firmly that this was just another chimney, albeit a big one. Every chimney could be swept if one was determined enough—and could find the right way to climb it.

Mr. Chuckwick was clad today as an additional chimney sweep—he even managed a bit of the smell—and this certainly helped clear a space round us. Ned was busy diving here, there and everywhere, reporting back on every suspicious person he saw in the crowd—which was a great many. I only hoped he hadn't been helping himself to the odd wallet on the way. Time enough to find that out this evening, but meanwhile we had a job to do that transcended even wallets.

A roar went up as the procession got under way. All six carriages were open, and so every now and then I got a glimpse of the royal couple as they turned into Old Kent Road toward London Bridge. It was then I realised there was going to be trouble with these happy crowds, as I had feared. All the people crammed outside the terminus were determined, as I was myself, but with more cause than they, to follow the procession every step of the way they could manage. They swarmed after it to join the mobs already lining Old Kent Road and Great Dover Street. The cheers, the dust, and the sheer mass of people were threatening to overwhelm me, both mentally and physically, but luckily Giant George pinioned me to his side as he ploughed his way onward. Grateful as I was, I had to gasp instructions from time to time.

"The bridge," I cried feebly. "We must reach the bridge." I did not think the attack would come as early as this point, but we had to keep up with the procession. As we were forced on past St. George's in Borough High Street, I thought of my Maria buried in the churchyard, and of how much she would have liked to see this day. I remembered Jack too, and vowed that Eve Grünfeld, who had been responsible for his death, should not triumph today.

Then we were swept along Borough High Street toward London Bridge, deafened by the sound of shouting and yelling as the crowds pushed towards the line of carriages and horsemen. At last came the wonderful sight of London Bridge with its imposing and glorious decorations everywhere. I was relieved to see that the roadway across was guarded by a double line of soldiers.

"It won't be here then," I shouted over to Mr. Chuckwick, who was pinioned to Giant George's other side as well as hanging on to Ned.

I might have spoken too soon. Once the carriages were on the bridge, the mass of people following behind from Borough High Street swarmed onward in the procession's wake and then pushed forward to squeeze their way into the crowds already waiting on the bridge. The soldiers were unable to prevent them, because of the sheer weight of their numbers. The Guards became separated from each other in the crowds, and I could see only the occasional bearskin bobbing up and down. Each guard was isolated, left fighting his own way through to protect the carriages.

Then I saw my first Union Jack in a cap and then a Danish flag in another—and felt relief that Billy's and Dabeno's men were indeed here. All around me I could hear snatches of "For he's a jolly good fellow," meaning the Prince of Wales, not Billy and Dabeno. Princess Alexandra was also a jolly good fellow, it seemed. Their carriage and then those in front came to a standstill, unable to move forward for the mass of people around them on the bridge, and we were there for thirty minutes or so until the police and soldiers managed at last to clear a path for the procession to continue. Thanks to Giant George, I was up quite near the royal carriage and could see the princess smiling through this ordeal—though a trifle nervously, I felt. I saw the Prince of Wales lean over to take her hand more than once.

I was in agony in case the assassin should strike at any moment, but nothing happened. This situation was too unexpected for Eva Grünfeld to have planned anything here, and there would be no chance for the assassin to escape from a bridge as he might well be able to do in a street. Was this a consolation? No, for it meant the uncertainty would continue.

At last the procession moved on, by which time I was dizzy with noise and tension. All the way over the bridge were statues of the kings of Denmark, who seemed to be looking down at me, each one ordering me to prevent whatever was going to happen to his successor, Prince Christian, and I tried to regain my strength so that I did not disappoint them. As we half-walked and were half-carried under the arch at the end of the bridge, and into Adelaide Place, my fears grew.

Someone grabbed hold of me, and to my amazement it was Young Nipper. "Sweep," he shouted in my ear on the far side from Giant George. "Seen anything yet?"

"No. Have you?" I gasped. Who was he working for? Billy? He'd no Union Jack in his cap. So it must be Sir Laurence? Or could he be the assassin? It was all getting too much for me.

"Loyalty, Mr. Wasp," Nipper yelled at me, probably seeing my confusion. "We're all on the same side. Where do you reckon he is? Whoever's doing this job ain't running by the side of the carriage waiting for a chance to pop up, is he? He'll have something in mind."

"Where though?" My mind was whirling.

"Mansion House is my bet. I'm off there."

I agreed, but then had doubts again. Were we all wrong about that being the most likely place? The crowds seem to be getting thicker and thicker, as the police tried to sweep us back toward the Borough. The crowd had a mind of its own, however, and was still pressing forward. I expected our little gang of four to be swept onward too, so I had to be sure over this.

"Ned," I shouted over to him. Mr. Chuckwick still had one of Ned's arms firmly in his grasp, and now Giant George had released Mr. Chuckwick's in favour of Ned's other arm. "If you wanted to pick someone's pocket, what do you do first?"

Ned shouted back the answer to that easy question. "Wait till the cove's busy with something else."

But that would imply Mansion House was the place too. I couldn't think clearly for the noise and the frightening crowds, but I had to force myself to do so, as we (the crowd and I) were swept into King William Street, which leads up to the Bank of England and Mansion House. I could hear women screaming and for a moment I thought the worst had happened, until I saw the carriages going on ahead of us unharmed. Their children must be getting crushed or lost. This alarmed me, and I shouted at Ned to get over to the side of the crowd by the buildings, and stay there. Ned didn't move. Mr. Chuckwick agreed with me, so

I told Ned he'd done his bit. He shouted back that he wouldn't go, so Giant George gave him such a shove into the crowd that he shot through it like a cork out of a bottle.

As we were being swept along by sheer numbers up toward the Mansion House, my mind cleared at last.

"If they're going to try soon," I yelled at Mr. Chuckwick, "it'll not be at the Mansion House, but *just before* it. That's when everyone will be thinking about the left turn before them to the Mansion House and the stop ahead. The escort, the police, the people in the carriages, everyone will be concentrating on that."

There were only about fifty yards to go now. I could see the Bank and Royal Exchange ahead, as I was now, thanks to Giant George, right behind the royal carriage, save for half a dozen guards and police. There was an important-looking pigman on a horse completely surrounded by the crowd, unable to move, and so few police around him that the crowds were having it all their own way, with him imprisoned in their midst.

Any moment now the carriages would be turning to the left. On the right just ahead of us was the grand church of St. Mary Woolnoth, its turrets proudly visible high in the air. It seemed to be a warning to me. Suppose the assassin was watching by the side of the church, ready to hurl himself at the Prince's carriage from our right, just as all eyes were fixed on the left turn it was about to make?

Miraculously, Young Nipper momentarily reappeared at my side. "There," he said, pointing to that very spot. "I reckon he's *there.*"

For a moment I agreed, but realised that was wrong, as he plunged through the crowd to check that side of the church. The Prince of Wales was on that side of the carriage, but I was sure it was Prince Christian the assassin would be after. So sure that I pummelled Giant George to take us to the left side of the royal carriage.

As we reached its rear, Prince Christian looked right at me with mild interest. If only he knew why I was there. By now, only one soldier and a single policeman were able to protect the carriage at this point, as the crowds pressed around it.

I heard a shout of victory go up: *"Der Tag!"*

I turned to see a face I knew: to my horror Carl Weber was climbing onto the back of the carriage behind the princess.

I yelled at Giant George who promptly dropped me and plunged back to haul him off as Young Nipper rushed across to join him, with a dozen willing hands to help and half the police of London piling in behind them. I briefly caught a glimpse of Weber as they dragged him away—but to my horror I saw triumph in his eyes. Why? He'd been caught.

In a flash I realised Weber was only a diversion. There was someone else, and here I was alone by the carriage—just as another figure dashed up to it in front of me, his hand already in his pocket.

"Mr. Chuckwick!" I called out for help, even as I threw myself forward to grab the hand holding the pistol. Then Mr. Chuckwick was at my side, taking the pistol as I hung on to the assassin's arm, just as two soldiers and a policeman saw what was happening and arrived to tear him away from us. The terror on the princess's face, and indeed on those of the parents and of the Prince of Wales, was only brief, before the smiles returned and the carriage moved on.

It was only then that I looked at the would-be assassin whom Mr. Chuckwick, Nipper and I had caught.

It was the man whom I had helped get released from Newgate: Erich Mayer.

Epilogue

Sweeps often appear at weddings, as we are thought to bring good fortune, but it's not often a real sweep gets invited to a royal wedding.

I was. On 10 March 1863, I was among the spectators at Windsor Castle to see the Prince of Wales married to Princess Alexandra. The prince had written on the invitation handed to me by Sir Laurence that I'd already brought them good fortune, but perhaps I'd like to come to the wedding anyway.

I would, and I did.

Ned was not forgotten either. Sir Laurence explained that, apart from other rewards, he had a special present for him, to thank him for his part in saving England from this difficult situation that Mr. von Bismarck wanted to put us into. The emperor of China was most obliged, too, because Ned had taken such an interest in his porcelain figure, although he was glad he had it back.

Sir Laurence had bought Ned another bird. Another linnet, in a golden cage, who sang almost as sweetly as Jack. Sir Laurence said the bird had had a few days with the china lady to get accustomed to singing. What would Ned call her? he asked. It wasn't a Jack, but a female bird, Sir Laurence explained tactfully. He had realised that nothing could replace Jack.

Ned looked surprised he should even ask.

"Her name's Kwan-yin."

ABOUT THE AUTHOR

Tom Wasp and the Newgate Knocker is the second in the Tom Wasp series, following *Tom Wasp and the Murdered Stunner.* **Amy Myers** (www.amymyers.net) is also known for her Auguste Didier series of crime novels with a Victorian master chef sleuth, and for her current modern series featuring Peter and Georgia Marsh. She also writes short stories, appearing in *Ellery Queen Mystery Magazine, Alfred Hitchcock Mystery Magazine* and in anthologies. She and her American husband currently live in Kent, about forty miles from London's East End where Tom Wasp carries out his chimney sweeping (and sleuthing) duties.